TEN DOLLARS AND A DREAM

$10 AND A DREAM

HAZEL JAMESON

POLESTAR
BOOK PUBLISHERS

Published and Distributed in Canada by
Polestar Press Ltd., R.R. 1, Winlaw, B.C., V0G 2J0, 604-226-7670

Distributed in the United States by
Slawson Communications Inc., 165 Vallecitos De Oro,
San Marcos, CA 92069   619-744-2299

Published with the assistance of the Canada Council and the
B.C. Cultural Services Branch.

Canadian Cataloguing in Publication Data
Jameson, Hazel, 1914—
Ten dollars and a dream
ISBN 0-919591-29-9
1. Depressions - 1929 - Alberta - Fiction. I. Title.
PS8569.A43T4 1988   C813'.54   C88-091282-0
PR9199.3.J36T4   1988

Acknowledgements
Ten Dollars and A Dream was designed by Jim Brennan and
edited by Stephanie Judy at Polestar Press in Winlaw, B.C.,
typeset by Phantom Press in Nanaimo, B.C., and printed by
Gagne Printing in Louiseville, Quebec in October, 1988.

Ten Dollars and A Dream is the third title in the Polestar First
Fiction series, a series that showcases new Canadian writing
by presenting the first book of fiction—a novel or collection of
short stories—by a Canadian writer.

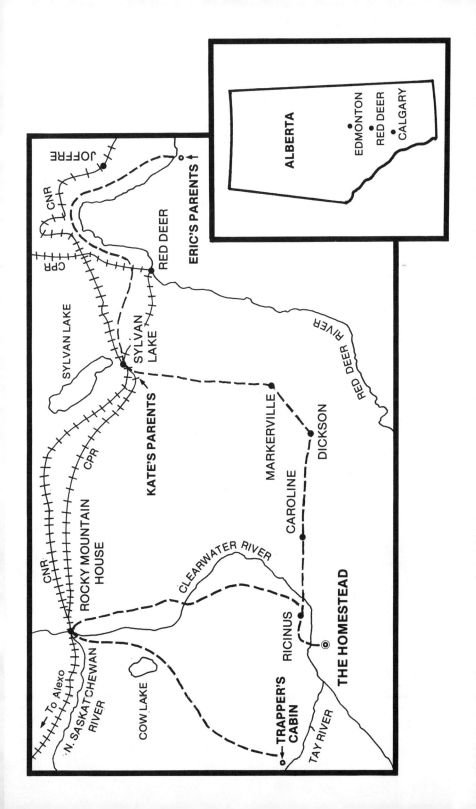

1

Kate heard the scrape of a window being opened and she tensed, waiting for Granny's white head to poke out, for the whine of her mother-in-law's voice.

"Kate! You'd ought to take the baby in out of that hot sun. He's a red-head you know—burns just like you do."

"Yes, Granny."

Kate's weary mind read an accusation into the words. Yes, I do burn sometimes, smolder at least. You say take him in. Pa comes along and tells me to get him outside in the fresh air.

She looked down at Robby cutting his teeth on a handful of sand, his shirt front drool-grubby and his other outfit not yet dry on the line. She picked up her son, dug the sand out of his mouth and put him down in the shade of the truck. The window thumped shut.

Kate and her husband, Eric, were sharing an old, rented farmhouse with Eric's parents, Pa and Granny Morgan. Kate found the arrangement hard, but they didn't have enough money to rent a house of their own. There was little work for a carpenter in Alberta in 1936.

Eric appeared at the kitchen door, pausing to run his hand through his thick dark hair. He needed a hair cut. His six foot frame was prematurely stooped from avoiding doorways. He came out with a tin dipper in his hand and sat down on the saw buck by the door, shifting over to make room for Kate.

She picked up the baby and sat down beside him, feeling the warmth of his long lean body. He had been so quiet lately, almost withdrawn, looking so much older than his twenty-five years. Silently he offered her a drink of the lukewarm water. It had been fresh and cold two days before when they

9

had hauled it from the spring down on the Red Deer River. Now it tasted of the wooden barrel. Kate sipped it slowly, her tongue guiding it away from the cavity in her wisdom tooth. She knew he had something important to say. He always moved his lips like that as if rehearsing the unsaid words. At last he looked up.

"How would you like to go homesteading?"

"Homesteading?" She stared at him. "Where?"

"Out on the Clearwater, west of Innisfail. There's a few quarters left for the taking. We can file on one for ten dollars and have five years to prove up."

"How far?"

"About a hundred miles."

Kate felt a stir of hope. A hundred miles seemed a long way, but not as far as her folks had come. They had driven from South Dakota to Alberta at the turn of the century, to settle first on the prairie in southern Alberta, and then in Sylvan Lake where they still lived. Eric's parents, too, were early settlers along the Red Deer River. Both families had come from the United States with their horses and wagons and ploughs. But she and Eric had nothing, and after two years of marriage it had begun to seem they would *never* have anything. In 1936 the economy, like their spirits, was low.

"We couldn't get everything in the truck."

Eric paused, his fingers drumming slowly on his knee.

"We'd have to sell the truck. We'd have those threshing wages, but we'd have to go right after that. We could get an early winter."

"What would we live in?"

"We can borrow Miles's tent until we could build a little cabin."

Eric's older brother, Miles, and his wife, Leah, lived less than a mile away on a rented quarter of land. Kate would miss Leah if they went. She wouldn't miss much else—not the constant worry about rent, or hauling water, or the two-room addition they lived in. Her mind went racing ahead. Her ancestors had all farmed. Maybe now it was her turn for a piece of land.

"It's sure worth a try, Eric. Let's go in. I'll make some tea."

She wiped Robby's chin, put him down on the floor and gave him a spoon to play with. She measured the water for tea and sat down. With her hands folded in her lap, she looked around the kitchen. It was a shell of rough boards and weathered siding on the bare studs. Only the north wall had been sealed with beaver board. The room had once been a brooder house for chickens. Fels Naptha and Lysol had made it livable. She pictured a cabin of clean logs, warm in winter, secure. They drank their tea in silence, random thoughts, half formed, outrunning the reality of the present.

Kate watched Pa Morgan come across the yard, a heavy-set man, the straps of his faded bib overalls lengthened with loops of shoe lace. He stopped at the woodpile to stare at the few sticks of kitchen wood and pushed back his sweatstained felt hat. He pumped the handle of the double-bitted axe to work it free from the chopping block, put the axe over his shoulder, and strode off to the school section in search of willow. There would be wood out there on the Clearwater.

That night Kate and Eric lay listening to the gnawing of a mouse in the corner, the faint rhythm of a cow bell, and the silent call of adventure.

Eric took her hand. "It'll be hard, Kate. We have no horses, not many tools, nothing but ourselves to rely on."

"It's hard here, too. I want a home of my own." Robby stirred and flung an arm against the iron bar of his crib. "Maybe we can give him a chance at something better."

Miles and Leah came over the next evening. They sat around Granny's kitchen table poring over maps. With a stubby pencil, Eric traced the blue line of the Clearwater and put an X on the bend of the river. "Right here. There's still some quarters open on the south side."

Pa tapped out the cold ashes from his pipe and began the story about his own parents' wilderness cabin. Granny joined in with her family history. Kate had heard the tales before, but tonight they were told with a sense of uneasiness. She could see Granny's face in the yellow lamplight showing worry.

"My mother told me about a family in a lumber camp in Michigan who lost a baby even older than Robby, there," said Granny. "This big cougar came in daylight and snatched the child right out of the yard!" Granny nodded her white head, full of grim warnings.

Kate shifted her thin body on the hard kitchen chair and held Robby a little closer, defiantly. If a cougar came for Robby, he'd have the busiest fifteen minutes of his life. She was going homesteading and her mother-in-law could stay here and preach about danger all she wanted, all by herself.

Kate had taken the bread out of the oven and was covering it with a dish towel when she heard Eric call. "Can you help me here a minute?" He had the hood of the truck up and was standing with a wrench in one hand and old dishpan in the other. "I have to take the oil pan off again and tighten that connecting rod. There's still one shim left I can take out. I'll drain the oil first."

Kate stood looking at the truck. It seemed as if Eric spent half his time working on it, patching inner tubes and tightening up things. Maybe it was better to sell it before it fell apart any more. It wasn't really a truck, anyway. They had cut down the body of a 1928 Chev sedan and put a box on the back for hauling water barrels. Kate hoped it would hold up for just one more trip—to look for a homestead.

When the last bolt was tightened, she went about her own work, getting ready to leave the next day. Ten yards of flannelette only made up into thirteen diapers. Washing was an endless chore. There was still a little water in the slough behind the house. She took a pail, a dipper, a straining cloth and three clothes pins to the edge of the pond. She took off her shoes and waded out past the weedy growth where the beetles and skippers hid. Dipping and straining, she got a pail full of amber water that smelled like cold vegetable soup.

She always hung Robby's diapers on a short line behind the

house because the stains never came out completely. Eric always told her to stop fussing. He assured her the sun and air would take out what his son and heir had put in, and laughed as he said it, putting his hand on her shoulder. Eric was reserved, often lost in his own thoughts. Kate knew from these flashes of humour and affection how much in him had been subdued, held under. She hoped a homestead would give him more than just land.

With the truck half full of gas, and a borrowed tent, they set off the next morning from south of Joffre to look for their land. Kate felt like one of her own ancestors. They drove across country to Innisfail and on west. The scenery changed gradually, from park land to poplar hills and willow flats. A few evergreens appeared, a few log houses. Occasionally a new frame house sat parallel to the road, square with the world, while the original log one stood along a creek bank. Kate would have settled for one of the old log houses if it could be her own. They passed another, bigger truck that had stopped to fix a flat tire, and farther on, a wagon, both piled high with household goods. Maybe she and Eric were too late to get a place. She hoped the people in the wagon had one, for she could see three youngsters on the load and a baby on the woman's lap. Kate waved to her. The woman waved back.

They drove through Caroline, a small village with its general store and service station. The Post Office was in a private house. Scattered evergreens stood out against the bare poplars. Farther on, the road dropped down to cross the Clearwater at the bend where the river swung north toward Rocky Mountain House. There was a store there with a sign: *Frazer's Trading*. Gas pumps and barrels sat in front, and the two big windows revealed the backs of display cards meant to be viewed from inside the store. Eric bought two more gallons of gas, and a small wedge of cheese to go with their bread and butter sandwiches.

"We're on the north side of the river, now," Eric said.

"If that open land is on the south side, why did we cross the bridge? Why don't we just go up the south side?"

13

"There's no road up there, Kate."

"No wonder the land's still open over there. I guess we don't need a road anyway if we sell the truck." Kate managed to laugh and hoped she didn't sound angry.

"We'll get by." He smiled at her.

They passed Ricinus Post Office and went on about three miles, Eric judged, from the fence lines they saw. The mileage gauge on the truck didn't work.

The make-shift cab shuddered as the road grew rougher. They stopped at last and put up the tent in the water willows beside a small stream. The sound of the river to the south grew louder as the late afternoon air cooled into evening. While Kate warmed up potatoes and beans, Eric consulted a map. He looked at first as if he was in one of his dreamy moods, but then he suddenly sat up straight: "The land that's open is just here, across the river. I'll have a look at it in the morning."

After supper, Kate put Robby to bed while Eric stared into the fire, absorbed in his own thoughts. When they had banked the fire with ashes and slapped down the last hardy mosquito in the tent, they crawled under the patchwork quilt and lay listening to the chuckle of the nearby creek and the distant roar of the river. Such a wealth of water in this new land! No more hauling it two miles in barrels. No more saving the baby's bath water to rinse out his diapers or to wash the floor. Kate held these thoughts close, then turned to Eric and put her arms around him.

Kate was awakened by Eric calling out. "Where's the coffee pot? It's getting daylight."

She opened her eyes and saw the gray canvas, heard the crackle of the fire, and remembered. She scrambled out of bed, the cold striking her back where Robby, despite his extra diaper, had wet the shirt she had worn to bed. She put on her coat and joined Eric at the fire. He was squatted with his back to the flames. "I froze out. There's frost on the grass out here."

By the time they had eaten and Eric was ready to leave, the

sun was shining and the sound of the stream had subsided in the warming air. He put a sandwich and the map into his pocket and turned to Kate.

"I don't know when I'll be back. Depends on what I find over there."

"How will you cross the river?"

Eric picked up the axe. "Maybe I can find a tree to cut down. I may have to wade, but I'll find us a place."

"Be careful."

Kate stood with folded arms, hugging herself and watching his long-legged stride until he was out of sight. She washed the baby's clothes in the creek, rinsing them three times, and hung them over a bush to dry. She spread the quilt in the sun to air. It was hard waiting, wondering if Eric would find a place where they could make a home. Would there be trees to build a cabin? There would be wild meat out here, and they could have a garden. She gathered driftwood for the campfire and piled more into the truck to take back home for Pa and She sat beside the stream with Robby and built sand castles for him that looked more like log cabins.

It was mid-afternoon when Eric returned. He sat down heavily on a log by the fire while Kate poured coffee from the pot on the embers. Eric lit his cigarette with a glowing stick the fire before he spoke.

"Well, Kate, I think I've found a place for us right across the river. I walked six miles down to the Raven through pine and a tangle of alders, and the best place I saw was right back here. There's a little land we could break up, when we get some horses of our own, and lots of timber for building logs. There's a spring creek there, too."

His calm voice belied the pride she saw in his eyes. He had to offer his wife and child.

"How did you cross the river?"

"Cut down a tree across a narrow channel."

"But how will we get out if we live over there?"

"Same way until I can build a bridge."

Only a log for a bridge? The river with its promised

abundance of water was asking a fee. The distant mountains, hidden beyond the timbered hills, issued both life and peril its streams. Kate ran her hands down her slim thighs and wondered if she could carry Robby and keep her balance on a narrow log.

Eric went on to describe the location. He had found a corner stake. Township and range lines didn't mean much to She wanted to hear about the place they would build the house.

"Can we go back across? I want to see it. It's early yet."

"I think we should leave right away for Rocky Mountain House, in case someone else has seen that timber and files on it first. It's only about thirty miles. We can get there before the Land Office closes."

Kate's eagerness to see the quarter immediately became a desire to reach Rocky Mountain House in time to file. When they loaded the tent, Eric saw the wood in the truck and added another piece to it.

On the way to Rocky, they crossed a long muskeg and corduroy flat. Unmindful of Kate's urging feet on the floor boards, the old car ploughed and boiled its way slowly through to the highway and the town. They found the Land Office and went up the wide steps into a small entryway. A black arrow pointed down the high-ceilinged hall to a door that said

LAND OFFICE

Walk In

As Eric opened the door, the clerk was straightening the papers on his desk. A map on the wall showed south-west Alberta, with little squares of red and squares of green scattered across it. Kate wondered which colour stood for the land still available. She hoped the green; there were more of them. She was trying to pick out the Clearwater River when the clerk looked up.

"We want to file on a homestead," Eric said.

The young man, wearing a bow tie and eyeshade, glanced up at the clock on the wall. "It's closing time."

16

Kate shifted Robby in her arms and sat him down on the corner of the desk. "We've driven over a hundred miles and ..." The young man looked at the child and the dark stain of dampness between its legs. He reached into a drawer for a book.

"All right. What's the numbers?"

Eric told him, and the clerk turned to the map on the wall. he studied a list of names and numbers for a long time. The sun shining through the venetian blind streaked the big desk brown wainscoting behind with bars — bars that imprisoned Kate in fear that someone had already filed on their quarter.

At last the clerk pushed the paper across the desk. "All right. Fill out this form. The fee is ten dollars."

While Eric filled out the blanks and signed his name, Kate a safety pin and unbuttoned the flap of her shirt pocket. She out a fold of one dollar bills, uncreased them and put them on the desk in a neat pile. The clerk picked them up, licked his and snapped each one as he counted. Satisfied, he made out receipt and handed it to Eric.

When they were outside again, Eric folded the paper in half and offered it to Kate, smiling. "You want to hold it for awhile?"

She took it, put it in her shirt pocket, buttoned it and pinned down the flap. She remembered how easily Eric had sold his old rawhide saddle to get the ten dollars for the filing His confidence then outweighed her uncertainty. This final exchange swept away her doubts. The precious document gave them the right to live on a piece of land and someday make it their own, a toehold on the future.

As they drove back down the main highway toward home, Robby's constant fussing turned to howls. Kate could not pacify him. She offered him a piece of bread, but he shook his head and cried louder.

"What's wrong with him?" Eric asked.

"He wants some milk and the last of it went sour. Maybe we can stop at my folks at Sylvan Lake and get a little for him."

"That's another thirty miles down the road. Doesn't sound

like he can wait that long." He slowed the truck and motioned toward a farmhouse beyond some trees. "I'll see if I can get a for him over there. Give me that empty sealer."

He crossed the ditch, crawled through the fence and disappeared. Before Kate had finished changing the baby, Eric was back with the sealer half full.

"How did you do that? That house must be a quarter mile away."

"I met up with his cows in those poplars and helped myself. They'd probably given me some anyway. Here, fill him up."

They stopped briefly at Kate's folks at Sylvan Lake. Jim and Wilson wanted them to stay the night, but both Kate and Eric eager to get home.

Kate looked back at her parents standing side by side and Her mother's salt and pepper hair was still cut in the boyish of the 20's. Convenient, she said, for a farm woman who had behind dusty harrows or leaned her head tiredly into the flank of a cow as she milked at five o'clock in the morning. Her Jim Wilson, whose broad-shouldered body stood half a head shorter than his wife, always said there was nothing wrong with looking up to a good woman.

It was late that night when they arrived back at the farmhouse. Granny was still up.

"You put Robby to bed, Kate," she said. "Then come in and have some tea. The kettle's still hot."

Kate responded with a warmth she seldom felt of late. Her hand went instinctively to her shirt pocket, checking the paper it held.

2

Eric brought in two square panes of glass. "Do you want to wash these up a little? I'll make frames for them. They'll make good windows for the cabin."

"Where did you get them?"

"They're the back windows from the sedan when we cut it down."

Kate compared the flawed panes in the farmhouse with the clear glass of the car windows. "Look how thick and strong they are."

Eric smiled up sideways. "Bear-proof, too."

She knew he had been amused by Granny's stories about marauding bears and cougars. She had, too, if only in the daylight hours.

That evening Kate and Eric sat alone in their kitchen and talked of their plans. Eric took his banjo down off the wall and played "Isle Of Capri" and "Love Letters In The Sand." He ended with the lively "Under The Double Eagle." He hadn't played like that for a long time. Kate couldn't stop tapping her feet.

The warm September sun had finally dried up the slough behind the house. Kate rinsed Robby's diapers a second time in water dipped from the barrel. She suspected it was a residue of Naptha soap that had chafed him when she had to use the hard spring water. His skin was so fair. She had finished hanging his clothes on the line when Eric's mother came across the yard.

"You'd ought to hang his things in the sun. They'll whiten up a bit that way."

"Yes Granny." It seemed pointless to mention the fact that the clothsline was in the shade. She bent to pick up Robby playing beside the porch and take him inside. Pa Morgan sauntered past.

"The kid ought to grow," he commented. "He's wet and dirty enough."

Kate didn't answer. She knew his frequent remarks were an attempt at humour, but they hurt, probably because there was usually some truth in them. Why didn't he say things like that when Eric was around? She suppressed her anger, remembering that he had offered to drive them with his team and wagon to their land on the Clearwater. Anything was worth the chance for her and Eric to have a home of their own.

A week of rain had delayed the harvesting until the middle of September. While Eric was gone, Kate began sorting their things for the move. It was a simple task for they had so little. The big trunk her mother had given her would hold their dishes and linens and still leave room for their few good clothes. There was Eric's black pin-stripe suit and the blue, bias-cut crepe dress she had been married in. It had been worn only a few times. There was no place to go. As she sorted things on the curtained shelves, she hesitated over her tennis racket, then slipped it into the bottom of the trunk. It was all she had left of her high school days.

It was the end of September before they could leave for the west country and their new home. They had sold the truck for thirty-five dollars, and when it was added to the threshing wages, they had fifty-nine dollars to start homesteading. From Eric's brother, Miles, they made their first purchase on credit—thirty dollars for a red cow called Clarabelle. He included six chickens and a rooster. Leah shared the bounty of her garden. The mound of vegetables was topped by two orange pumpkins. To Kate they were symbols of plenty, like promises. She knew there would be hard times ahead, uncertain times, and lately she had sought these omens of good fortune—a four-leafed clover, or the first star of evening to wish on.

The day before they were ready to leave, Eric, who was making a crate for the chickens, reluctantly offered to watch Robby while Kate walked over to see Leah. She promised to be back in two hours. Kate did not feel guilty about leaving the boy when Eric was busy. She knew Granny would take over in a case of such obvious neglect. Kate smiled to herself as she trotted along the dusty cow path, crawled under the fence and cut across the pasture to Leah's brown, weather-beaten house.

Leah was on the back porch, her fair head bent over a dish pan as she stripped corn cobs of their kernels for drying. She looked up and waved a cob as Kate approached. "You look like you're running away."

Kate sat down on the steps, breathless. "I am in a way. I know we have to do something, and this homesteading is likely the right thing, but it scares me, Leah. We have to build some kind of house before winter—and with Robby so young!"

Leah looked at Kate, hearing the near panic in her voice. "Come on in. I'll make us some coffee."

They sat at the kitchen table, the sun bright across the white oilcloth. "I can't stay. Eric is keeping Robby. But I had to talk to someone. I know Granny means well with all her advice, but I'm getting edgy about everything from cougars to moldy bread."

Leah laughed. "It does get to you, doesn't it? Once you have some kind of shelter built, you'll be all right, and there'll be neighbors somewhere near to count on in an emergency. Just a minute." She went into the other room and came back with a tan wool pullover. You take this, Kate. It's too small for me now. Too many washings in hard water, I guess."

"Thanks, Leah. It looks warm." Kate held it against her cheek. "I brought you something, too. When I was packing, I found that narrow, red silk scarf you liked. I'll have no place to wear it out there."

Leah took the scarf and knotted it around her neck. "I always loved this, you know. I wish we were going with you,"

21

she confided. "We can't stay here forever, renting pasture for the stock."

As they talked over their coffee, most of Kate's fears retreated, and they spent the time in intimate talk until it was time for Kate to go. "See you in the morning," Leah called as Kate looked back and waved.

Kate sat up in bed, groping in the darkness for the clock. Eric's arm reached up and pulled her down beside him. "Well, this is the day, Kate. There's no hurry yet. It's only a quarter to four. I just lit my lighter and looked." She nestled her head on his shoulder. "Lay here a minute. We're in this together. Let's start it together." His arms held her close.

The rattle of stove lids in Granny's kitchen finally started their day.

By sunup they had added the last box to the pile on the porch. Miles and Leah came early to help with the loading of the hayrack. They tied their horses to the corral and walked toward the house. Miles, though heavy like his father, had Eric's almost awkward stance. He stopped to talk to Pa, shortening the side straps of a halter for the cow. Leah followed, a tall, raw-boned woman with skin browned to the shade of her short, sun-bleached hair. She took off her wide-brimmed hat and carried it in her hand, waving it gently like a school girl. She went to Kate's door, through the kitchen and into the bedroom where Kate was untying the sagging cord from the window frame.

"Hello, Leah. Thought I'd better take this string and nails, too. We'll only have what we take across the river with us."

"Anything I can do?"

"Not until we eat, I guess."

Their voices echoed faintly. Kate might have felt the emptiness, might have been reluctant to leave these two rooms, had the unknown not held more promise than the past. Granny called them to breakfast and they sat down to a big platter of hotcakes and eggs.

"We should make Sylvan Lake and Kate's folks in two days,"

said Eric. "We'll get an earlier start on the road tomorrow morning. "What do you think, Pa, three more days from there, then?"

Pa considered, his fingers counting. "We'll swing south from Sylvan Lake, go through Markerville and Spruce View, keep to the dirt roads, off the gravel. We should make good time there. It's fairly level across those flats. Three days, I'd think."

Kate listened to the men planning her future, saying noth. ng, having nothing to say. Her thoughts ran to other things. They'd have to camp near water for the horses, and she could wash for Robby that way. If she put his milk in a sealer and buried it in the hay on the load it would keep all day even if the sun stayed hot.

At last Eric scraped back his chair and stood up, tucking his shirt back in across his narrow hips. "Time to move." He turned to Kate, hesitated and asked, "Can you manage in here? We have to start loading the rack." He seemed both reluctant and eager to start.

"Yes, just a few last minute chores."

The men put the big trunk and the household things in the bottom of the rack and piled hay on top. When it was rounded high with sweet-smelling, upland hay, they nestled holes for the chicken crate and the camp box. Another box with blanket and pillow, was wedged in to be a bed for Robby. The precious windows and Eric's banjo were stowed beside it. Clarabelle was tied behind the wagon and the team brought out and hitched. The family gathered around the wagon.

"Be careful along that river," Miles told them.

Granny's white head bobbed sideways as she cautioned. "Take care in the woods and watch out for bears. Stay warm and don't overdo. Remember you'll be over thirty miles from a doctor."

"You'll write to us, won't you," Leah said.

"Yes, of course I will. Thanks for everything."

The baby was passed from one to another in loving farewell. At last all was said and they stood in awkward silence. Pa Morgan took the lines and crawled atop the load. When Kate was ready to climb up, Granny came out with an old-fashioned sewing rocker and put it down in front of Kate. "Take this with you. It will help with the baby. And remember, don't take his bottle away from him. He'll wean himself soon enough." She brushed a strand of hair from her face, her pale blue eyes misty.

"Thanks Granny." Kate had always wanted a rocker. She held the old lady in her arms and felt the slight body tremble under the faded cotton dress. Why did this moment come only with parting?

"I'll miss you," said Kate, her own eyes filling with tears as Granny's arms tightened around her.

Eric picked up the rocking chair and lifted it up onto the load. Then he held Robby as Kate climbed up and took the boy. She settled herself in the hay by the boxes and Eric took his place beside his father at the front. The team leaned into the harness and the wagon began to move. She waved Robby's limp arm at the group waving back from the yard.

At the turn of the road, the farmhouse passed from view, and Kate turned her eyes and her thoughts to the future. Like their forefathers, they were moving on to a new way of life, settlers on the raw land, and yet, when a big shiny car passed them, rolling up dust from the dry country road, Kate knew they belonged to a bastard breed of pioneers, destined to grub out a primitive living rubbing elbows with the semi-affluent. The nineteenth century had caught up to the twentieth and was staring it in the face.

Pa Morgan was driving the team. When the first dust had settled, Eric crawled back to where Kate was sitting with Robby. He picked up his banjo, struck a few discords and sang in a twangy, sing-song voice, "Oh, We're Leavin Hungry Valley." Then he leaned the banjo against a bedroll and put his arm around Kate.

"We'll have a car like that some day."

She didn't care if they never had a new car. Sure, some day another one, maybe, one a little better than the old Chev, but it was the change in Eric that lifted her spirits now. Ever since they had returned from the Lands and Mines Office in Rocky Mountain House with the written promise of a bit of land of their own, he had been like his old self, the man she had married two years ago. She leaned her head against his shoulder and closed her eyes, aware then of her muscles as they tightened and relaxed, keeping her balance on the jolting, swaying load.

3

The steep hills rising up and away from the Red Deer River made travelling slow. They rested the horses after each climb of benchland until noon found them on the top. There would be easier travelling ahead. They pulled off into a bluff of poplar trees. It had been hot and Robby was fretful. While the men tended the horses, Kate put Robby on a blanket on the ground and fanned him with a lid from the dish box. He took his bottle and slept fitfully while she set out the lunch.

Pa pointed downhill to a small ravine with willows lining the steep banks. "Looks like there could be water down there. I'll lead the horses down for a drink. You start a fire for coffee. Give me the milk pail. I may have to carry some up the bank."

Eric handed him the pail. "Bring back some water to put out the fire before we go."

Kate had brought a quart of cold tea and a two quart sealer of water to make coffee. She put out egg sandwiches and filled the coffee pot with water to heat. They had drawn the wagon up so the taller trees shaded the chicken crate on the load. Before long the hens had ceased their open-beaked panting and were squawking and cackling. Eric climbed up and found an egg that had slipped through the crate and was lying in the hay. He held it up triumphantly for Kate to see.

Pa came back with only a little water in the pail. "It was far down to reach the water. They really didn't get enough."

"Want me to take them back, Pa?"

"No. They'll be all right until we get up to that slough south Joffre. It's good. Spring water feeds it."

After lunch the two men smoked and talked while Kate tended Robby and gathered the cups to repack the camp box.

By one o'clock they were again on the road. The sun had lost some of its intense heat and a few clouds gathered in the west. A vagabond cloud broke away and drifted across the sky, hovering above the wagon long enough to pelt them with a dozen big drops of rain. Kate watched the horizon. The loosely formed bank of clouds seemed content to shift about in the distance. As the air cooled into late afternoon, Robby was less restless and played in the hay, watching the chickens in their crate.

They made only twelve miles that first day. Kate was tired. She had been up since four and was glad when they stopped at last and camped near a farmhouse. They were setting up the tent on the road allowance when the farmer came out, a black collie following close at his heels. He nodded to Eric.

"The Morgans aren't you, from down the river? Heard you was leaving the country. I'm Ole Kime."

"Yes. I'm Eric and this is my wife, Kate. We're heading west to a homestead on the Clearwater."

Pa Morgan came around the wagon and shook hands with Ole. The Morgans from the river settlement and the Kimes from the top land considered themselves neighbours although they seldom met. The men stood talking while Kate changed Robby. "My barn's full," Ole said, "but you can tie your stock in the machine shed. I got a few oats to spare. It's a long drag up from the river bottom. You folks come in and have some supper."

Kate was grateful. Her head ached and Robby was fretful. She followed the farmer into the house and through the summer kitchen where his wife, a short woman with iron gray hair, was stirring the fire in the range. She turned as her husband spoke. "Nora, this is Mrs. Morgan from down river. They're going through to their homestead. They'll stay for supper with us."

Kate shifted Robby in her arms and brushed back the hair from his damp forehead. "We don't want to trouble you Mrs. Kime. There's three of us besides the boy."

"No trouble at all. There's plenty of spuds. I'll just shuck a little more corn." She bustled about putting more plates on the table. "Do you want to put the baby down on the couch?" Robby cried and clung to Kate.

"I'll fix a little supper for him," Nora Kime said. She poked about in the bubbling potato pot and came up with one that was cooked enough to mash with a fork. The brown beef gravy she spooned on the top smelled heavenly to Kate, and her stomach growled in anticipation. She shifted and tightened her stomach muscles as Mrs. Kime added turnips with a generous dot of butter to the plate.

By the time the men had come in, had gotten washed up and were ready to sit down to the table, the baby was sleeping soundly on the couch in the living room. Kate accepted the offer of a second helping and ate slowly, savoring each bite while Pa and Ole Kime exchanged stories of their early days.

After a final cup of tea, the men went outside, Ole to his farm chores, and Pa and Eric to make up their beds in the tent beside the road. Mrs. Kime opened up the Winnipeg couch in the living room for Kate and Robby, and hung a blanket over the backs of chairs for privacy.

Eric had brought the cardboard suitcase in from the rig, and Kate found dry clothes for Robby. She was busy pinning an extra diaper around the boy when Mrs. Kime came in with a heavy brown paper. "Don't worry about the mattress. My grandchildren have it well broken in, but you can put this paper under him if you want. You get him settled and you can wash out a few things if you like. There's warm water in the reservoir. His things will dry by morning."

How thoughtful she was. From the supper conversation, Kate knew the Kimes had raised six children of their own. Pictures on the organ and sideboard showed them in all stages of growth and maturity. Kate looked closely at a photo of a girl in nurse's uniform and cap and thought of her own almost forgotten dream of being a pharmacist.

Once in bed she lay looking at the hanging spider plant silhouetted in the west window. Someday she would have a house like this. Her tired limbs ached and she wanted to shift around, but the springs creaked with every movement.

Robby cried intermittently throughout the night. To soothe him, Kate sat up and rocked him in her arms, shivers of cold and weariness running across her shoulders and down the backs of her arms. When she heard Mrs. Kime moving quietly in the kitchen, she got up and folded the blankets of her bed and rolled Robby's wet diaper in the heavy brown paper.

After an early breakfast, Kate thanked Mrs. Kime, gathered the dry diapers and went out to the wagon to wait for the men to bring the team. Robby was feverish and crying as she arranged the boxes on the load. She put her finger in the side of his mouth and rubbed his swollen gums where his incisors were coming through. Eric came and called Kate aside.

"Pa and I were thinking maybe you should take the train to Sylvan Lake to your folks. We'd get there with the team tomorrow night."

She hesitated and looked up at the rack, the milk pail hanging from the side, the handle of a pitchfork slanting eastward toward the cloudless dawn. "I hate to give up. What would Granny think of me? She came all the way from Iowa in a covered wagon."

"She was fifteen, and she didn't have a baby."

They both looked at the boy, his nose and cheeks red from sun and tears, his curly hair damp against his forehead. She realized she had been indulging in romance at his expense.

"Can we afford the ticket?"

Eric's father dug deep in his pocket and pulled out a dollar bill. He put it in Kate's hand and turned away before she could protest. She watched him walk away. She had been so angry with him for his barbed comments, but underneath he was a generous, sensitive man. She could have, should have laughed with him sometimes. There really wasn't much laughter in his life.

Eric urged, "What about it? Ole will take you to Joffre in the car. The morning train will be along soon. It doesn't stop at the little station unless you flag it down. Ole will do that for

29

you. You just stand on the platform and wave and they'll stop."

"I guess I'd better go. It would give Robby a day of rest. I feel like I'm deserting you."

Eric kissed her cheek. "Not you." He looked at Robby chewing his fingers. "I don't know how you stand it. This way I won't have to worry about the both of you."

Nora Kime had packed her a lunch for the journey that day. It was only after they were speeding away in the car toward Joffre to catch the train that Kate remembered she had put it up on the loaded wagon. She had the suitcase with fresh milk for Robby. That was the important thing. They would be at Sylvan Lake by noon, anyway.

They reached Joffre and pulled up beside the platform. Ole shut off the motor. Into the silence came the sound of a train whistle. "Just in time," Ole said. He put Kate's suitcase down and helped her to the ground. The engine was in sight. He stepped onto the track and waved his arms. Two short whistles from the train told them his signal had been seen. It rolled to a stop and Ole helped Kate up the steps.

4

Kate got aboard the train wearing the clothes she had saved out for the wagon journey—a pair of Eric's pants and Eric's shirt and deerhide vest. Her canvas shoes, bursting at the sides, carried her purposefully up the aisle to the green plush seat. She stowed the battered suitcase, a leather strap securing the broken clasp, on the rack above. Some of her confidence ebbed away as she watched the dust from the retreating car and heard the mournful steam whistle as the train jerked and began to move.

There were only a half dozen passengers on the coach. Conscious of her clothes, she chose a seat near the back, and settled down. Robby stood supporting himself with one hand, his fingers working convulsively in the deep pile of the upholstery, the other travelling from his mouth to the cool window pane. He watched until, mesmerized by the fleeting scenery, he slumped down and slept.

At the Y on the main track, the train switched onto the CPR line and backed into Red Deer, leaving the main line clear for the daily freight from the west. Kate did not change seats as some of the passengers did. She remained seated, riding backwards, watching the open parkland retreating from her.

At Red Deer the rest of the passengers got off. Kate changed the baby first, lining his diaper with a strip of oilcloth and an extra piece of cotton rag. The conductor helped her down the steps. "We'll be stopping here for two hours, today. The freight from Nordegg has been delayed. You'll have time to go for some lunch."

"Thank you."

She reached into her pocket and took out an aspirin box.

31

"Don't you feel well?"

"Yes. I'm fine." She opened the lid and took out her watch. "The crystal's broken. I keep it in here." She held it to her ear. It was still ticking.

"Well, don't be late."

Kate walked slowly along the street, her eyes picking out familiar buildings. She remembered coming to Red Deer when she was only five. Her parents had driven a horse and buggy the fifteen miles from Sylvan Lake to the Red Deer Fair. There was a picnic in the trees and her mother had dampened the corner of her handkerchief with her lips to wipe Kate's face before they joined the noisy crowd.

She remembered Red Deer as a teenager coming to the big arena where the couples ice skated cross-handed to music. The strains of the "Stein Song" marched through her head as she walked.

She remembered Paul Corbin. He'd lived up on Michener Hill and worked in the Bank of Montreal, and he'd taken her to see *Arrowsmith* with Ronald Coleman and Helen Hayes. She wondered what it would have been like if she had married him, and lived with him in the city?

She remembered the little coffee shop where she and Paul had gone after the movie, where he had held her hand across the table and said, "I think I'm falling in love with you, Kate." She couldn't remember what she had said. She tried to recall the feeling, but it had been swept away, submerged in her love for Eric. She sat on a bench at the bus stop awhile and put Robby down beside her, resting her arms, before she continued along a side street in search of the Blue Moon Cafe. She found it, the same blue painted store front. It was now a laundry.

Kate was hungry. It had been a long time since breakfast. With the extra long wait here and the time it would take to walk from the station to her parents' farm, Robby would need more than his milk. She had no money for lunch.

She decided to sell the small gold ring that had belonged to her grandmother. There was no other choice. The man behind the counter at the jewellery store looked over his glasses at her, taking in her garb and the baby straddling her hip. He may have thought her some poor delinquent leaving home with her unwanted child. He could not know the dreams and anticipation under those make-do clothes. He gave her forty cents for the ring. She felt no guilt for having parted with the keepsake. If as the Bible said, *the dead know nothing*, her secret was safe, and if by chance Grandma Eliza Jane was up there watching her, the pioneer lady would surely understand.

Kate bought a box of arrowroot cookies for Robby, a doughnut and coffee for herself, and put the extra ten cents into the aspirin box with her watch. When she returned to the train, the coach was empty. As she sat fixing Robby's bottle, the conductor came back and sat across from her.

"Going to Sylvan Lake? Do you know any one there?"

"My parents. I was born there."

After a pause, he said, "I remember you. That was two years ago. You and your husband got off back there at Ferrant, that little siding. You started to walk across the field. It was snowing."

"Really? We'd just been married then. We were going to his sister's place. I'm only staying with my folks until the men catch up with the wagon. Then we're going on out to the Clearwater to our homestead."

"You have a home to go to then."

"No house. We have to build a cabin yet. But the land is ours, or will be when we prove up. There's timber on the place. We'll get a mill sometime."

He listened while she related some of their plans. The lack of shelter was of little concern, the land was the focal point. They could do the rest. The man looked worried. At first Kate thought it was an expression of sadness, that maybe he didn't have land of his own. Then, having lived all her twenty years in Alberta, she suddenly realized the cause of his concern, for it was now the first day of October.

"We have a tent, and it's a warm one."

33

He reached over to touch the sleeping baby.

"Well, good luck."

Sylvan Lake was Kate's home town, a small village strung out from east to west between the CN track on the south and the lake shore on the north. The highway through town followed the shore and was bordered with summer cottages. As the train began to slow for the station, Kate watched for familiar sights. The place hadn't changed much, a few newly painted houses, a few needing paint. Railroad Street was still only a back road and as full of chuck holes as ever. The lack of civic progress here comforted her. Some things stay the same, well known, safe. She hoped she could find the short-cut path from the tracks up to the farm. The train stopped and stood panting small puffs of smoke.

Kate took Robby in one arm and the suitcase in the other and jostled her way up the aisle and down onto the platform. She rested on the plank bench until the train had gone, then followed the rails on west until a well defined path through the dry weeds showed the way was still being used. It led past stock yards where she and her brother had played so many years before. They had often walked the narrow planks around the top of the corrals, not far above the milling, bawling cattle. She could still remember the smell of the stock and how the bulldog flies tormented them.

She put the suitcase down and shifted Robby to her other arm. The short-cut path took her through a stand of poplars and across a swampy spot where the yellow marsh marigolds bloomed every spring. The trail bordered the ball diamond, and it was only a short way home from there.

Through the row of spruce, she glimpsed the house, the narrow storey-and-a-half with its lean-to kitchen. The roof of the pump house showed above the lilac bush. She longed for a drink of that cold water from the well. Her mother had "witched" the well with a willow wand and found the stream in solid sand rock only twenty feet below the surface.

She walked past the flower bed where pansies and chrysanthemums still bloomed, and went up the steps to the screened-in porch. Lila Wilson came to the door, wiping her work-roughened hands on her hips, smiling.

"We didn't expect you until tomorrow. Where's Eric and his father?" She took her grandson from his mother's arms. "Come in. You look tired, Kate."

"I came on the train from Joffre. Robby's so fussy, his teeth, I guess. We'll go on with the outfit from here."

Over coffee, Jim and Lila Wilson made plans of their own. Kate was to stay with them until the men reached their final destination on the Clearwater. Then they would take her and the boy on in the car. Robby lay on the settee, sleeping fitfully.

"You go on upstairs and have a rest and I'll watch the baby. Sleep if you can."

Kate's arms ached from carrying the child. She climbed the steep stairs slowly, her foot automatically avoiding the center of the second step with its telltale squeak, the bane of her teenage years. Her old room was a kind of guest room now, with new curtains on the tall narrow window and a new bedspread of pink jacquard rayon. The hand braided rug was the same and the coal oil lamp was in its bracket on the wall. Faded ribbons she had won at school fairs still hung beside a Woody's Bakery calendar, a blue and white winter scene in papier-mâché, its sparkling snow tarnished now. One New Year when she was twelve, Walter Woody, with complete devotion had presented it to her. By February, he had bestowed a big heart-shaped box of candy on another girl. The past was nudging gently at her future, offering security and rest from the weariness and apprehension she felt when she thought of the venture ahead.

The next day Kate's father packed a box to be sent on with the wagon. Jim Wilson had gathered two tobacco cans of assorted nails and spikes, some bent, some rusty, all usable. He put in a wide chisel for notching logs. With that and Eric's own few basic tools they would get by. He added a coil of baling wire and part of a roll of stovepipe wire. He had saved the metal roof jack from their own kitchen when he put in the concrete chimney. They would need that, too. Kate and her mother sewed and mended for Robby. Lila's boxes would go when they took Kate and the boy out in the car to the homestead.

The men arrived that night. Kate saw them coming and ran out to open the gate. Eric jumped down from the load and hugged Kate. "Well, we made it. You all ready to leave in the morning?"

"Eric, the folks want me to stay a few days until you get there, and then they'll take me on in the car. I couldn't say no to them. It does make sense, except I really want to go with you and Pa."

Eric hesitated. "They're right, Kate. It sure was dusty today. We came the Burnt Lake Trail, and it'll be all dirt road from now on. It's shorter across country and easier on the horses' feet. We'll be three days on the road and it could rain."

The men were tired, and keeping farm hours, went to bed early. Pa was given the couch in the living room. Eric followed Kate up to her old room. She put Robby on the wool quilt on the floor, tucked him in, and turned to Eric. He had stopped in the doorway, looking around.

"At last. I've wanted to sleep up here with you for three years."

"We weren't married three years ago."

"I know."

"You're wicked," she said, giving him a stern look that dissolved into a sly smile as she unbuttoned her shirt. He helped her.

The men were ready to leave early the next morning. Eric said to Kate, "We'll leave a sign where to turn off the road onto the river bar." He climbed up and the wagon began to move.

Kate watched the wagon until it disappeared beyond the trees. She wanted to run after it, to go with them. This was her future, too. But the baby in her arms whimpered and chewed on his fist.

5

The sun was still bright the Tuesday morning Kate and her father and mother packed a lunch and started on west in the Graham-Paige.

The pile of boxes Kate's mother had assembled almost filled the back of the car. There was a quilt of hand carded wool, and some flour sacks to augment Robby's thin diapers. Mother Wilson had packed some fruit, too.

"You take these sealers of saskatoons. A big jar is too much for your father and me now."

Even the old farm dog made her contribution, a pup, half collie, with four white feet. Kate called him Boots.

Robby, on his mother's knee, enjoyed the car ride, faster than the plodding team, slower than the swift train. He pointed out horses and sheep and was excited by the burning straw pile in a field.

When they left the main highway and turned south, Kate began to recognize bits of the country she and Eric had seen when they came in the truck to find their land. They crossed the long stretch of corduroy road. At the bend in the river was Frazer's country store. They went west again. Kate began to worry. What if she couldn't remember the place where they had camped? The roadside all began to look the same with its small spruce growing in the ditches. She hadn't remembered so many of them.

"That house." Kate pointed. "Look. I remember that house, the steep roof. It can't be far now," she told her father.

A half mile farther on they saw the marker, a stake and arrow pointing out the faint wagon trail leading to the river. They drove through the shallow creek where they had camped that first night, went on and stopped on the river bar. Kate looked to the south and thought, *My home is over there, all that land, all those trees, all that water!* She saw the river for the first time. It looked harmless enough flowing swiftly in its rocky bed, but she could see the old channels and jam piles from previous flood water, the big rocks piled high along the bank, and she had a feeling it was a sleeping giant that could take as well as give.

The car horn broke into her musing. After a second long blast, she thought she heard a shout mingling with the roar of the river. She could pick out the place on the other side where the trail emerged from the water, angling up the bank and disappearing into the willows. Piercing the horizon were the tops of tall evergreens, timbers for their cabin.

Above the sound of the water she could hear the thump and grind of wheels on rocks even before the wagon came into sight. Eric and her father-in-law waved as the horses entered the river, picking their way over the boulders, the water seething between the wheel spokes. Kate saw the water rising on the wheels until it reached the hubs, then receded. She let out her breath. The river really wasn't very deep at the ford. The wagon drew up and stopped beside the car. The pup bounded gleefully around the wagon and horses.

Eric jumped down and came over to the car. He picked Robby up and pointed across the river. "That's your new home, son, across there. You'll be a little bush ape from now on."

The boy took his fingers out of his mouth and reached up to touch his father's face. Eric wiped his cheek with the back of his hand. "Here, you take him. He's wet on both ends."

Kate took Robby and pointed across the river to the stand of timber. "Is that on our place?"

"Most of it. There's more where we're going to build. I found a place on a bench in the pines above a spring."

Eric put his arm around Kate as she stood looking beyond the swift water to the jagged outline of tall spruce. Still entranced by the distant sight of their own land, she turned

slowly back to where her parents were unloading the car.
Kate was relieved to know there was timber enough for a house. It was their first need. They all climbed into the empty hay rack, Eric holding Robby, Jim Wilson trying to quiet the frightened pup, while Kate and her mother hung onto the sides and onto each other.

Kate looked at her mother for assurance and saw fear in Lila's eyes. She's afraid! And I have to live over here! This will be our only way out—and we don't have horses. Kate's muscles tightened against the jolting rack. She tried to ignore the sound of the tormented water. She kept her eyes on the willows on the far shore. When they were finally across, Lila smiled at Kate, a shaky, grateful smile. "It wasn't so bad, was it?" she said.

The horses plodded on down the small flat with its willows and alder and rotting driftwood logs, evidence of floods many years before. A few blackened pine snags stood proudly above the rest. Fire had also swept this flat at one time, but it had regrown with smaller trees. The sight of so much fuel warmed Kate. The days were over when they would have to scrounge the scanty diamond willow to feed their voracious cookstove. She unbuttoned her coat and loosened the baby's blanket, smiling, remembering how Eric, before leaving the old farm house, had scraped the last of the chips from the wood box for a fire to warm Robby's bedtime bottle.

The wagon trail entered a heavy stand of spruce and came out at the benchland with its pines and the high hill beyond curving protectively around it. Eric pointed ahead. "It's right up there in the pines."

They crossed the spring where a few late yellow leaves drifted slowly. The team drew the wagon up the bank and stopped. A campfire smoked lazily in front of the tent. Eric helped Kate down to the ground.

"Well, here we are. This is where we'll build."

Kate looked up at the tall trees, their plumed branches a canopy of green. She breathed deeply of the resin-scented air, and although a great peace settled over her, knowing no sacrifice would be too much to make this their home, there was urgency, too. September was already spent, the first snow was not far away. She turned to Eric.

"It's a beautiful spot, Eric! The trees, the spring, all that clean water."

"It took a little time to find the east line. We can start cutting logs tomorrow." Eric stirred the campfire and moved the gray enamel pot closer to the flames.

While Eric and Pa and Dad Wilson strolled toward the big timber to look for house logs, Kate and her mother busied themselves with unpacking. Lila Wilson could hold back her fears no longer.

"Watch Robby closely, Kate. That spring is deep in some places and the timber so close."

Kate had thought of all these things, but to be here at last, to be standing on their own ground gave her confidence.

"He won't be walking outside until spring. Eric will put up a fence by then. But I'll watch him, Mom. You know I will."

The Wilsons stayed long enough to help arrange the tent. It covered only the mattress and a pallet for Robby. They moved the trunk outside and covered it with the oilcloth from the table. These chores finished, they sat around the fire lingering over a last cup of coffee. Lila took a snapshot of them with her Brownie box camera, then handed the camera to Kate. "You keep it here, Kate. Take some pictures of the cabin and yourselves. You'll be glad for them sometime."

It was already late afternoon and time to take the Wilsons back across the river to their car. Kate's mother called her aside and slipped some coins into her hand.

"Now if you ever really need us, you have someone telephone and they'll send someone out to the farm with the message."

"A delivery costs extra."

"It's only twenty-five cents. You take this, Kate. I had some eggs to sell this summer."

The horses were hitched again and the wagon drawn up before the tent. Jim and Lila Wilson shook Eric's hand and turned to kiss their daughter and grandchild. Kate clung to her mother, assuring her they would be safe and well, and that she would write as soon as she could.

Eric helped Lila up into the rack and the wagon moved away. Kate watched them until, with a last wave, they entered the timber trail and were gone. Was this how her mother had felt when she saw her and Eric leaving for their one-night honeymoon after their wedding? There was loss on both sides this time.

Eric took Robby and led Kate to where they could look across the flat toward the river. The land would be easy to clear of small poplar and willow. They walked to the edge of the spruce timber along the edge of the bank, and Kate marvelled at their size and height, their straight trunks. They were standing beside the clear spring when they heard the wagon returning. Eric shifted Robby and put his other arm around Kate. "All this will really be ours one of these days, Kate."

That night, with Robby asleep in the tent, Kate, Eric, and Pa sat by the campfire, the stars bright overhead. They had searched out the north star and put up stakes to guide them in laying the first round of logs for the cabin. Kate wanted the door to face west, to turn her back on the past and always look to the future. She could already picture herself sitting by the door in her rocker watching the sunset. The men, too, seemed lost in thought. Eric's fingers drummed slowly on his knee; short puffs of smoke from Pa's pipe drew to the upward draft of the campfire.

The next morning Eric and Pa began skidding spruce logs, clean and straight. Kate gathered firewood, moved the cow on her picket rope to fresh graze and took her to the spring to water her. There would be no more hauling water here. The spring ran clear and strong.

Wood was not hard to find. The flat was scattered with pieces of dry alder. For the campfire the length did not matter, but for the cookstove she found she could dash the rotting alder to the ground and it would break up into short lengths. "Squaw wood," she called it.

Kate couldn't take the boy with her while she gathered wood each day, so she put him in a cardboard box under a big tree. The pup kept him company, romping and licking his face. When Robby learned to rock the box until it tipped over, she fastened a rope to the straps of his overalls and tied the rope to a tree. Robby hated being tied, but Eric couldn't stop to build a play pen. They were racing against time and the first snowfall.

Kate became exasperated with cooking outside when a sudden shower put out both the cookstove fire and the camp fire. *I'll make my own kitchen,* she thought. She constructed a teepee of poles and moss, shingled with bark and the hard shells of rotting logs. It leaked a little when the moss became saturated, but it was better than nothing.

Their meals were simple—a pot of beans or boiled vegetables. Once Eric shot a partridge. Rabbits were plentiful, but that year they were afflicted with watery blisters under the skin, making a valuable food source unfit to eat.

"Hot cakes for lunch?" Eric put two on his plate and spread them thinly with buter. He passed the basin of cakes to his father who was sitting on the end of a log.

"I didn't have time to make biscuits and there's only a little bread. I saved it for Robby. I'll bake tomorrow."

She started the bread that night, putting the kettle in the tent and covering it with a coat. The dry Royal yeast cakes required the sponge to be set overnight. In the chill of October it refused to raise. She tried all the next morning to coax it to life by setting the kettle in a dishpan of warm water. She had no success and baked it, anyway.

Eric hefted a loaf in one hand. "Make good corner blocks." He continued to laugh until she threatened to throw the other loaf at him. "The chickens will eat it," he said. "We're nearly out of feed for them. But it was a good try."

Every day after that, Kate stopped her other chores to make a huge batch of biscuits. Hot, with Roger's Syrup, they were dessert as well as bread.

The days grew colder. Their bedding was limited. Kate heated rocks in the ashes of the campfire, wrapped them in Eric's other shirt and put them in Robby's bed. The first night a coyote howled from the ridge behind the cabin, Boots deserted his shelter and nosed his way into the tent. To keep him from waking Robby, Kate shoved the pup down into their bed where he slept every night after that. He was tent-broken, and only for that virtue did she endure his wet little feet as he squirmed his way into their bed every night.

It was the tenth of October before all the logs were skidded. They had the first round of them laid out when Pa had to leave for home. Kate gave him a letter for Granny. It was short and told of the beautiful setting for the cabin, the trees for building logs, the spring. She did not mention her fears of the river and the deep timber, the threat of snow. Granny would have her own worries.

"I'll write more once we're settled," she told Pa. "It's only three miles to the Post Office at Ricinus. I won't mind the walk, once I get across the river. I don't like the thought of having to walk that log, though."

"I'll make a footbridge as soon as I can," Eric promised.

Kate watched her father-in-law's wagon out of sight and stood listening until she heard the sound of wheels bumping on the rocks. He was safely across. Eric had already turned back to his notching. She remained a moment longer, the sleeping child in her arms, and took in the tent, the teepee and the pile of moss covering the vegetables. This was their home now, their whole world. It seemed to have shrunk noticeably, with only the sound of chopping and the cowbell clanking.

6

It was already dusk when Kate secured Robby with the rope fastened to his overalls while she went to bring in the cow. When she returned, all she found was his clothes tied to the tree. He had unbuttoned the straps, discarded the garment and crawled away.

She looked around. He was nowhere in sight, not near the smoldering fire or the dog's abandoned shelter. She ran to the tent. It was empty. She had to tell Eric. He was straddling a log, head down, busy with his work.

"Eric! Come here! Robby's gone." Kate shouted.

"Gone? Where was he?" Eric clambered down from the half finished cabin wall and saw the rope under the tree. "Maybe he crawled into the tent."

"I looked there!"

They ran in a wider circle around the small opening. It was getting too dark to see scuff marks in the path.

"You go to the spring, Kate. I'll take the trail into the timber."

They raced away and returned, silent in their dread. The one path the boy could have crawled along led through a tangle of alders. They turned and ran down it, the pup following. They heard sudden joyous barking and turned back, plunging into the thicket. Only eight feet from the trail, Robby was sitting up, rubbing his eyes, trying to fend off the pup's devotion.

Kate scooped up the child and held him close. Her tears of relief turned to sobs of fear for what might have happened. How was she going to protect him from all this, the deep woods, the darkness held back only by the light of a campfire?

"Oh, Eric. I don't know if I can stand this any more. What if we didn't find him until it was too late?"

Eric silenced her self-accusations. "It's all right now. You can't take him with you all the time in that tangle of brush. We'll have to take turns watching little Houdini."

After that they put the boy inside the cabin with Boots. He howled when he couldn't see Kate, but they knew he was safe there, and after a while he accepted his confinement and played with the round blocks Eric cut for him from a small dry pole.

Each night they scanned the sky for snow clouds. The weather held as if God, watching over them, could not make up his mind if they were children or fools. Kate was setting out lunch the next day—a sealer of milk and another pile of biscuits. She stopped abruptly and listened.

"I hear voices," she said. She had grown used to the silence of the woods. The murmur of human voices was a foreign sound, a welcome one.

Eric put down his axe and turned toward the river as two men came into view. Denim clad, boots scraping on the rocky path, they climbed the short rise before the camp. Their dark heads showed white lines between deep tans and recent home haircuts.

They had a pole across their shoulders, and swinging from it was the hind quarter of a moose. They stopped and put it down. The shorter of the two men nodded to Kate and looked up at Eric working on the cabin.

"I'm Fred Hanover." He motioned toward the younger man. "This is Tim. We live across the river. We heard there was a new family over here and thought you could use some meat."

Eric climbed down and shook hands with the men. "Eric Morgan," he said. "And this is my wife, Kate."

Eric shook his head. "That's the most steak I've seen all in one place. We'd better get it in the shade. How did you cross the river?"

"We found the log you cut down," Fred said. Boots came

around the corner, and wagged to a stop in front of Fred, who cut off a piece of meat and gave it to the pup.

Kate stared at the huge haunch. All that meat and they were strangers to these men! She was so grateful she could hardly speak.

"I don't know how to thank you. We were going to have lunch. Will you have a cup of coffee with us?" She turned to stir the coals of the campfire.

The men put the quarter of meat into a potato sack and pulled it up with a rope into a tree by the spring.

"The flies won't bother it up that high," explained Tim.

Kate watched, her imagination racing. Steaks! Brown gravy! There'd be bones for soup, too.

They sat on the pile of logs to have their coffee. Tim spied Eric's banjo hanging in a tree.

"Do you play that?"

"Some."

"I sure like the banjo. I play a little guitar myself."

Eric's dark head nodded slowly, his long fingers formed soft fists as if grasping and holding something precious. "We'll have to get together sometime and try a few tunes."

Fred looked around and said, "You folks are pretty isolated over here. There's only one other family, the Durhams, on this side of the river. Jess has the quarter cornering yours."

"Any women folk?" Kate brightened.

"Sure, his wife and her mother. The old lady's not very well. They keep to themselves, but Jess'll be a good neighbour."

The two men stayed to help Eric with a round of logs before they left.

The cabin rose steadily as Kate peeled the logs and Eric notched the corners. It was late October, the sap had gone down and the bark no longer slipped off easily. Her axe strokes missed often as she chipped away at the dry bark, and her back ached from bending over. Kate finally threw down the axe.

"I can't use this thing. I never hit where I'm looking."

Eric came over and picked up the axe.

"You have to use a long stroke." He sliced at the log. The blade hit a knot and bounced up. He sighed, squinted one eye and sighted down the axe handle. "It's warped for one thing and too dull, anyway. I need the other one. Why don't you use the draw knife? You can sit down that way."

She took the knife, straddled the log and worked, pulling the blade toward her. They had settled now for peeling only the top and bottom sides of the logs. Even so, she raised a dozen blisters on her hands.

A few days later, Tim Hanover came over with a homemade tool for peeling logs. He called it a "spud"—a piece of blade from a crosscut saw fitted into the end of a split pole handle. Since it was designed to be pushed, it merely reversed the method by which Kate was acquiring blisters.

Robby played more contentedly now in the enclosure. They always had their lunch and short breaks from work down in there with him. They sat on blocks of wood and planned the arrangement of the house.

"The door should go in the middle of that west end," Eric said. "That makes room on both sides for the stove, there, and the table over there."

"Let's have a window on the north by the stove and the other by the table then." Kate motioned to the east end. "It won't matter if the bdroom end is darker. There's just our bed and Robby's crib and the trunk to go there."

Two wooden chairs and the sewing rocker comprised the rest of their furniture. Kate's imagination built in shelves and a closet for their clothes.

After the sixth round, Eric and Kate could no longer lift the logs into place by themselves.

"How are we going to get the rest of them up?" Kate asked. "I wish I was a man."

"I don't." Eric leered at her. He leaned back on the handle of the axe and considered their next move. "We'll have to use a barrel hitch, I guess, and roll them up."

"Up what?"

"A couple poles. I'll get poles and you find the rope Pa left. He hung it in a tree somewhere."

Eric slanted two stout poles up to the logs and put a few wraps of the rope around the center of the log on the ground. Then he stood on the top of the structure and pulled on the rope. The log turned and began to roll slowly up the poles unwinding the rope as it came.

"Now you block both ends with those wedges and I'll take up the slack."

After the last round was notched into place, they cut a doorway in the west and openings for the two windows. Kate went inside and looked all around. Now it looked less like a log corral and more like a house, her house. She would make curtains for the windows, hang them on the logs beside the glass. There would be little enough light when the roof was on. It would make the room look bigger that way, too. She was still dreaming when Eric called, "Come on, Kate, we have to get these gable ends up."

They built gables of smaller logs. Kate stood on a scaffold at one end and helped lift the long ridge pole into place. With it balanced on her shoulder, and on tiptoe, she was an inch too short to lift it into the notch. When she tried to bounce it into place, the whole gable end toppled. As the ridge pole shot past her, she dodged and jumped, grabbing a branch of a small pine behind her as she leaped to the ground. Eric was there almost as she landed.

"Damn it," she cried angrily.

"Are you hurt? Where are you hurt?" He knelt beside her.

Kate stood up. "I'm all right. The branch broke my fall. But look at that. Now we'll have to start all over."

"Oh, to hell with the house! Are you sure you haven't broken something, Kate?"

"I'm sure. Listen. I hear Robby in the tent. We woke him up. Let's make some coffee."

They built the scaffold higher and had the ridge pole up before dark. The collapsing logs had been a setback, a waste of precious time, but the ridge was up now and the two other beams ready for the roof. As they sat by the fire that evening, a cold breeze swept along the ground and stirred the pines overhead.

Kate looked up at the dark structure etched against the night sky. If they could just get the roof on, she would feel safe. The days were so short now, their work time so limited. "What are we going to use for a roof?" she asked.

"I've been thinking about that," said Eric. "We could buy some second slabs and tar paper, but we need our money for flour and feed for the cow. A dirt roof, I guess. Tomorrow maybe you should start gathering some moss."

The next morning Eric cut small green poles and began nailing them close together for the roof sheathing. Kate left Robby at the cabin and went into the timber. Moss was abundant under the spruce, two and three inches deep in places. She found she could lift and peel back patches of it a foot square and make small piles to carry back to the cabin.

By late afternoon, she had enough to pack into the cracks between the poles. Her hands were chapped from the cold, and sore from the sharp, dry spruce needles embedded in the moss. The next day they put on a layer of clay, carried by the pailful from the hill beyond the camp. A light snow had fallen in the night. It melted in the morning sun, but remained all day in the shaded places. After supper they built a bonfire and worked on into the night.

At last the roof was finished. That evening Eric brought out his banjo and played softly, "I'll String Along with You." Kate sat in the rocking chair under the pines and continued to rock Robby long after he had fallen asleep. Beyond the flickering firelight she saw the outline of their cabin, the roof completed, the windows in. She looked up at the starlit sky and murmured a prayerful wish, "Let everyone be as fortunate as we." She smiled then to think of how much, yet how little she was asking.

On the first of November they moved into the cabin. The chickens and the cow inherited the teepee. With a roost pole across the back, there was only room enough to shelter one end of the cow at a time. Clarabelle usually chose head and shoulders, suffering the indignity of such proximity with chickens, a situation she would have scorned a month before.

The cabin, twelve by eighteen feet on the inside, looked grand to Kate. They had room for all their possessions. The metal roof jack did not fit the pitch of the roof, and so the stove pipe slanted up in a kind of Toonerville fashion. The smoke from their first fire in their new house ascended unhampered. She stood outside and watched it curling white against the background of green; there was something about smoke rising from a stove pipe that meant a home and belonging.

There was no door as yet, only a blanket hung over the opening. They had brought some scraps of lumber with them to make one, but it would have to wait. The cracks between the logs had to be chinked with moss. Eric's gloves were too long in the fingers for Kate, curling over at the ends, pulling the moss out as fast as she stuffed it in, so she worked bare handed and developed a full set of hangnails to go with her blisters.

They both worked at the urgent needs. Kate chinked the cracks in the cabin walls. Eric built a small barn with one stall for the cow and a roost for the chickens, which had quit laying now. The roof, like that of the cabin, was poles, moss and dirt.

When the cow and chickens were sheltered, Eric began to build a proper door for the cabin. They had brought some rusty strap hinges and a lock consisting of the handle and mechanism from the window winder on the back door of the old Chev. When Eric had the door swinging freely, Kate opened and closed it a few times, letting the metal bar fall into place with a satisfying and secure click.

7

With the door on at last, the urgent work was completed. They had time to walk out to the river. The water, low in November, had left signs of former flooding, driftwood on the bars, jam piles of logs in dry beds where the wayward river had changed its course several times. They stood on the cottonwood log and looked down at the swift water.

"Try walking across," Eric urged.

"I can't walk across that!"

"You'll have to if you want to go to the Post Office."

"I don't think I can."

"Sure you can. If it was on the ground you could run across it."

There was some logic there. Kate had always won when she and her brother had competed to see who could run the farthest on the rail of the train track without falling off.

"Just don't look at the water. If you do you'll lose your balance. You tend to lean toward it."

He was not helping much.

"I'm going to take off my shoes and try it in my bare feet."

"Sure. Go ahead."

Kate walked over to the other side and then panicked, because she realized she had to go back again. Eric's words of encouragement were lost in the roar of the water. Robby, in his father's arms, waved happily at her. They were both out of their minds! She looked again at the swirling water, then sat down, straddled the log and hitched herself across, her auburn hair blowing across her face. Some one had once said if you want to keep your wife at home, keep her barefoot and pregnant. Well, she wasn't pregnant and she still had a pair of

51

rubber boots, but this river with its boiling torment and log jams amounted to the same thing.

Eric worked for two days tail sawing for Sam Levy who had a mill across the river. He took his wages in lumber, enough to put down a floor in the cabin. It was green lumber, planed and worth twelve dollars a thousand, two dollars more than rough cut. They used flattened poles for joists. They had only a few feet of the floor down when Robby let go of the wall and took his first steps alone, teetering, arms outstretched like a tight-rope walker. He ran the last few steps and collapsed into his father's outstretched hands. Eric tossed him, laughing, into the air.

Despite the shimming Eric did on the pole joists, the corner of the room by the table slanted a trifle toward the wall. He nailed thin pieces of wood on two of the table legs to keep the gravy from running off their plates. Eric worried over the imperfections, but Kate was thrilled. The new floor transformed the cabin from a shelter to a home. The eaves of the cabin were wide and the sun of late November was low behind the timber. Kate opened the trunk and took out a small hand-braided rug to brighten the dark end of the room.

Kate's mother had told her how her own parents and their six children had come to the prairie and lived in a tent. They had built their house around and over it. They'd had horses to work with, and there had been two uncles to help with the building, but they had to haul lumber for miles and plow fire guards around their dwellings to protect against prairie fires. Kate wished her mother had told her more, had written some of it down.

She took a page from her lined writing tablet and wrote.

DIARY OF KATE MORGAN
Nov. 30, 1936: My own home at last. How thankful I am. What a difference the floor makes, those spruce boards so white and clean, no more of that awful dust. Robby walked alone today. I wish he had some shoes. Eric has built a little barn for the cow and chickens. It makes me

*feel better to know they are warm, too. I hope we can get
a horse next summer. I hate to see Eric carrying those
long poles out of the woods on his shoulder. I know he is
young and strong. I want him to stay that way.*

Kate had left the washing on the line, hoping it would dry a
little more, but only the dish towel moved limply in the cold
breeze that had sprung up from the north-west. She put on
her sweater and brought it all in, Eric's long underwear a stiff
ghost, now growing limp over the back of a chair. She hung
the clothes up beside the stove and breathed in the freshness
as she rubbed her fingers to tingling warmth again. Eric came
in with another armful of wood to pile high in the box. He
turned and put his arm around Kate as they stood in the
doorway watching the tops of the heavy spruce bending to
the wind. The pines on the benchland moaned as the gusts
reached them. Robby left his play and squeezed between his
parents. Eric picked him up.

"It's going to snow," Eric said, "probably our deep winter
snow. I think I built the barn just in time."

"It should be warm, dug into the sidehill like that. Maybe
the hens will lay again now."

"I'll make a chicken house in the spring, make it big
enough for a dozen or so hens. Then when we can raise our
own feed, maybe we could sell a few eggs."

"That would help," Kate agreed. "Maybe we can build onto
the house sometime. It would be nice to have a real
bedroom."

"The roof's pretty low for a lean-to, but we could always
build on the east. We'll have a whole new house someday.
There's lots of logs."

An owl came to sit in the dry snag by the spring. His hooting
echoed against the wall of timber. Kate pulled her sweater
around her.

"It has a lonesome sound."

"He's company, though, like that squirrel that teases the
pup."

Kate nodded. She had come to depend on these wild things for company.

Robby squirmed and clung to his father.

"He's cold, Eric. Let's go in."

They went inside, still planning buildings and fences and gardens.

With the cow and chickens now sheltered for the winter, they turned their efforts to their own needs. The ground was frozen deep, so they built a fire to thaw it where the outhouse was to be. The work was hard and slow. On the morning they saw their efforts covered with a foot of fresh snow, they gave up. Eric nailed a pole between two jackpines and they built another teepee around it. The permanent structure was consigned to "next year"—that elusive milestone pioneers know so well.

In December the weather cleared and turned cold. Eric came in from hunting, tossed a rabbit to the dog and held up a squirrel hide.

"They're getting prime, now. Look, only the odd one a little blue behind the front legs. Tim said they were getting ten cents apiece for the hides in Rocky."

Kate put the beans to soak and Eric began shaping stretchers for the squirrel hides from fire-killed pine. He looked up. "Think you can learn to skin squirrels?"

"I could try."

Kate learned to skin squirrels. It wasn't so bad once she got the hang of it, and with a little practice, she could do one in two minutes flat. Eric encouraged her in her record setting. She wondered just how much was in the interest of her self-competitiveness and how much was pure strategy. Gradually, she took over the skinning while he fleshed and stretched the hides.

One evening they were adding the day's catch to the skins drying along the wall, when Robby wakened and lay crying and rolling around in his crib.

"Teeth again?"

"I don't think so." Kate picked him up to soothe him. "He's

not feverish." She sat him on her lap and began to undress him. "Look here, he's got white spots all over him."

Eric examined the boy.

"I thought kids broke out in red spots." He took the baby's shirt and picked out a rusty-red particle that moved when he dropped it on the white oilcloth.

"Squirrel flea."

"Fleas!" Kate shifted and scratched her armpit. "Don't they bite you, too?"

"No, just crawl around. Robby's more tender, I guess. What can you do for him?"

"Soda paste, I suppose."

She bathed him and applied damp soda to the bites. After awhile he slept.

Kate soon found that the fleas bit her, too, the first bite sending her to peel off her clothes and search frantically for the offender. It was too cold to do the skinning outside; they had to do it in the cabin. Eric hit upon an effective scheme. He held each squirrel over the stove until the fleas deserted the cold skin and appeared on the surface of the fur. Then he flicked them off onto the hot stove where they exploded like popcorn.

When they had a hundred skins dried and ready to sell, they tied them in bundles and hung them along the ridge pole, their rusty, black tipped tails making bouquets of colour moving gently in the rising air from the stove. Eric nodded approval.

"At ten cents apiece, we should have ten dollars for Christmas. I'll see if the Hanovers are going up to Rocky tomorrow. I should have another trap. I saw mink tracks along the river."

"Are you sure?" Kate looked up eagerly. "One of those would bring a good price."

"It was mink all right. They look like big weasel tracks only they go in and out of the water. They were on the shelf ice along the river bank."

"Get another trap, then. We can have a nice moose roast for

Christmas, and Robby's too young yet for presents. Maybe some candy or nuts would be nice."

Early the next morning, Eric packed the squirrel hides in a bundle, carefully reversing each layer to keep their tails from breaking off. He slid them down into a gunny sack and tied the top. "If Fred isn't going into Rocky today or I can't catch a ride with a lumber truck on the main road, I'll be back in a couple of hours."

Kate watched him go, the sack slung over his shoulder, turning back to wave as he reached the spring. She hummed to herself as she made the bed, happy with the thought of mink to trap. By dusk, Eric hadn't returned. Kate took Robby and the lantern and went to wait for him at the river. They had two logs across now, side by side, easy enough to negotiate in daylight, but it was getting dark. She fingered the matches in her pocket and waited.

She lit the lantern when she heard a car coming, its lights flashing through the trees as it wound its way along the rocky road. The car swung around to shine the headlights on the logs. Eric walked easily across, a box balanced on his shoulder.

"I was worried, Eric. It was getting dark."

"Fred went to Rocky this afternoon, so I waited and went with him. Then we had a flat tire on the way home and had to patch the tube. Here, let me take the lantern."

"Did you get another trap?"

"No. Furs are down, Finberg said. I only got eight cents apiece. I had to buy some .22 shells." They walked along by the swinging lantern light. "Hanovers asked us over for Christmas day."

"That was really nice of them." Kate paused. "Let's have a small tree at home, though."

"Sure. I got a few peanuts for us and some suckers for Robby."

Eric brought in a small spruce and fixed a crosspiece on the bottom so it would sit on the shelf by Robby's crib. Kate trimmed their little tree with stringy moss and bits of red and green yarn. Eric cut out a star from a bright tin can. It caught the lamplight and shone its message from the dark corner.

Christmas was still a few days away, but Kate began to get their best clothes ready. She opened the trunk and found her green crepe dress with the patent belt and Eric's suit and white shirt. The shirt needed washing—he wore it so seldom. There was nothing special for Robby to dress up in. He had so few clothes. Kate had to wash nearly everything he had every day. She took out a flat cardboard box and considered it. "Aunt Fanny, forgive me," she murmured as she laid aside eight of the twelve linen table napkins, the big, chin-tucking kind, a foot and a half square. The napkins and a silver plated tea service had been Aunt Fanny's legacy to Kate. The next day, under overalls, Robby wore linen. The absorbency was minimal; they merely strained, but they kept him covered. Kate felt regret, but also some pride at having made do yet again.

Christmas day came, and Kate dressed carefully. She had straightened the hem on the flared skirt of her dress where it sagged at the side seams. The mended runs in her stockings hardly showed. Her winter coat was one she had had since high school and it was still good except where mice had chewed a hole in one shoulder. It had a big collar which she kept turned down over the patch. Eric thought this was foolish.

"Put the damned thing up, Kate. You'll catch cold like that."

"I'm wearing a scarf."

Eric had made a toboggan for hauling wood from a timber-bound spruce growing out of the sidehill. Although cumbersome, it slid easily in the loose snow. They rolled Robby in a blanket, put him on the toboggan and laced him down. At the logs across the river, Eric unlaced Robby and took the sled across. He came back and held Robby while Kate crossed, then took the boy over and put him back on the sled. They walked the half mile up the rough river bar and turned onto the trail through small evergreens, making their way past the barn and up to the big, two-story house.

Fred greeted them at the door. "Come in. Glad you could come." He turned to his parents, standing behind him in the warm kitchen. "You've met Eric before, and this is Mrs. Morgan and little - "

"Robby," Kate prompted.

Mary Hanover, a stately woman, with a bright appliqued apron over her ample front, nodded to Kate and smiled at the child still rolled in his blanket, his red hair curling out across his face. "Robby? A good name," she said with a faintly Scottish accent. In Pete Hanover, graying and slightly stooped, Kate saw Fred's facial features and heard an echo of his son's jovial laugh.

Mary Hanover took their coats, and Pete directed them with a wave of his hand toward the living room. "Go on in. You know Tim."

The living room was large, the walls hewn and chinked to a flat surface. A gas lamp, hanging on a hook and wire from a beam, hissed steadily, its white light seeking the farthest corner, highlighting the O'Cedar shine of an old upright piano. Fred, at the spraddle-legged, gas-barrel stove was putting another long block into the fire. The puff of wood smoke mingled with the tang of spruce nedles from the gaily decorated tree in the corner. Kate sat Robby on the rug in front of it and took the easy chair Tim offered. She sank into the luxury of its softness. Robby crawled toward the tree, reaching for one of its bright ornaments.

"No, Robby. You mustn't touch."

Mrs. Hanover took a yellow stuffed toy cat from under the tree. She handed it to Robby. "For your Christmas." Robby examined the cat's eyes and long tail and settled to play, looking up now and then to stare at the fascinating, forbidden tree.

Tim helped his mother put another leaf in the table at the far end of the long room. As they spread the big, white linen table cloth, Kate's truant thoughts speculated on how many diapers one that size would make.

Kate was self-conscious as they found their places around

the table. She wanted to hold Robby on her lap and feed him off her plate, but Mary Hanover insisted he have a seat of his own. He was soon enthroned beside her on four thick books of Charles Dickens's works piled on a chair. Bibbed with a dish towel tied around his neck, he sat wide-eyed and quiet. The dinner was a golden-brown turkey and wild cranberry sauce. There was an extra dish of oatmeal dressing, a tribute to Mrs. Hanover's Scottish ancestry. Kate ate slowly, savoring each bite.

After the table was cleared, they sat around the living room, the men talking hunting and fishing for a while. Kate looked around. Why, they could fit their whole cabin into this one room. She saw the wood box cut into an outside wall, one that could be filled from the porch, no chips, no tracks across the room. A place like this would be so easy to keep clean. She felt a surge of envy. Why did some people seem to have everything? She looked at Eric sitting with the men, sated and comfortable, their conversation lagging.

Eric's eyes strayed more often to the piano. At last he got up, wandered over and stood looking down at it, unaware of the silence his move had created.

Fred spoke. "Do you play?"

Startled out of his reverie, Eric turned. "No. Well, I play at it a little." He indicated the music on the rack. "I can't read music."

"Play something, anyway," Mrs. Hanover urged. "It's hardly been touched since our daughter married."

Eric sat down and ran his fingers gently over the yellowed ivory keys. He began haltingly, his right hand chording and his left hand picking out the melody in single bass notes. He faltered out "Easter Parade" and "The Old Spinning Wheel." Tim took his guitar down from its peg and began strumming an accompaniment. Eric turned, a smile lighting his face, his body moving in rhythm as he swung into "Ain't She Sweet."

Kate fought back tears of shame at her rebellious thoughts. These people had worked hard for what they had. When she and Eric were the Hanover's age, they would have something, too—before that, Kate hoped. She looked again at Eric playing easily, turning his head to nod encouragement to Tim. Robby was asleep on the rug by the tree, the soft cat clutched in his arms. Kate leaned back and closed her eyes, letting the music, Eric's fulfillment and friendship fill her with gratitude.

As Kate and Eric approached their own cabin that evening, the owl hooted its welcome. Its vigil done, it flapped away toward the timber. They stood a moment, their arms around each other in the frosty air.

They carried the toboggan inside and unwrapped Robby. He rolled limply in sleep as Kate undressed him. Eric built up the fire, and they sat by the stove, both reluctant to end the day. In the heat they grew drowsy and finally got into bed. Kate rested her head on Eric's shoulder, and he smoothed her hair, letting the curls bounce back under his fingers.

"You looked pretty today."

8

The next morning when Eric checked the traps, they had the best Christmas gift of all, a mink. While Eric made a stretcher for it, Kate stroked its sleek fur, with only slight regret for having taken its life. When the hide was hanging on the wall away from the heat, he picked up the carcass and turned it over.

"Could I have a little lard?"

"Good God! You're not going to eat it!"

"Well, hardly. The lard's for mixing bait. Come here. Look at this." He pointed with the knife blade to a doughnut shaped gland around the anus. "That's a scent gland, the best bait for mink when they are running in the spring."

"Well, don't puncture it in here. It was bad enough when you skinned it."

In January the temperature dropped. They had no thermometer, but estimated it was either *cold* or *damn cold*. The frost built up knobs on the nail heads and painted tropical scenes on the windows. It rimmed the willows along the spring with feathers of white. Trees in the woods boomed and cracked with the frost that struck down through the protective layer of moss to freeze the vegetables in the pit. Kate left them frozen and dropped them into boiling water to cook. They were fibrous and tasteless, but with milk gravy they sufficed. Eric ate slowly.

"I've heard the saying that what won't fatten will fill, but I never thought we'd have to prove it," he said.

Squirrels went back up to ten cents after Christmas. Eric hunted daily. As they acquired cardbaord boxes, Kate cut them in strips with the butcher knife and nailed them over the moss-stuffed cracks between the logs like she had in the little cabin her father had built for a play house—only this time she was not playing.

Robby was thirteen months old. It was time to wean him from his bottle. He saved Kate the trouble. One night, instead of going to sleep, he stood up in his bed, took the bottle by the nipple and swung it around his head like an Indian Club. The first revolution missed the iron bed post. The next one beat her call, "Stop Robby," by a fraction of a second. The bottle shattered across his bed. She shook the shards of glass from his bedclothes and rocked him to sleep. He slept for an hour and woke searching for his bottle. His whimpers turned to cries of frustration. Kate rocked him again. He slept fitfully, the rest of that night and the next, during which she contemplated emptying the vanilla into a pint sealer and letting him use the vanilla bottle. They both perservered, but Kate won.

Only three months and we have the cabin snug against the winter cold. There seem to be lots of squirrels. If we can make it through this first winter we may be able to hang on. The Hanovers have adopted us into their family. It was kind of them to give Robby a present, but it hurt to know we couldn't buy a gift for our own child on his first Christmas. I hope someday Eric can have a piano. Music means so much to him....No more bottle for Robby. He uses the engraved, silver baby cup that was mine. Linen diapers and a silver cup. He's my little prince.

By February the weather relented. Warm days left the snow filled with water, and the cold nights froze it into crystals. Kate melted snow for washing. The soft water saved on soap. She filled the tub with the heavy snow one morning, then discovered it was too heavy for her to lift. She was standing still, listening for a sound of Eric's whereabouts, when a succession of short blasts from a car horn came from the river.

She knew that horn, that signal. It was her parents!

She called to Eric, already coming in from the woods, smiling at her excitement. He put the axe up out of Robby's reach. "Sounds like we have company. We better go over to the river and help them across the log."

"You go, Eric. I have a few things to do here." She wanted to go with him, but she needed time to think. What was she going to feed them? It was nearly noon; they'd be hungry soon. There was no meat left, and it was too late to cook beans. She couldn't give them frozen vegetables.

She saw them coming across the flat, her father and Eric both with boxes in their arms. She picked up Robby and hurried to meet them.

Kate need not have worried. Lila Wilson had brought a whole meal—fried chicken, potato salad, saskatoon pie, and a transparent excuse: "We didn't let you know we were coming. I thought you might not have baked this week." She took out a sugar cookie and gave it to Robby.

"You can stay overnight, can't you?" Kate asked. "You can have the bed. Eric and I will sleep on the floor, or we can put the bench along the side of the bed and all sleep crossways. Our feet might stick out a little—that's all."

Jim Wilson smiled at his daughter's enthusiasm. "No, Kate, we can't stay. We couldn't get anyone to do our chores. We'll have to start back before dark. We did want to come, though, even for a few hours."

There was so much to say in the short time. Kate took their coats and put them on the bed. Her mother's warm jacket was new, but she had worn only her second-best town clothes for the day. Her father, as always, wore a tie. Kate saw Eric relax when he stripped it off and hung it over a nail on the wall.

"It's cosy in here," Jim said. "I see you got an airtight heater."

"Yes," said Eric "A good fire in the cookstove kept the place warm, but Kate could never get near enough to it to make a meal or bake without burning something."

Kate's mother studied the cabin. "You've done so much in

four months! I was so worried those first weeks before you got into the cabin. I prayed every day the good weather would hold." She sighed. "Now I know how my mother felt when Jim and I started married life in a tent at Sylvan Lake." Kate knew her mother wouldn't worry as much now that they had seen the cabin. She looked at Robby bouncing up and down on his grandfather's foot and thought, *It takes a long time to raise a child.*

The hours passed so quickly, and by five o'clock they were at the river again, waving and watching the car disappear across the river bar. They walked slowly back to the house, both thoughtful and content.

Back at the cabin, Eric took Robby and went out to the wood pile. Kate heard him whistling as he picked up the axe and started out the trail into the timber. She went inside and closed the door on the lingering presence of her parents. As the aura faded, she pushed the tea kettle to the front of the stove to hum away the silence.

At nightfall one evening in early March a soft snow began drifting down, settling on the wood pile and throwing a halo around Eric's figure as he carried the lantern from the barn to the house. He came into the warm kitchen where Kate was undressing Robby for bed. The child stood holding onto the back of a chair before the open oven door, his cheeks red from washing and shiny with vaseline. He pointed to the dark window pane streaked with white.

"Snow!"

"Sure is, and cold."

Eric reached out his fingers, threatening to put them on the boy's bare neck. Robby squealed in laughing protest. Eric put down the milk pail and turned to Kate, blowing on his fingers.

"We have to get more feed for that cow or she's going to dry up entirely. She's not due to calve until May, so I guess I'd better take those hides we have left to Rocky and see if I can get some greenfeed somewhere."

He left the next morning with the furs in a pack, hoping to

catch a ride at least part of the way. While he was gone, Kate emptied a cardboard box of sealers and arranged them on a shelf Eric had put up above the bed. She cut more strips from the box and finished covering the cracks between the logs in the far corner of the cabin. The cardboard helped to discourage the blue flies that wintered in the moss and came out whenever the cabin was warm.

Eric always cringed when she cut cardboard with the butcher knife. He said it dulled the blade worse than when she cut kindling. When he was around she dutifully cut with tinsnips, using both hands to manipulate them. But now, since he was away, she used the kitchen knife. She had to laugh to herself how Eric was forever sharpening it and complaining about the poor steel in it.

Eric was back within an hour. She heard his step on the path and quickly reached for the tinsnips. He came in, nodding approval at her work and tossed the furs on the bench. "Kate, I ran into a guy on the road. He wanted someone to help buzz up some wood, a day's work, maybe. He wanted to pay me in lumber, and I thought about that outhouse we have to build. When I asked about feed for the cow, he said he could pay me in greenfeed bundles instead. I guess the little house will have to wait."

Kate thought how something always had to wait. This time the milk was more important.

In late March, Kate's folks drove out again. Although only a sixty mile trip, it had to be planned carefully between too much snow and too much mud. They suggested Kate go back with them for a week, and Eric urged her to go, saying it would do her good.

Kate packed a box of mending to be done on her mother's machine. The suitcase held both Kate's and Robby's clothes since he only wore diapers at night now. Before fastening the strap, she opened the suitcase again and slipped in her diary.

Eric went to the river with them and carried Robby across the logs. The February thaw had left the river open below the bridge, a deep pool of swirling water. Animal tracks in the last fall of snow were melted and frozen in a line along the bank. A coyote. Eric had told Kate how to distinguish them. A dog's tracks were staggered, but a coyote stepped in a straight line. This wilderness knowledge had become so much a part of her life, a kinship. She always took part of the feeling with her when she went away from it, just as she brought remnants of her former life back with her to her homestead. It was a blending of two separate ways of life.

As they approached the farm gate, the rows of spruce trees Kate had helped plant as a girl seemed to stand guard around her childhood home, closing in its security, its warmth, just as the pines sheltered the cabin in the woods. She glanced around, beyond the protective trees. Out there was another world, uncertain and vaguely hostile.

Only when she was stretched across her old bed upstairs, did she relax completely, breathing in the trunk smell of stored bedding and the clean odor of freshly washed, sun-dried pillow cases.

Everything at the farmhouse was the same except for the radio. Kate's parents had sold the old open-faced machine with its morning glory speaker and had bought a new one with a power pack battery.

"Yes, it is a nice one," said Kate's mother, "but the Department of Transport is making us pay two dollars and fifty cents for a radio licence! They're calling us private receiving stations. Anything to raise a dollar. I expect there's a few radios in attics they don't know about." She laughed. "Your dad didn't complain too much, though. He'd have a fit if he had to miss his Saturday night hockey games."

Kate smiled at the memory—*Now back to the gondola and Foster Hewitt.*

The radio brought Kate into first hand contact with the world. At the cabin she had only second- and third-hand news from the Hanovers or the Durhams, and much of its impact had been lost in her daily routine of getting by. Since German's pacts with Italy and Japan, the murmuring threat of war had now become a reality.

She listened as the world heard a king abdicate the British throne: *I have found it impossible to carry on the heavy duties and responsibilities and to discharge my duties as King as I would wish to do without the support of the woman I love.*

Kate suppressed a giggle. Only two nights ago Eric had said practically the same thing to her in his own halting, endearing way, and she had felt like a real queen.

The broadcast continued. On the side of domestic progress the Automobile Workers of America had been granted a five cent an hour wage increase, and Wallace Carothers was seeking a patent for nylon. The newscaster's voice droned on—*The natural gas explosion that wrecked the Consolidated Public School in New London has taken the lives of 294.* Kate was glad her child would get his education at the kitchen table in his own home.

She listened to the Prairie Bible Broadcast with Premier William Aberhart, that evangelistic economist: *You can't talk religion to a man who has had nothing to eat for three days.* His platform had been *Eliminate Poverty.* He proposed to do it with a basic dividend, giving every adult twenty-five dollars a month in the form of non-negotiable certificates. Kate wasn't sure she understood how it all worked. Her brush with economics on the larger scale was slight. You either had money in your hand or you didn't.

On the lighter side, the air waves were busy with "Gang Busters" and "Major Bowes Amateur Hour." There was more news of the Stork Derby, in which some bachelor lawyer was going to give $25,000 to the woman who had the most babies in the next ten years. Kate looked at Robby growing out of his clothes. God! Who would want that many babies!

Lila Wilson brought out a big cardboard box and put it down in front of Kate with an encouraging nod.

"Here's some things Aunt Clara sent over for you, some of your cousin Marcie's things. You know how that girl is about clothes. Spends every last dime she makes on them! You can take it upstairs and look through it. There may be some things you'll want to make over on the machine while you're here."

The box was heavy. Kate carried it up the steep stairs, put it down on the rug in front of the bed and opened it up. She was grateful, of course, but wished the dark haired Marcie didn't wear so much pink. The rose wool cardigan on the top clashed with Kate's hair. There was another sweater she could make over for Robby and a pair of brown and white saddle oxfords for her, a little big but almost new. There were some cotton gloves and three pairs of silk stockings with only short runs.

She hummed a few bars of "Alice Blue Gown" as she lifted out a faded, flowered, blue voile dress with a circular skirt. In the bottom of the box were two pairs of men's fleece lined underwear, only a little thin in the knees. Aunt Clara had pinned on a note. *Maybe you can make something for the boy from these.* Kate answered the message aloud, laughing. "Thank you, Aunt Clara, but I think Eric will wear them a season or two first." She suspected Aunt Clara knew that already. She repacked the box and picked up her diary.

I think about Eric out there alone on the homestead, but knowing I won't be staying long, I can enjoy my stay. Aunt Clara's box will be a big help. I wonder if I will ever have clothes that someone else has not worn first. From the quality and style of Cousin Marcie's clothes everyone knows I could never afford new ones like that. Maybe next winter, when Robby is bigger, I can hunt a few squirrels and have some money for myself. I don't want expensive things, just something of my own. I hear Mom calling me downstairs for coffee and cake. Kate Morgan, be thankful for what you have!

On the last day of Kate's visit, Sylvan Lake caught the edge of a southern chinook, shrinking the snow banks and filling the ditches with water. The morning news reported a half-load road ban for trucks on the main highway. Jim Wilson turned to Kate.

"I'm kind of worried about taking you home. The frost will be going out of some of those side roads, and my car doesn't have much clearance. A good freeze would help. You're welcome to stay longer, you know."

She smiled up at his worried face. "I know, Dad."

Kate went upstairs and sorted through the clothes box again. She laid aside a navy skirt and blouse, and she stuffed paper in the toes of the shoes until they stopped sliding on her heels. Now she would be dressed up enough to go down town and see her friend Eileen Rathdorf. Eileen had gone to Normal at Camrose and was teaching this year in Sylvan Lake's new school. As she mended a pair of the silk stockings, she wondered why all the snagged runs were above the knees. Cousin Marcie had always been a little on the wild side.

Kate walked down town and along the board sidewalk toward the white and brown house on the east crescent. A late-model black car drove up and stopped in front and Eileen Rathdorf got out. She looked at Kate, hesitated, and then came toward her, holding out her hands in welcome.

"Kate Wilson!"

"Hello, Eileen."

"It's Kate Morgan now, I guess." Eileen looked at her closely. "I'm just back from shopping. Come in."

She led the way through the heavy front door and down the hall to the kitchen. The pale yellow walls intensified the sunshine through a window over a white enamel sink. Little shelves on either side held plants and ornaments. In the corner away from the stove was a breakfast nook like a booth in a cafe. One whole wall was cupboards. Through a large glass door, Kate saw a gleaming china service in Willow design. Kate wondered if it was original or one of those good imitations.

Eileen was bending down, putting the contents of her hand-woven shopping bag onto a lower shelf already half full of cans. Linoleum in gray and yellow squares covered the floor and ran down the hall. Kate followed Eileen back into the living room. This must have been the way Dorothy felt when she followed the yellow brick road, thought Kate.

Eileen, chattering happily, showed Kate through the house. She and Jack were buying it, she said. It had two bedrooms and a sun porch. In the living room, a pale green rug almost covered the polished hardwood floor. Eileen's high heels clicked around the edge of it as she served tea.

In grade one, Eileen and Kate had shared a double desk and a gray-green blob of plasticine. In grade three, they shared whispered secrets. In high school, Jack had taken turns dating them. Kate liked Eileen and hated herself for being envious. Imagine having both a hardwood floor and a rug!

Jack came home from his insurance office while they were having their tea. He had grown stout with a hint of double chin, and he had given up the fashionable pompadour for a low part on the left side of his thinning hair. His smile was still engaging. He settled into an over-stuffed chair and asked with seeming interest, "Just what are the requirements for filing on a homestead!"

Kate laughed. "Canadian citizen, ten dollars and a sense of humour."

She gave her answer lightly, but it was prompted by envy. She'd have given a day of her life for any one of Eileen's conveniences. The phone in the hall rang, and after a short conversation, Jack excused himself, said good-bye to Kate and went out. Kate and Eileen continued their reminiscences.

"Remember the time we decided to play hookey?" said Kate. "We got cold feet and came back."

Eileen bobbed her dark head. "Yes, I do remember." She laughed. "I still feel like playing hookey sometimes, don't you?"

Kate wondered if Eileen really meant it, if she was dissatisfied with her seemingly perfect life. Kate was still thinking about Eileen's words and her own moments of rebellion as she prepared to leave.

"Come and see me again, Kate, whenever you come to Sylvan Lake."

"I will. It's so good seeing you again."

By the time Kate returned to the farm, her feet ached from Marcie's ill-fitting shoes. She wanted to go back to her own cabin and Eric, so close in miles, yet so far removed from Eileen's life in town or even the comforts here at her parent's farm.

When she entered the kitchen, her mother was sitting on a low stool, hand-carding raw wool for a quilt. She made a few more jabbing swipes at the matted wool, then took two reversing, releasing strokes and held up the finished batt, waving it at Kate as she spoke.

"I've been thinking. The roads may only get worse from now on, so why couldn't we travel at night on the frost? The truckers do, even on the banned roads, sometimes."

"Sure we could, but you'd be awfully late getting back."

"I know, but it would be better than risking some of those mud holes!"

Kate took Robby upstairs, put him down on the bed and jiggled the coil springs until he lay quiet. She lay on her back beside him and looked up at the familiar ceiling. It was thin, pressed metal her father had salvaged when he helped tear down an old grain elevator. Each piece had designs of interlocking squares and circles. When she looked at it one way, it was only squares and circles, then suddenly, it would change into four-petaled flowers, then back to its geometric design.

She had looked at these changing patterns through her childhood. They had been there above her bed all through measles and scarlet fever and even the smallpox outbreak of '28. Her life was like that changing design, a constant pattern of making do, with a sudden flash now and then of success or beauty.

They left the next night after chores, and it was ten o'clock when they reached the river.

Jim Wilson gave two long blasts of the car horn, repeating them every few seconds. They waited. Before long they saw a faint light bobbing across the flat. Eric appeared out of the darkness into the car lights shining on the log bridge. He put down the lantern and walked across to the other side of the river. He talked a few minutes with his in-laws before he lifted the drowsy Robby from the car and carried him back across the bridge. Kate followed and held Robby while Eric went back for Kate's boxes. They stood and watched the car swing away and heard the horn in farewell.

Eric took Robby in one arm and put the other around Kate as they waited for their eyes to adjust from car lights to the feeble glow of the lantern.

"It's good to have you home, Kate."

She laid her head against his chest and closed her eyes. She could smell the wood smoke on his jacket.

That evening, Kate and Eric had talked and grew silent with the pleasure of being together again. Kate made a pot of tea and took down her diary.

It's so good to be home. Here in the cabin with Robby asleep in his crib and Eric playing his banjo, town life, even the farm, seems so far away, and that other world of radio almost unreal. I've had enough of town luxuries for awhile. There are other luxuries.

9

Kate sat at the table looking at an old copy of *Life Magazine*. She knew the pictures by heart. Above the rustle of turning pages, the monotonous tick of the alarm clock, and the constant squeaking of the stove pipe nudged by the spring breeze, she heard a soft swishing sound behind the curtain in the corner. It was the coat hangers again.

She had brought with her only six good hangers as part of her dowry. Then one day Eric had made a great find—a tangle of discarded telephone wire in the brush along the main road. He had brought it home, cut it into five foot lengths and shaped them into hangers. When tired of its burden, the soft No. 9 wire drooped its shoulders and dumped the clothes on the floor. Somehow it was the last straw.

> *The squirrel season is over now that March is here. Will all winters be this long and lonely? Unless Eric gets some work away from home, it looks like hungry months ahead. Robby's cold hangs on despite everything I do. I sure would like someone to talk to, something besides Robby's constant "What's that?" and "Why?" I miss Granny more than I thought I would. We did have some good talks. I liked to hear about her younger days in Iowa. I guess some of my resentment and rebellious thoughts were just an attempt to convince myself I could run my own life. I don't seem to have done very well. I hate being cooped up in the cabin.*

She put aside her diary, picked up the clothes and laid them across the bed. She went out to the wood pile where Eric was shaping an axe handle from a piece of birch.

"Could you do that in the house and watch Robby for a few hours? I want to walk to the Post Office for the mail."

"That's a six mile walk there and back. You'd probably only get a catalogue, anyway."

"I don't care, I just want to get out of the house! I can't stand being cooped up much longer! I'd walk to China the way I feel now."

Eric laughed. "I didn't think. You go ahead."

Robby cried and clung to her as she put on her coat and rubber boots. Eric took him and gave him a curly wood shaving to play with. He threw it on the floor and screamed louder than ever. Kate hesitated, guilty and furious at the same time.

"Go on. He'll be all right as soon as you're out of his sight."

She went out the door with her guilt still nagging, and felt resentful again when his crying turned to laughter before she reached the path to the spring.

Once away from the cabin she relaxed and took in all the bright March day had to offer. A moose had crossed the trail and continued on up the river. Partridge tracks ended abruptly with wing marks in the snow where some raptor had scooped up its prey and made off with it. There were signs of rabbits and burrowing shrews. The world was full of living things, unseen and silent.

She ran for a short way on the main road, sending her blood racing. Filled with the beauty of the outdoors, she felt renewed determination to get the patent on the land and feel secure. She panted open-mouthed, until the cold air started her hollow tooth throbbing with every heart beat.

At the Post Office there was a letter from Eric's brother, Miles. It was addressed to both of them, so she read it as she walked back along the main road. She hurried to bring Eric the news, excitement sending her thoughts racing.

When she reached the cabin, she gave the letter to Eric, then told him everything that was in it before he had a chance to read it, looking eagerly over his shoulder.

74

"They're coming out. Miles and Leah are coming out! They're going to settle here, rent a place."

"Good! Maybe we can borrow a horse and work up a garden spot." Eric was enthusiastic, but borrowing horses was not the only thing on Kate's mind. She wanted a garden, too, but most of all she wanted someone to talk to, woman talk.

Kate was sifting wood ashes into a can to scour her blackened pots and to polish her Rogers silverware. During her long engagement she had been able to collect a setting for six with the Poker Hands given out in Imperial tobacco. Her pots and pans were Nabob, and her dishes, premiums from Cobb's General Store. Kate's dowry was a series of advertisements.

She put the tobacco can and the screen away when the dog barked. She saw the two riders coming across the flat, only their heads bobbing above the willows. It seemed an eternity before they were close enough to recognize. It was Miles and Leah. Eric's sister-in-law rode with an easy grace Kate envied. Kate had only ridden a work horse in from the field a few times, sitting atop the harnessed horse and hanging tightly to the brass balls on the hames.

The women exchanged waves, and Eric, who had been sharpening the axe, leaned back on his heels and rolled a smoke. How could he be so calm! They were having company, real company! Kate ducked into the house, pulled off her ragged blouse and exchanged it for the patched one with the pink flowers.

Robby ignored his kin. "Horse! Horse!"

His elation was complete when Eric handed him up and Miles let him ride in front of him in the saddle and hold the dangling ends of the reins. Eric walked alongside, head upturned, in deep conversation with his brother as he led Leah's horse to the barn. Kate watched them with some concern.

"They can't put the horses in the barn. The roof is too low. We built it for the cow and chickens."

"They'll tie them outside. Miles brought a few oats in his saddlebag."

The women went into the cabin. Kate's delight at seeing Leah checked her speech, hoarding conversation so long denied. Leah talked easily.

"The place we've rented is ten miles up the road on the other side, but I'll ride down once we get settled in."

At last, as Kate prepared the noon meal, the words came tumbling out.

"You asked about neighbours? There's only one family over here, the Durhams a mile east. They have a boy about ten. We don't see much of them. Sometimes they cross the ford out here. I talked to Martha Durham one day out at the river. Her mother stays with them. I don't think the old lady is very well. Martha said she is very confused at times. Maybe when we get a horse I can get out more. I guess I'll have to teach Robby. The nearest school is fifteen miles away across the river. Martha Durham teaches her boy, Chuck.

"Just knowing you are there will help. I think this fish is ready, Eric. You can slide the bench over closer to the table. I'll use the apple box." Kate began to wonder if she was talking too much.

An hour later, they lingered over stewed prunes and coffee.

"The folks are planning to come out here, too," Miles said. "Pa's dickering for a place right across the river from you, an abandoned homestead with a few buildings on it."

Eric nodded. "That's great! With their team and wagon and plough, they can make it. I'd rather starve out here than back there. At least there's lots of wood to burn."

"There was nothing wrong with that feed of fish, either."

They sat and talked a while longer before Miles and Leah left. Kate watched them ride across the flat, Leah's red scarf fluttering over her shoulder.

Leah here at last. And Pa and Granny coming, too. I really will be glad to see them. I don't want to quarrel, but I have learned to speak my mind a bit more, so Pa and I should get on better now. And I won't have to get by next winter on old magazines. Reading is good, but real talk with real people is better.

As spring approached, Eric hunted spruce grouse—fool hens, as they sat stupidly in the trees overhead. They had been feeding on pine needles and tasted like it. The ruffed grouse had become targets when they sat on a log and drummed out their invitation to the hens, and the dog feasted on rabbits Eric shot.

When the cow calved in May, they were elated to find the calf was a heifer. They groomed and petted it, planning their future herd. They had no fences, so Eric put a halter, a long rope and a drag pole on the cow. Sometimes in the night when they heard her bell in one place too long, they went out with the lantern to untangle her rope. She grazed at night and stood most of the daylight hours in the smoke from a smudge fire to ward off the mosquitoes hovering in a gray cloud above her.

For themselves, they smudged out the cabin each evening with a pail of smoldering chips through the house.

Eric carried the pail and Kate herded. "Take a cloth and wave them out of the corners. Then we can shut the door and kill off the rest."

Kate flapped a towel into the dark corners. "I think they hide until the smoke clears. Can't you just see the little devils with their heads in the moss holding their breath?" She attacked like a bullfighter with the towel.

Eric coughed. "This place is going to smell like a smoke house."

"I don't care," said Kate testily. "We've got to get some sleep. We're both getting cranky, and Robby may get sick from those bites."

"If the smoke don't get him first." Eric coughed again.

Kate watched uneasily as the river rose, the undertow sucking greedily at the floating debris. In early May it rose with the local run-off, then went down a little. But when the snow began to melt in the distant mountains, the river rose higher than ever. The Hanover boys had said this happened every spring. They said the real high water never came until June.

It was the sixteenth of June when Eric came in with the news. "The foot bridge is gone. Washed out. Come out and have a look." He picked up Robby and started back down the trail. Kate could hear the grind of driftwood being forced into jam piles, the thump of rocks being moved deep in the river bed. She wasn't sure she wanted to witness the power of that monster which had cut her off from her family, from the Hanovers, from the whole world, it seemed.

"Where was the bridge?" She saw only a wide crest of churning gray water carrying driftwood and a few trees, some with green leaves still on the branches. Eric motioned with a nod of his head. "Across there. The current took out the point of that bank."

"How will we ever build another bridge across that?"

"We can't. Have to wait until the water goes down."

They stood on the bank and watched trees being undermined. Down here in the valley, the water level was always high and even the bigger trees had shallow roots. The swirling current tore at the opposite bank until the tallest spruce leaned down to touch the surface, then was torn out of the earth, swept downstream, around the bend and out of sight.

Eric shook his dark head. "All that good timber wasted. There was enough in that last tree to make one round on a chicken house."

Kate thought only of their isolation. Maybe they had been foolish to choose this side of the river, away from the main road and the rest of the community. She knew, however, they could never have worked land without horses, and there was timber on the place. The Durhams had chosen to live over here. As she thought of them, she decided to go up and see them soon. She needed reassurance.

Robby, playing in the sand beside Eric, pointed up the

river. "Cow! Look, big cow!"

"That's a deer, darling."

The current caught it and rolled it over. Stiff legs stuck out from a bloated body. It tumbled on and lodged in a jam pile, was drawn under and appeared again downstream.

"Let's go back, Eric," said Kate.

They walked slowly toward the house. No wonder there was so much land available over here. The river guarded it jealously.

At the spring they stopped short. The water was gray with silt. The river had overflowed somewhere upstream and was running into the spring. They followed the stream toward the house, but the dirty water had nosed its way through the clear spring as far as the cabin.

Eric picked up a pail. "We can always use the creek water and let it settle. It's only silt."

"After that dead deer? Heaven knows what else died in there!" Kate looked back toward the river, her brown eyes again close to tears.

"There's a small spring up in the timber," Eric consoled. "The river won't reach that. Let's go up and see." He took her hand and they made their way through the undergrowth. Deep in the moss, the spring bubbled up. Eric dipped the pail carefully to avoid the bouncing funnel of sand.

"Oh look, Eric. Look at these." Kate was on her knees, her fingers cupped under two wild orchids, delicate mauve and white ones. "They're like little old ladies all dressed up for church!" Eric smiled and touched her hair.

She picked one of the flowers to take home, to brighten the kitchen table and make herself forget about the rising river.

The next morning, Eric started building a cooler box to put in the spring. Kate left Robby with him and walked up the long hill to see Martha Durham. She lingered on the path where clematis wound its way into the alders. She held the vine to her nose, but the four-sepaled, blue flower had no scent, only the freshness of spring.

The path led into a clearing. On one side was the low, sprawling, log house, a wisp of smoke beckoning. The yard had a slab fence, high enough to keep out the three goats standing on a sawdust pile, heads cocked in curious interest. The gate's hinge complained as she opened it, and Martha Durham came to the door, a short woman with dark hair piled in a knot on top of her head. She moved quickly to hold open the squeaking screen door.

"Mrs. Morgan. Come in. I thought it might be Jess. He and Chuck went off to get fence posts. Come in."

The main room was large, kitchen and living room combined. On the far wall, a bookcase held dozens of books. Kate took an involuntary step toward it, then stopped, aware of her action. Martha noticed, and her pinched face brightened.

"You like to read? I do when I get time. Books are all that kept me going those first few years before Chuck came along and then Mother. I was so homesick and lonely."

Kate liked her right away.

They turned toward the kitchen where Martha's mother sat nodding in her chair. She wore a large print apron with bits of paper and string showing from her pockets. An empty cup sat on a box beside her. Martha motioned Kate away to the far end of the room. She took down a rose patterned tea pot from a high shelf on the wall and made tea for them. Martha seemed grateful for the company, and they passed an hour in talk.

Kate saw the texts and workbooks on a low table in the corner. "How do you manage teaching Chuck?"

"He's taking correspondence, grade four this year. He's bright enough and could do better, but there are so many interruptions. He helps his dad a lot. It's hard for me to organize his work." Martha looked out of the window and frowned, hesitated, then said, "I don't think Jess realizes how important schooling is for a child these days. Jess only had grade seven. We're doing all right here now, but it won't be enough for the boy when he leaves home. And he will some day," she added. "This won't be enough for him always."

Kate had already begun to worry about teaching Robby. Martha's words made her uneasy again. Eric, too, had been raised on a farm and had only grade school. He had often said high school was a waste of time. Eric, with his manual skills and common sense, would always get by. But Robby was growing up in a different society.

They talked a while longer, and when Kate had said good-bye, she started slowly back down the hill. The Durhams had stock, cows and horses, pasture and hay to keep them through the winter. Still, Kate knew the women were as trapped by circumstance as she was, Martha obligated to care for her mother, and the old lady, house-bound and living in the past. Kate ran the last way down the hill to free herself from the rebellion rising in her. Not me, she decided, suddenly. Yes, I like her, but not me!

As she reached the cabin, she found Eric still working at the spring. Robby came running to her with a jangling noise. Eric had tied a sheep bell between the boy's shoulders where he couldn't reach it. Eric looked up.

"How do you keep track of him and get anything done?"

Damn the mosquitoes! Damn the river! Will every summer be like this? I don't think I can stand much more of it. If Leah hadn't come I'd take Robby and go back home. No. No, I wouldn't. I would never leave Eric, and he's having a hard time of it, too. He's so determined to see through and is so patient with me. Maybe next summer we can get some screens for the windows, and there are always more trees to drop across the river when the water goes down—if it ever does....I visited Martha Durham today. We have a lot in common. She made me see that my lot is not as bad as I see it sometimes. They have stock, are better off in that way, but Martha is more isolated than I am. I must go up to see her again soon.

While the river flood wore itself away, Eric and Kate cut and burned brush on the flat between the shore and the cabin. There was too much timber on the place to prove up with breaking and cropping the land, and the quarter would never support the seventeen head of stock if they chose that option, so they aimed at the alternative, a combination of ten acres broken, eight acres in crop, and ten head of stock for which the land had to be fenced. They worked in the cool mornings and the evenings, sometimes long after dark, lacing Robby to the toboggan and leaning it up against a tree where he could watch the fire until he fell asleep.

The first year was slipping by. They had four more years to get the patent, but they had only one cow and a calf and a small patch cleared. With short periods of work and rest they were able to keep going on a diet of bread and milk and fish. Their bodies were lean from long hours of work. Robby's eyes always seemed too big for his small face. When Kate cut his hair short it seemed to fill out his cheeks. She knew he hadn't changed, but he looked better and it made her feel better.

Kate stopped cutting brush and put her hands on her aching hips. Would they ever make it, she wondered?

Eric looked up at the sun. "About dinner time isn't it?"

Kate didn't answer.

"What's wrong?"

"There isn't anything in the house but a little bread and no baking powder to make bannock. I can't cook beans and be out here, too. They burned last time, remember?"

They walked in silence to the creek that bordered the flat. The water ran slowly in a wide bed crossed with sunken logs. Eric had caught a Loch Levin trout in the river and put it in the pool, where after a time the usually wary species became accustomed to them walking by. They called the fish Angus. It lay there on the shady side of a log, its fins barely moving in the water. Eric stopped, smiled and licked his lips.

"Not him," she said. "No. I'd rather eat Boots."

"I hear in China they do eat dogs. O.K. I'd never catch a fish in that river now. I'll go down to the little creek. The fish are small, but I can get us a feed if we can hold off a couple hours."

They walked on. At the house Kate asked, "Do you want me to dig some ant eggs for bait?"

"No. I'll make some."

She watched as he rolled bits of stiff flour and water dough into round balls, wrapped them in a piece of paper and put them in his pocket. "They won't know the difference until they grab the hook. By then it'll be too late. Where's your fish pole? I left mine at the river."

"Leaning up behind the house."

He tied the green cotton line to the saskatoon pole and went whistling off on the two mile walk to catch their dinner. Kate was sure he would bring home enough fish for one meal, anyway. If there were a few extra she would make fish patties for supper. There was an egg left over for that. They always had ground wheat porridge for breakfast. But tomorrow was another day. Some of her depression lifted as she gathered chips and started the fire. The faint gnawing on her insides was only hunger now.

Eric returned with enough brook trout for several meals. Kate divided the bread and Eric searched for the tiny bones on Robby's plate. Kate thought of the five thousand by the sea of Galilee who were fed on bread and fishes.

10

It was March of 1938, a year and a half of living day to day. That first winter, when squirrel hunting had been their only income, there was never enough money to pay the debt for the cow, so Eric poached beaver on a backwater. They had no other buildings except the little barn, so they skinned the beaver in the house. The floor boards absorbed the grease and smell. They stretched the hides on frames and shoved them under the bed. Company was rare, but even so, Kate always kept a pot of coffee handy to boil up in a hurry to mask the distinctive beaver smell. It was a battle of odors.

To signal Eric, if someone came while he was tending traps, Kate hung the cloth milk strainer on a line by the door. She never thought of the rich beaver fur in terms of a coat, only that old Clarabelle would soon be paid for. Other women in other places would wear the coats.

It was early April when Eric's parents came. They settled on a place across the river from the homestead, less than a mile north of the main road. Eric was helping Kate cut up some fresh deer meat when they heard a wagon crossing the river, the breaking of shore ice, the sound of churning water, more ice, then silence. In a few minutes the wagon emerged from the timber trail. Granny waved, and Kate came out of her mental forest to greet her and Pa with delight. Established now in her own home, resentments of the past were forgotten. Like most of the people in this west country, they lived for the future, however uncertain.

Pa had brought a bag of his favorite blue potatoes. "I'll plant a few this spring," he said. "There's a big garden spot by our house, gone back to sod, but I can break it up with the walking plough. Your cabin looks pretty good, Eric." He walked around inspecting the notched corners and pointed up to the door frame. "You should have put in a piece of wood along the top so you could take it out when the logs settle. There's a joint opening up already under the eave."

"Yeah, I know," Eric admitted. "I never thought at the time. We were in such a hurry to get into it before it snowed again. A tent gets pretty damn cold in October."

"It's cosy in here now," Granny remarked, taking Robby on her knee. "My, he's growing so fast."

Robby, now two, sat on his grandmother's lap and reached up to touch her white hair as if recalling a far off memory.

Pa and Granny stayed most of the afternoon. Eric gave them a big piece of venison and rode out to the river with them when they left.

By May the last of the beaver money was gone, so they sold the new calf for four dollars, Kate thickened up the potato soup and watered down the coffee. Sitting by the window, she watched one of the hens busy in the pine needles. A kindred spirit—scratching for food. A sudden flash of slate-blue wings, and the hen was snatched from the ground and carried off, squawking. Kate ran outside, shouting, but the hawk had risen above the trees and was gone. Tears of rage and helplessness seared her eyes. They could have eaten that hen.

She beat her fist on the log wall and swore aloud. She hated the way people equated temper to red hair. It just wasn't so. Any raven-haired woman would have done the same. She looked around for a possible audience to her display. Finding only a red squirrel bobbing and scolding in reprimand—or sympathy—she laughed, her sudden anger slipping away.

After that, Kate tried to watch the chickens, but one by one they disappeared, until there was only the rooster and one hen left. Eric killed the rooster and they ate him. The hen quit laying, so they ate her, too. Kate watched Robby's face as he dipped bread into the rich soup. She smiled as she recalled her father's favorite saying when times were tough. *To hell with poverty. Kill the hen!* Sometimes the truth was like a new shoe—to stretch it kept it from hurting.

Eric had brought the mail and was sitting at the table checking the fur prices at the final spring sale in Edmonton.

Kate opened her mother's letter carefully so as not to drop the stamp Lila always enclosed to assure a reply. She thought of the times that this 2¢ stamp had been their only cash asset. The letter was short.

Dear Kate and Eric,
There isn't much news. We are over our colds and busy with the garden and chores. Sarah had twin lambs yesterday. I've saved some raw wool for you. Dad wants to write a note to Eric. Love, Mom

Hello Eric, my neighbour wants a garage built. I told him about you and he said he'd pay 30¢ an hour. His money is good. You won't have to wait for it. If you come, bring Kate and the boy. You can all stay here.

Dad

Kate passed the letter to Eric and watched his face as he silently considered the offer. She hoped they would go, and not just for the money. She wanted to get away from the small cabin and the constant torment of mosquitoes.

"I should go," Eric said at last. "If I can get Tim to drive me out there, you and Robby can come, too. I'd have to give Tim most of what we've got for gas."

"What about the cow? She's milking good now."

"I'll take her up to Pa's, her and Boots."

Sylvan Lake was at its height of summer activity. The beach and dance halls were crowded, and preparations for the Wrigley Swim were underway. Kate had never cared much for the water. She never progressed beyond a splashing dog paddle, partly from lack of time to do much swimming, but mostly because her bathing suits were all hand-me-downs and several years behind the times. When black wool suits were in, she was still wearing navy cotton with red binding. By the time she had a wool one, the rage was thin rubber suits that fit any figure and snagged, leaving the wearer embarrassed after a trip down the slide. She spent only one afternoon of their visit at the beach with Robby.

Jim Wilson looked up from his newspaper. "I see Arv Solenen is having a farm sale. You two want to go, Lila? I think I'll run out and see what they have."

"No. You take Kate if she wants. I'll keep Robby. But don't go buying a lot of junk. We've got enough around here already."

"Now Lila, you know those grab boxes always have something we can use. There was a good pair of pliers in that last one I got for ten cents. Want to come, Kate?"

"Sure."

The sale was posted for ten o'clock. By nine-thirty people were arriving, whole families in cars and wagons and Bennett buggies. They walked around inspecting items, men checking machinery, women leaning over with outstretched arms, bouncing the mattresses of beds to test the spring. Children ran, looking back over their shoulders at pursuers, tripping to sprawl in the yard dust. Mothers scolded and farm dogs fought, walking stiff-legged in defiance until the fray was broken up.

Kate had always enjoyed farm auctions where neighbours hailed each other and met to talk. She wandered around looking at things and listening to partial conversations.

"—and he's selling her good dishes."

"He's going to move back east after the sale. It costs to ship. Maybe it's best he don't see her things every day."

"I guess Gerda would understand. She suffered so."

Kate walked on past the household goods, past the man with his hands in his pockets and grief in his eyes, as he watched his team of matched Percherons inspected and sold. Noon lunch was served in paper bags, a bologna sandwich and store-bought cookies. The coffee was hot and strong. Kate went back for a second cup and found her father talking

87

to a man about calves. He had bought a box of assorted nails and hinges—and his prize of the day was a farrier's knife. Jim Wilson beamed.

"All for two bits."

Before the auction ended he made another purchase, a dust-laden Edison phonograph and a box of cylinder records. "I wanted to buy it for you, Kate. I wasn't sure I could. I bid a dollar and a half, then everybody dropped out. It works good. I tried it. Wait until you hear some of those old records."

"Thanks, Dad. I sure miss the music. Most evenings Eric is too tired to play his banjo."

Robby was delighted with "Uncle Josh Buys an Automobile" and "The Preacher and the Bear." A military band played "Over the Waves" and when Van Epps, the banjo king of his day, performed "Alexander's Ragtime Band" Kate saw Eric's fingers forming chords on imaginary strings as he listened. There were sad songs—"The Vacant Chair" and "Tell Mother I'll Be There"—and a slightly naughty one called "O Helen." All the singers rolled their r's; it seemed the high class way to speak, Kate decided.

After they heard "I'll Take You Home Again, Kathleen" and "Let The Rest Of The World Go By," Eric sat a moment, his foot still keeping time to the rhythm in his head. Then he went to gather his tools, for his job building the garage was finished. Kate's father offered to drive them home on Sunday.

When Robby was asleep, Kate and Eric sat on the bed and counted the bills as he smoothed them out across his knee. "Twelve dollars." He handed one of them to Kate. "You take this and get that tooth pulled. It's not going to get any better. Dr. Gilbert pulls teeth right in his office here in town."

Kate put her hand up to her bottom jaw. The throbbing had been faint but constant for many weeks.

"I'll go down in the morning. Dad said he could take us home Sunday, so I should be toothless by then."

Dr. Gilbert's office was in his house. He was in the back yard bending over a flower bed, snipping the dead seed pods off the pansies. His wife called him and he came lumbering, his rolled up sleeves and sandaled feet revealing the deep tan of a gardener. There were tufts of dark hair on his toes. He smiled, showing even white teeth. Kate wondered if they were real. He had picked a velvety, purple flower and handed it to his wife as he passed her.

"A tooth, eh? I suppose it's way at the back and only half there."

"It's a wisdom tooth and it has a hole in it. And it hurts."

There was a dentist's chair in the office. She sat down as the doctor indicated by a wave of his hand, while he, whistling softly, selected instruments from the painted cupboard. He put them in the sterilizer and picked up a syringe. Kate looked away. Next to a toothache, she hated needles.

Dr. Gilbert talked to her while he plunged the needle on both sides of the tooth and at the back of her mouth where there weren't any teeth. "The Clearwater River?" he said. "I hear there's good fishing out that way. I always meant to try it." He continued to talk of fishing, how the pike were biting in the lake off Third Point.

Kate answered in monosyllables as the hot prickly feeling crept along her lip. There was more one-sided conversation while the doctor probed and pulled until the tooth was out. He smiled at her. "There. That should feel better."

With her mouth full of cotton, she thanked him, handed him the dollar and walked out to find Eric waiting in front in her father's car.

"I thought you might not feel like walking home." He handed her a small, brown paper bag. "For being a good girl."

She opened the bag and smiled at him with compressed and bloodstained lips. It had been a long time since she'd had any jelly beans. It was almost worth having the tooth pulled.

"Where are we going?" Kate asked, as Eric turned the car east along the lakeshore road.

"Just thought we'd take the long way home." He drove slowly and stopped opposite a secluded, sandy beach, a familiar place where they had walked and dreamed five summers ago. Eric put his arm around her. She wiped the corners of her mouth and leaned against him, both silent with memories.

"Seems like only yesterday," he said, as he turned the key and the motor throbbed away the years. "We'd better go back."

Kate's father gave Eric some hinges and a can of assorted nails from his bargain boxes. Eric looked at Kate and grinned. "An outhouse!" With that her father rummaged in a box in the corner of his workshop and came up with a keyhole saw with the tip broken off.

"Here. It's a little rusty, but it'll work. You'll need it for those magic circles and the half-moon in the door."

Kate had a box of treasures, too. Hers contained a white flour sack for a pillow case and a printed cotton one for a good apron. There was a bracelet Lila had gotten with a soap box top from the Ma Perkins radio program, a brown Eaton's envelope with Sweet William seeds her mother had saved— and her jelly beans.

On their way home, they skirted a drying mud hole with its half buried brush and rocks. Kate thought how nature heals the earth's wounds. A scarred pry pole lay beside the road. It had lifted more than one high-centered car, with its wheels spinning helplessly in the deep mud. It was like the few dollars in Eric's pocket, vaulting them over their last involuntary fasting. She felt renewed hope as they approached the cabin. They still had a little over three years to get the title to the place.

Eric built the outhouse of logs stood on end and chinked with small poles. He split out shakes for the roof. It was the popular country style two-holer with a lower seat for Robby, who was three that summer. They made it extra big so they could store boxes and tools on one side.

Eric surveyed their work. "Well, it ain't brick, but it sure is sturdy."

I never get tired of fish, brook trout so fresh they curl

up in the hot pan—a good thing, I guess. I hated to sell the calf. We had counted on it to start our future herd. At least the cow is paid for at last. The job at Sylvan Lake came just in time. No more toothache, and the phonograph—Robby loves it. He is beginning to show some musical ability, singing along with the records. I can see Eric is pleased....I must take another picture of Robby. He's growing so fast. And at last an outhouse! So private, so closed in after all that fresh air. I was almost claustrophobic. I confess I left the door open the first few times....

While Eric went across the river to help Miles put up some hay, Kate had a young girl stay with her. Beth, who was from a large family, had gone out to work at an early age, most of the time for her board and a few second hand clothes. There Kate could help, for the trunk offered a few garments which needed little making over for Beth. The girl helped Kate put up a hem and Kate cut Beth's hair, sunbleached and splitting at the ends, enjoying the friendship and laughter.

They had been sitting by the window looking at the Eaton's catalogue. From there they could see Robby playing nearby, and watched as he began to cry and throw the sticks he had been piling up.

"Time for his nap," Kate said.

"I'll get him," Beth offered.

Beth brought him in and Kate sat down in the rocking chair. At three years, she still rocked him to sleep, as much for her own sake as for his, preserving the closeness the three of them needed to survive their isolation. His head was nodding when Beth called out.

"There's a bear! Look, right where Robby was playing!"

"Here, take him, Beth! I'll get the rifle."

The south window was hinged. She swung it open, aimed at the retreating animal, fired, and kept shooting until it climbed the hill and disappeared. The air was filled with the acrid smell of gun powder.

What would it have done if Robby had still been there? Kate's stomach knotted in fear as she tried to reason with herself. It had already been turning away at the sight of the cabin. Bears in the wild usually avoided human habitation, Eric had said. She went to the slop hole at the bottom of the bank and found the animal's tracks in the soft earth. She'd get Eric to dump ashes there. That might discourage it. Kate turned to Beth who had come up behind her, Robby in her arms.

"I know I hit him once, but these little 32.20 bullets wouldn't stop him. I'll bet he won't come back, though."

"I've heard bears will stuff moss in a wound and keep right on going," Beth said, wisely.

"He'd look kind of silly doing that," Kate laughed. "I hit him in the hind end as he went over the hill."

As they returned to the cabin, Kate strode along, the gun over her shoulder in mock military fashion. She'd won that skirmish. How did her grandmother cope with marauding animals around her prairie home? Kate wished they had told more stories, had written them down. The past was slowly slipping away. Her diary became more important to her. Someday Robby might want more than vague memories. With each generation the records would become more precious.

The haying was finished, and Miles brought Eric home, riding on the load of hay Eric had taken in exchange for his help. When Miles went back, Beth went with him. Kate had enjoyed Beth's company, but knew there would be little privacy for any of them in the one-room cabin. She knew, too, that Miles would be able to give the girl a small wage for helping with the chores. Kate gave Beth a sweater from the trunk and a hand crocheted hat that would be warm for her in the fall.

One August evening Kate watched Eric lift a piece of dirt out of the butter dish with his knife. He looked up. "We got to get another roof on here. I never know whether I'm eating something with legs on it or just plain dirt."

"What can you do? You can't make shakes for all of this."
She looked up at the pole and dirt roof.

"I could get some second slabs. We could put them down
first and cover the cracks with plain slabs."

They bought bark-edged boards and the Hanovers gave
them the slabs. After they had moved out what furniture they
could, Kate covered the rest before they began to tear off the
roof. As they removed the pole sheathing, there was no way to
stop the moss and clay from falling inside. They had it about
half done when Kate heard a car horn at the river. Her folks
had come! She surveyed the mess and looked up at Eric for
consolation.

He smiled. "Hope they brought a shovel."

While Eric went over to help them across the log, Kate fixed
up the fire they had built outside and hung a pail of coffee
over the flames. She washed Robby's face and waited.

They came at last with a big picnic lunch which they ate in
the shade of the lone spruce. Eric threw some green grass and
leaves on the fire for a smudge to drive off the mosquitoes.

While they sat catching up on news, Robby fell asleep with
his head in his grandmother's lap. They put him in his crib
under a tree and returned to work. Lila stood in the doorway
and looked at the clay and moss covering the floor and stove.
"I always knew you hated housework, Kate, but I never
thought I'd have to shovel out your kitchen."

Their laughter lightened their task as they dragged away the
loosened poles and cleaned up the floor while the men
nailed down the roof boards. By mid-afternoon they were
almost finished.

"I wish we could stay longer and help," Lila told Kate, "but
there's more chores now with haying coming up." And so
Kate watched as they left, waving across the river.

After her parents were gone and she was putting away the
left-over food, Kate nibbled on a piece of bologna. How good
it tasted! The square of cheese would flavour a big pot of
macaroni. She stuck her finger in the top of the catsup bottle
and licked it. She could eat sawdust if it had catsup on it.

It was dark before they had the roof finished and the beds, clothing and dishes brought back inside. The cabin looked bigger, now, with the lamplight on the boards overhead.

At first Kate enjoyed the freedom from the dirt sifting down until she discovered they had traded dirt for raindrops. After a week of hot sun on the green boards, some of the knots fell out. Eric made plugs for the holes and smeared them and the rest of the knots with spruce pitch from the blazed trees in the timber. When the cooler days came they kept the door shut more often, and she began to feel closed in.

"I wish we could have a window in the door."

"It's still kind of dark in here, but when the snow comes the reflected light will make it better. Remember last winter?"

"It isn't that," Kate said. "It's light enough. I'd like to be able to see out the front. It would help me keep track of Robby. He's outside most of the time, now."

"I'll see what I can do," Eric promised.

He came home with a big square of glass Fred Hanover had given him from a shed he was tearing down. "It's pretty big for the door, but maybe I can cut it down."

"No! You might break it. Let's put it in the other end of the house over the bed. Anyway, look what I found in the trunk."

She held up a tall narrow picture she had received at her bridal shower. It ws one of those popular frameless ones with only a strip of narrow black tape holding the picture to the glass. It depicted a scantily clad woman, who for some reason, was sitting behind some bullrushes, making dramatic gestures.

Eric looked at it. "Well, it is about the right size, but I hate to give up that picture."

"Don't worry. We can hang it up without the glass. I don't think she'll mind."

Kate removed the lady and tacked her up on the bumpy log wall, where, viewed from certain angles she looked quite pregnant. They called the little glass their picture window.

11

In mid-August a few chokecherries had ripened along the river and Kate made jelly. She held a jar of it up to the window and tipped it sideways. It hadn't set, but chokecherry jelly rarely did. They could dip their bread in it or eat it with a spoon. There was real, genuine beauty in the garnet glow of chokecherry jelly, a liquid jewellery, a ruby gift. She wiped the jars until they shone in the faint evening light and set them in a row on the table for Eric to see when he came in. He had taken the rifle and gone out to the flat. Sometimes the deer came at dusk to feed on the new growth in the clearing.

Before Kate washed the dishes, she wound up the gramaphone and put on a record for Robby. He never tired of listening to it. She put on his favorite, an instrumental number, a late nineteenth-century lullaby "Berceuse." He seemed more interested in the first part of it. After watching his face as she played it over and over, she discovered the exact moment of elation, a progression of organ chords which transported him far away from his cross-legged position on the floor to—she wondered where. How little she knew the workings of her child's mind!

Sometimes Eric played his banjo along with some of the selections, "Sweet Adeline" and "Claire de Lune," retuning his instrument each time to the pitch of the record. Although the phonograph had brought some of the outside world into the cabin, she still liked the winter evenings when Eric played alone, filling the room with marches and polkas, or when he hummed along to a tune they had danced to before they were married.

As the last song played to its end, with Kate dreamily

nodding, a shot boomed out from across the flat, and within minutes Eric came in, his eyes bright with success.

"Got a small buck. Can you come out with the lantern and help me? It won't take long. Put your coat on, Robby. There's a cool breeze on the river."

They walked to where the deer lay, and when they had it dressed out, Eric decided to take half of it up to his folks across the river. It was nearly midnight when he returned. Kate was still cutting meat to be canned, sawing bones for soup, preparing salt brine for meat to be smoked. She looked up. Eric seemed taller and darker in the lamplight.

He put his hand on her shoulder. "Leave the rest for tonight," he said. "I'll help you in the morning. I had to get that fresh meat up to Pa while it was still dark. The hunting season doesn't open for another month, yet."

They were up again before daylight to pack the sealers and start them cooking in the wash boiler, and put the big pieces in the crock of brine. When the salted meat was ready, they would hang it up in the teepee and smoke it with a fire of willow roots. Eric took the rest of the fresh meat to the earthenware crock in the spring box. It would keep a few days there and they could enjoy it.

They had meat again now, enough to do them until the whitefish began to school up in the river in September. They would take the fish with a long pole and gaff, or a "round hook" of brass wire, but until then it was deer. They were living off the land as generations of their ancestors had done.

Kate felt proud as she watched Eric cut a thick slice from the roast and slide it onto Robby's plate. She smiled up at him and waited her turn. Although she was not one to say grace as a ritual, she silently gave thanks when they sat down to a meal like this.

Kate walked out to where Eric was cutting fence rails. He put aside the saw and sat down on a moss covered log. Robby ran to him, and Eric took his son between his knees and ruffled the boy's sun-bleached hair. Kate picked a blue columbine growing spindly in the shade of the heavy spruce. She sat down beside Eric and turned the flower slowly on its stiff stem. She enjoyed these quiet moments of sharing, and so they just sat for a while, happy together.

Eric spoke first. "Yesterday when Tim and I went into town he was telling me about the new ranger up at the station. Said he was a real tough one and planned to clean up the poaching around here."

"He can't do anything to us. I canned all that fresh deer we had left."

"I was thinking about the Durhams over here. When we were in the store, their kid came riding in alone and bought some rock salt and a package of saltpeter. Looks like Jess might be wanting to cure up some fresh meat. Do you want to walk up there with me this afternoon? I'll just mention the new ranger."

"Sure. Martha doesn't get out much."

When they reached the neighbouring homestead, Jess Durham, a short man with bushy beard, was building an A-coop for the late hatch of chickens.

"Silly fool," he commented, indicating a buff coloured hen herding her brood through the grass. "She always steals away and hatches a second batch this late. They'll make good eating come Christmas. Go on in Mrs. Morgan. Martha'll be glad to see you."

Kate could smell the fresh bread before she entered the house. Martha Durham came to the door, wiping her hands on her apron.

"Mrs. Morgan. Come in."

Robby hung back. The old lady in the rocking chair by the stove beckoned with a gnarled finger.

"Come here little boy. I won't hurt you." Her thin laughter crackled across the room.

Martha turned to Kate. "Not one of her better days." She handed Robby a hot bun from the table and said, "Chuck's off fishing. Do you want to go outside and play in the yard?"

The women were having tea when the men came in. "Like I

was saying, Eric, I'd have to let my brother know right away. The job starts first of September."

A job? For Eric? Kate knew it would be some time before they could support themselves on their acres without going away to work. The job, if there was one, would be just in time. Kate wanted to hear more, but nothing more was said while the men finished their tea. Robby stood, glancing furtively at the old lady dozing in her chair. When Eric and Kate arose to go, Eric thanked Jess and said he'd let him know right away.

"And thank you, too. We all have to eat."

Kate could barely contain herself until they were out of hearing. "What job? What was Jess talking about?"

"His brother is quitting his job at Alexo and going back to the farm. Jess thought I might want to apply."

"Where's Alexo?" Kate frowned.

"A coal camp west of Rocky. Bull cook job."

"You can't cook!"

"That's just a fancy name for roustabout. It pays seventy-five dollars a month and lasts until May."

Kate's mind was racing. Eight months. That would be six hundred dollars! They could buy a horse, maybe two, and some chickens, maybe even buy another car. She couldn't wait for Eric's usual thoughtful decision. She had to know.

"It sounds too good to be true. What do you think?"

Eric nodded. "I'd better apply for it. We sure could use the money. Jess said to phone his brother. He'd know about it. I'll catch a ride into Caroline tomorrow and phone. There's lots of traffic on the road now."

He left early the next morning and wasn't home until almost dark. The dog barked and Robby ran to open the door. In the dusk Kate could see the smile on Eric's face. He came inside and put his arm around Kate.

"I got the job. It starts Monday. We haven't much time."

At supper they talked of the possibilities and the problems. It would mean leaving the place for almost a whole year. There was so much to be done. This was already Tuesday night.

$600! It looks like our big chance to make it. Eric is
excited, although he doesn't show it. I think he's afraid to
count on it until we're really there. It will be good for
Robby having other children to play with.

I hate to leave my home for eight months, and I'm kind
of scared, too, moving into another new community. I'll
just go with the same hope and trust that has sustained us
this far.

Kate began to sort and pack some of their things. They
didn't have many clothes, and some were too patched to
wear, even in a coal camp. She put the ones to be left at the
cabin in the trunk, safe from mice. From her jelly bean bag she
sorted out three of each colour, put them in a glass jar and hid
the jar on the top of the clothes closet for good luck until she
returned. She knew she was being silly, but she'd seen Eric
blow out a match and strike another to light a third cigarette
for Miles and Leah and himself.

She packed one small box for herself, her few trinkets, her
Bible and the little red *Collins Gem Dictionary.* She wondered
if people would pass on magazines and lend books there.

She considered her Moirs "Pot of Gold" chocolate box of
poems cut from the farm papers her mother saved for her. The
ones by Edna Jaques were her favorites, along with some by
Florence Janson and a few more sophisticated ones from *Red
Book,* although she never cut them from the books she passed
on, for Martha liked them, too. They had talked of it one rainy
day. Maybe some day Kate would write a poem about their
wilderness home, this new way of life. Maybe she would
portray the woods as Edna Jaques had captured the prairies.
She tied a string around the box and put it in the bigger one.

Eric was busy, too. He sold the cow to Hanovers to pay for
the truck to move them and to buy a box of grub to take along.
Granny had said she would keep Boots. Pa was to haul their
stuff across in the wagon, although the trucker had told Eric if
it rained he wouldn't go. There were too many hills and a lot
of bad road west of Rocky. Kate prayed it wouldn't rain.

She stayed up late, doing the last of the packing, and when she did go to bed, she couldn't sleep. She dozed off, awakened by the sound of rain on the board roof. She nudged Eric. "It's raining! If it rains we can't go. The job starts tomorrow!"

Eric sat up and listened. "Not raining much. That won't stop him. Go back to sleep."

She lay thinking until a finger of light through the newspaper blind pointed out a cobweb above the stove. They needed work so badly! She had already mentally spent the first month's wages. She slept then, taking comfort from the saying, *Rain before seven. Quit before eleven.*

12

The rain stopped before ten o'clock. By noon the sun came out briefly as Pa hauled their things across the river to meet the truck. As they waited, Kate looked back across the river to their land. The whitefish would soon be schooling in the deeper pools, and then the first snow and trapping, and deer for meat. If only they could support themselves without having to go away from all the good things. She heard the truck coming and turned her attention to the long trip ahead.

It was late afternoon when they reached Alexo and went down the row of houses to the one allotted to them. It was a small, old, log building with an even smaller frame addition for a bedroom. Even so, it was almost twice as big as the cabin on the homestead. The walls and ceiling were hung with heavy building paper sagging in places. The only furnishing was a white enamel stove with warped grates, and a table that leaned tiredly against the wall.

"Well, what do you think of it?" Eric pushed the paper up on the ceiling. "We can tack that up."

Kate was not looking at the sagging paper or the bare board floor. She was looking at those wonderful electric light bulbs hanging in the middle of each room. There were cupboards against the wall, crudely built, but still better than the ones she had at home. There was a pantry in the corner with lots of shelves. She pulled her cap down tighter over her red hair against the cobwebs.

"I'm glad we came," she said, "cobwebs and all."

They put up their beds and cooked their supper. Eric started work the next morning at five, milking the cow and delivering milk in three-pound lard pails. He came home at six for breakfast, and at twelve for lunch, then went back until five in the afternoon.

The air compressor at the mine throbbed erratically day and night, until Kate's head throbbed with it, but after the third day she was no longer aware of it. It was not as easy to disregard the coal dust which seemed invisible at first, but appeared with each wipe of the scrub cloth as she cleaned the windows and the pantry shelves.

Eric tacked up the sagging ceiling paper in the kitchen and put up a rod for a curtain on the bedroom door. When they got some money, Kate would send to Eaton's or Simpsons for some material for it. The company store sold only staples, food and clothing. Robby followed his mother from one room to another as she worked, asking endless questions, finally venturing outside to play in the back yard. He missed his dog.

The place clean at last, Kate had time to explore the camp. They lived on the upper level, above the mine mouth and the slag heap. The officials lived down the hill near the train station, with white fenced yards and lawns. That was a switch, she thought. Most places the elite lived on the hill.

Mail came in twice a week, to the Post Office in the train station. The station master called out the names on the letters and parcels, and the people all crowded into the small room and stood waiting around for their name like children at a Christmas concert. Those standing at the back received their letter hand over hand until it reached them. Going down for the mail was an invigorating walk, and a chance for everyone to mingle and to reveal to the whole camp the extent and nature of their correspondence.

Going to the company store was a daily routine for the miner's wives. Kate, who had been used to shopping once a month or whenever their income dictated, soon fell into the same habit. Although she had met only a few of the miners, she nodded to them all as they came off shift, for they all looked alike with only the whites of their eyes and teeth showing in their blackened faces.

After watching Robby so carefully in the woods, Kate was disturbed by one of the camp customs: mothers let their small children traipse off to the store with any mother doing her shopping. Besides being responsible for the forced supervision, the shopper was expected to buy each child a penny sucker. With milk at nine cents a can, Kate was resentful.

I have some time to myself these days, time to read. Robby is sleeping in the afternoons again. Playing with other kids for the first time exhausts him. There's no living with him until bedtime unless he has his nap. Eric seems more relaxed these days. His work brings him in contact with people at the kitchen and bunk house. The coal smoke reminds me of the trains when I was a child living beside the train track. But I long for the smell of wood smoke. Coal gives a fierce warmth. Wood is so gentle.

The concert in the school house was the highlight of the coal camp Christmas; every child in camp received a present. The committee took up a collection and the men in the bunk house gave generously. Some married miners were separated from their families by miles, a few by a continent, and they reached out to the camp children with all they could afford. To Robby and all the three year olds, Santa brought a sleigh with metal runners. Now he could slide down the hill with the rest of the children.

Eric gave Kate a navy suit with a trotter-length coat she could wear separately with a dress, and she bought him a jacket of dark green Melton cloth with zippers on the pockets. Robby's toy was a brightly painted Mortimer Snerd in a wind-up car that wobbled across the floor. The grandparents sent him a set of barnyard animals and a bag of coloured glass marbles.

There was no room in the small kitchen, so they put up their tree in the bedroom next to Robby's crib. After breakfast Christmas morning, Kate and Eric sat on the bed with their coffee, watching their son herding both animals and marbles into kindling stick corrals. The marbles were his sheep.

At last with a few cents to spare, Kate sent away the film she had saved for so long. When the pictures came back, she studied each one. There was the picture her mother had taken, the campfire scene with the tent in the background—her home then. Robby looked so small sitting on her lap. There was the one of him sitting on the pile of logs for the cabin, his feet in slippers she had made from a worn-out pair of Eric's red and white German socks. He'd had no shoes. There were more pictures of Robby and one of the little barn in the sidehill.

They'd come a long way since then. She read the hope and resolve in their faces, the determination that had brought them through those first years. There was one Fred Hanover had taken of her holding Robby, with Eric's arm around her, standing by their old log bridge. She had known even then they would survive.

Kate adjusted to life in the camp. The coal dust was insidious. Every cut or scratch became inflamed unless kept scrupulously clean. Clothes were left on the line only until they were dry. The miner's wives had a back line where they hung their husband's work underwear, always gray with imbedded coal dust.

In truth, Kate hesitated to hang some of her sheets on the line, not because they were not white, for they had been boiled and hand washed on a scrub board, but because most of them had been sewn up from hundred pound flour bags. Her neighbour offered to let Kate use her clothes line when Kate's was full, but requested Kate not hang her personal underthings on it because *she* never did. If modesty had prompted the request, it seemed to Kate to be defeating its purpose, for anyone interested enough to take notice might wonder whether or not she ever wore any at all.

Social life was limited to leaning over the board fence at the outdoor hockey rink to shout encouragement to the local team, or attending the occasional dance in the school house where the cliques congregated according to their status. Since Eric sometimes played his banjo at these dances, Kate, as bull cook's wife, sat alone most of the time. She liked to dance, but she really didn't mind sitting and watching, wondering what life in this camp would be like if Eric could get steady work here, if she could afford to dress like other women.

She recognized many of the clothes from the pages of the catalogues. At one dance, three women showed up with the same satin striped dress, one in green and two in red. One was the mine manager's wife. Kate laughed to herself when the manager's wife went home to change.

In February, Kate began having a nagging pain in her side. Finally she went to the company doctor.

"Appendicitis," he said. "You may get over this attack. It's not too severe. But I've been out in that Caroline country fishing, and I know how bad the roads can be sometimes. You'd be wise to have the operation while you can. I work with the doctor in Nordegg at the hospital there. I can arrange for your admission."

Kate and Eric talked it over and decided to have it done. All the medical expenses were covered by the company medical plan to which they had been contributing a dollar a month. On Sunday Eric hired the timekeeper from the office to drive him and the boy to Sylvan Lake, where he left Robby with Kate's parents.

On Monday Kate went the twenty miles to the hospital in Nordegg by train. A car met her and took her to the big, old hospital on the hill. The large four-storey building was evidence of a once booming coal town. The hospital now employed only a cook and one live-in nurse on twenty-four-hour duty. There was only one other patient when Kate arrived. The halls echoed with their footsteps as the nurse showed Kate to her room on the third floor.

Since Nordegg was the final destination of the train, it stayed over night and returned the next day. Thus it was Wednesday before Kate's operation was scheduled. She lay looking out across the not-quite ghost town, its big blackened structures idle and silent. She watched clouds gathering up the steep ravines of the hills opposite. They came sailing out into the valley to disintegrate in the sunshine.

She had time to think and to worry. How was Eric managing? Would he wake up at four-thirty every morning? She wondered about the cabin on the homestead. Had it leaked? Were her things safe in it all winter?

Wednesday came and Kate was given an injection to relax her, they said. By the time the nurse came to take her downstairs, she felt weightless and floated down the steps to the operating room. She remembered breathing deeply when someone told her to—and then she was back in her room on the third floor. A local doctor visited her almost every day, and the camp doctor came up the twenty miles from Alexo twice a week on a speeder on the train track.

When Kate returned from the hospital, one of the miner's wives, a Polish lady she scarcely knew, came to the door, holding her gray hand-knit sweater around her plump body.

"I wash your floor for you. You shouldn't bend so soon you come home."

The woman's thoughtfulness stirred more than gratitude. Kate wanted to go home where this was a common thing, where people helped each other; she was finding the social hierarchies of the coal camp more and more disturbing. Eric had bought a second-hand electric iron and found a discarded radio at the bunk house which he fixed up with a new plug-in cord. She had learned to cook with the shiny, hot, anthracite coal without burning the bread. They had so many things they had never had before. But she longed for the sight of animals, even the blundering moose, and for the constant chuckle of the river when it was gentle in its bed.

Spring came at last. Each fresh fall of winter snow had been covered with coal dust until the melting snow bank behind the house looked like a huge, many layered cake with licorice filling. Dandelions bloomed along the bottom log of the house and chickadees called their spring song from the evergreens.

April. We'll be going home soon. I feel like a chipmunk with its cheeks stuffed with food, nourishment for a future time. Although I've hoarded a few material things, I'm full to bursting with determination to get a home we can call our own. I thought at times I had lost Eric to this easier routine, but last evening he was humming as he packed away a carton of .22 shells and a roll of brass wire in the box with his new mitts and blue felt insoles. I bought him some fish hooks for his birthday next month.

Eric came home at noon, carrying his coat over his arm. He tossed it on a chair and sat down heavily.

"If we weren't going home in two weeks, I'd quit this damned job. Do you know what the boss's wife had me doing this morning? Beating a carpet!"

He saw Kate's expression and smiled back. "Just call me Hannah. It sure will be good to see our cabin again." He got up and paced restlessly, running his fingers through his hair, brushing the dark lock back from his forehead until Kate put the meal on the table.

Eric drove home that night in an ancient truck with no cab, another Chev. It had scaly green paint and a cracked windshield.

"Where did you get that?"

"A fellow up at the kitchen wants to sell it."

"How much?"

"Sixty dollars. It runs good and the tires are in fair shape. There's a spare, too. What do you think? We could move home in it and be able to get around on our own, go to dances and get out to see your folks."

They did need a car. The neighbours had been good, but you couldn't depend on them forever. The look in Eric's eyes was enough to sway her.

"It sounds like a good deal."

"Want to take a ride in it? Where's Robby?"

"Out back with the kids. I'll call him."

Robby came running, climbed up beside his father and sat banging his heels against the seat to encourage some movement. Kate got in and took Robby on her lap. Eric drove out toward the highway and made a sharp turn onto a narrow rough road. The willows bordering it scraped against the fenders.

"Where are we going?" Kate clutched the boy as the truck bounced over a tree root.

"The garbage dump."

"How romantic!"

"There's something out there I want you to see."

He parked beside a heap of rubble and led the two of them to a big pile of one inch cable tangled in the weeds. "I had to bring out a load of cans this morning and saw this. You know, if we could take it home, we could put it up across the river and make an aerial ferry. We'd never be stuck that way."

Kate felt a strange surge of excitement. Both a car and a cable ferry! Now, she thought, I won't have to rely on the log bridge even in high water. I can learn to drive! She looked over the large coils of cable. "There won't be room enough for our beds if we take all that."

"I'll cut off what we need. It's a long one they used for hauling cars up from the mine and down to the tipple. There's more than enough here and plenty strong for a ferry."

They poked around some more and found a shovel and a pick, both with broken handles, and a bent crow bar. Eric piled them in the bushes with the cable. Kate walked around the young nettles growing up through the rusty cans and broken glass. When she came again, she would bring gloves and pick some for greens. A few yellow flowers she didn't recognize reminded her of the carpet of yellow dryas that would soon bloom on the river bar back home. She found a galvanized pail with no handle and held it up to the sun. There were no holes in it.

Robby had been busy, too. He stood defensively clutching

a rusty tricycle with a wobbly wheel.

"Can I keep it?"

Eric approved. They had never been able to give Robby the things he dreamed of. "Of course you can. I'll fix that wheel and paint it up for you."

"Red?"

"Sure! Red if you want."

Kate picked up a clay flower pot with only a small chip on the rim and put it in the truck. Maybe when they came back for the cable she could look around some more. How could people throw away so many good things, something someone else could use?

Eric picked up a tangle of wire. "This will be good to tie rails to the posts when we're fencing," he said. And so they went home, each with their treasures.

The next day, Kate tied up her hair in a kerchief and spent the day packing. Clothes and dishes that had come up in cardboard cartons went home in wooden powder boxes and carbide cans. She had plans for those boxes in her kitchen. The curtains needed washing, but they could wait until she could hang them outside in the clean air.

From the window she could see Eric's legs protruding from under the truck. He was wrapping a piece of stovepipe around a hole on the exhaust pipe where the heat had charred the truck box. It was makeshift, but it would do for the trip home. This was a typical Chev with a radiator that boiled without pretext and a vacuum tank that failed at will. Still, it had all the resiliency of the Morgans and their ability to survive on alternatives.

Eric directed the loading the day they left.

"Keep all the heavy things on the left side. There's a leaf missing from that right spring. I hope it holds out."

"I'll sit on your lap, then."

"I wish you would."

It was sunny the morning they started for home, the truck still listing a little and thumping down on the axle as Eric eased it in and out of the chuck holes. By the time they reached Rocky Mountain House and turned south, a few drops of rain had begun to fall. There was a blue sky behind the dark, fast-moving cloud. Maybe they would miss the worst of it as they drove south.

"Looks like a good shower coming."

Eric stopped the truck, and reaching behind the seat, pulled out a piece of binder canvas, complete with slats. It stretched from the stakes on the truck box and hooked over the windshield. It sagged low in front and he had to hunch down to drive.

Eric smiled. "Kate darlin', I always wanted to take you for a ride in a convertible."

A few miles farther on, he made an unwise choice in a series of chuck holes, and the canopy collapsed on their heads. They hung it up again and decided to have lunch, huddled under it. By the time they had eaten their sandwiches and Eric had rolled a smoke, the shower had passed.

They drove the truck as close to Pa's place as the spring roads would allow, and stayed the night. The next day Pa Morgan took their belongings to the river with the wagon. They followed with the truck, left it on the river bar and climbed into the wagon to cross the river.

The water was full of silt and still high even at the ford. Pa Morgan drove, standing spraddled against the box, and with tight lines and encouraging words, urged the horses into the fast water. Eric held Robby. Kate gripped the sides of the wagon box as the wheels lurched over unseen boulders. She felt the old fear of the river rising in her. Her stomach contracted and she held her breath until the water dropped away and they were across.

At last on their own land, she turned her thoughts to the immediate future. They lived by seasons. This summer it might not be as hard to get by until trapping time again, for she had hoarded staple foods with each of Eric's pay cheques. And there was still the sack of canned goods the camp cook had brought to the door one dark March night in exchange for the few dollars Eric handed him. The transaction had bothered Kate, but she said nothing. It would have bothered her more had she not been able to recall times in the past when she had carefully apportioned the meals—first share to Robby, the rest divided between Eric and herself.

Her heart beat faster as the cabin came into view, its wide eaves like arms waiting to welcome them. When they stopped in front, they saw the long teeth marks on the log above the door.

"Porcupine," Eric said.

A squirrel had built a nest in the top of a nearby pine and was defending it noisily. The animals were reclaiming their territory. A gray Canada Jay came to investigate. Kate tossed it a piece of bread from their lunch sack and it flew away with it, losing altitude and landing on the wood pile.

They climbed down from the loaded wagon and Robby and the dog ran to all the familiar places—his swing, the sand pile, the dog house under a big tree. Kate saw how much taller he had grown in those eight months.

Eric stepped over the weeds growing up through the doorstep, opened the padlock and swung the door inward. Stale air greeted them, stale with the smell of mice. Eric picked up a kindling stick and began to whittle shavings.

"It's damp in here. You open the windows, Kate, and I'll start a fire."

As they finished unloading the wagon, Kate turned to Pa. "Stay a bit. I'll go in and make some coffee."

Eric's father looked around and shook his head. "No. I'll go right back. The river may come up a little after dark."

"Thanks, Pa. I'll see you in a couple of days," Eric said.

Pa Morgan climbed back into the wagon and drove off. They were carrying the last of the boxes into the cabin when they heard the river roar louder at the ford. Eric looked at Kate. "He's across," he said.

By the time they had the beds set up, the coffee was ready. They went outside and sat under the trees, the hot cups cradled in their hands. They were silent, watching Robby pedalling the crippled cycle, listening to a squirrel defying the dog. From the stove pipe, white smoke rose slowly into the clear May morning. Kate took Eric's rough hand, its nails outlined with embedded coal dust.

"We're home," she said.

13

Water stains on the roof and board floor showed where the cabin leaked while they were away. Eric climbed up on the roof, and Kate, from inside, tapped out the places with the broom handle while Eric applied more pitch to the exposed knot holes. With the first heavy rain a few more drips appeared. Kate put cans under them. While she sat by the window, watching the rain coursing down the slanting board under the eave and into the tub, Eric picked up the cans and began pouring the water back and forth, re-arranging them.

"What are you doing? Why don't you just empty them?"

"Just a minute. Now listen."

The drops came plunk-plunk-plink-plink, playing a perfect tune "How Dry I Am." Eric waved a finger in rhythm and Kate laughed with him as he conducted for his imaginary symphony.

He missed music. Recalling the look in his eyes the times he played for dances, she knew the association with other musicians meant almost as much to him as the two dollars he received. His sacrifices to their homestead were more than material ones. She put her hand on his shoulder.

"The rain has let up," she said. "Let's go outside."

They walked out to the flat, Robby splashing along barefoot in the shallow puddles. The first pale leaves of the poplars had turned to summer green. Kate picked a rose bud and held it to her nose. Eric stopped and waved toward the opening.

"The grass is coming good. We could get a cow again now. We could put a drag on her until we get a fence up."

"Maybe Hanovers will sell Clarabelle back to us."

Eric hesitated. "They were going to butcher her."

"You knew that when you sold her?" Kate stared at him. Clarabelle had been part of the family.

"We didn't have much choice, Kate. Jess Durham has a cow he said he'd sell us. He wants fifty dollars, but she's part Jersey and only her second calf. I been thinking. We don't need to buy a team. We got no wagon, anyway. With one horse we could do some skidding and have it to ride across the river until we get the cable up."

Kate nodded agreement, still thinking of Clarabelle.

They bought a horse, a buckskin gelding they called Buck. With huge feet and shaggy mane, he was as rugged as the new cow was small and trim. Taffy's bull calf came with her. They bought six more laying hens and, at Kate's insistence, a rooster to go with them.

"One more mouth to feed," Eric teased. "Oh well, you can have your automatic alarm clock. He'll warn the hens of hawks and things."

They had milk again, and Kate made butter and cottage cheese. She let the skim milk sour and then warmed it until the curds separated from the whey. She put the curds in a thin salt sack and hung it on the clothesline to drain. By adding a little salt and cream it was finished.

She picked strawberries on the edge of the flat and put enough rhubarb with them to make three quarts. Eric picked up a jar and frowned. "It kind of spoils the strawberries, doesn't it?"

Kate defended her efforts. "But look what it does for the rhubarb!"

By the middle of July the river had cleared enough for fishing. Robby trotted behind his father as they walked back to the cabin with their catch of Dolly Varden. Kate followed, dodging the shoulder-high rose bushes along the path. As she jerked away from the brier that scratched her bare arm, she felt a pain in her leg. Her fish line had swung loose from the pole and caught the hook above her knee. With her leg tied to the end of the line, she limped along like a horse with stringhalt. She called out for Eric.

"You must have jerked it hard. It went in and out back through the skin again."

"How will we get it out? It hurts, Eric."

"I'll bet it does. I'll cut off the line and maybe we can cut the eye off the hook and pull it on through. The barb is already out the other side."

The prospect didn't cheer her. Free from the dangling line, her leg didn't hurt much, but she limped along, anyway, toward the house.

They had no side cutting pliers, only those loose-jointed kind that could be found under the seat of any old car. Their cutting edge just missed the eye of the small hook. She didn't ask about the alternative. She knew even before Eric began to sharpen the small blade of his knife, the one he used to skin squirrels. He tested the blade with his thumb, lit a match and held the sharp point in the flame to sterilize it, then wiped the blackened tip off on the leg of his pants. He sent Robby outside on the pretext of gathering chips for the supper fire. He gave Kate instructions.

"Now, you pull up on the hook as much as you can stand and don't look at it."

Like a good doctor, he used the diversion tactic. "There's a dance in town Friday night," he said, as he slashed the flesh and lifted out the hook.

Kate flinched.

"Does it hurt much?"

"No. Just stings a little."

The tiny cut in the fatty part of her knee oozed a drop of blood. Eric wiped the blade on his pant leg again, snapped the knife shut and put it in his pocket.

"Better get something on that, some iodine."

"That *will* hurt."

"Want me to do it?"

"No. You clean the fish and I'll fry up some spuds."

We have a horse now for skidding, but we still have to

borrow Pa's team and wagon for hauling anything.
Taffy's milk is so rich I can make a little butter. It's so easy
to shake up the cream in a two quart sealer. Eric usually
does that for me, keeping time to a tune on the
phonograph. Robby likes to watch the cream break and
the tiny specks of butter form into balls. With a few eggs,
mealtime is not such a challenge. I like to think ahead to
the time we can have a big garden, and raise our own
meat.... I worry about sickness or accidents, us being so
far from a doctor. I mean something really serious, more
than a fish hook in a knee. Funny, isn't it, how things that
seem so tragic can recede to the vanishing point in so
short a time. But how else could we survive? It is the good
memories we must keep alive. Eric brought me a branch
of ripe saskatoons today.

They lived close to the river, more than geographically. It
gave them food and fur, and it controlled their social life, for
each year it took out their log bridge, leaving them stranded
until the water went down. It would be better when they had
the cable up. They had the horse now to ride to the Post Office
and for small emergencies. That was some progress, although
each high water washed away a little more of the flat they had
worked so hard to clear. Kate and Eric lugged rocks to build a
pier, a construction like a long narrow corral filled with rocks
to divert the water. It helped some until the current cut under
it, spilling out the rocks, and in the end the river had its way.
They lost nearly an acre of precious land.

They began enlarging the clearing back toward the benchland, away from the threatening river. Kate rested while Eric
sharpened his axe. Her shoulders ached. Was this struggle
really worth it? When they had the place proved up on, when
she could no longer teach Robby, what then? She knew some
of the people who were on relief, had seen the hopelessness
in their eyes. If she and Eric ever had to accept that, she knew
they would go on living behind an armour of pride, beyond
the shame of defeat. Only that morning there had been a

sparkle in Eric's eyes as he told her of the saskatoon berries he had found down the river, not quite ripe yet, but soon. Another carrot on the end of a stick. She felt like a donkey—persuaded, plodding, rebellious.

One sunny morning in July, Kate stood looking at her flower bed beside the cabin, a three foot square of soil carried from the flat and fertilized with Buck's help to grow the Sweet William she loved so much. There was a sudden buzzing sound in the air, and then she saw it—a hummingbird, fragile, etheral. It hung there before her, and she drew her breath as the sun shifted the iridescent red of its throat before it ricocheted off thin air and was gone. She couldn't wait to tell Eric of this small but somehow terribly important event.

The summer seemed to slip away with little accomplished, their efforts divided between fencing, clearing land and finishing the root house. They found a spot up on the top land for a garden. The soil there was better and more protected from frost. They had been cutting and grubbing all afternoon. The growing pile of willow roots would be used for the smokehouse they had planned. Kate watched as Eric split and piled them to dry. A few had holes bored in them by those white, big-headed worms, pale and sluggish and flat like horseshoe nails. Kate stretched and straightened her aching back.

"I'll go down and start supper," she said. "Robby, you stay here."

She took the long way back, the old game trail along the top of the bank, and when she came to the opening in the trees where she could overlook the cabin, she stopped. It looked so small. Faded colours from the clothes line drew her eyes, the tattered patchwork quilt that served as a mattress for Robby's bed. His bedding and his bedwetting were diminishing together. He had outgrown his crib, and Eric had almost finished a small bunk against the wall. He would need a mattress for that. She walked on down, thinking of mattresses and gardens and humming birds.

The sun was still high above the stand of spruce when Kate finished up the dishes and checked to see that Robby was with his father at the wood pile. She took the water pail down to the spring. She set it aside when it was full and followed the stream where it skirted the heavy timber. The evening sun struck slanting rays through the tree tops and pointed out the moss-covered, leaning log Kate sought. She walked part way up the log and sat down. Up here she seemed to rise above the worries and depression of their constant struggle.

She had always had her secret places of escape. As a child she had crawled into the dark and dusty cubbyhole under the stairs to contemplate the Tooth Fairy: was she real, this magical older sister bringing money in exchange for baby teeth? As a teenager, when the stillness and monotony of the old farm house disturbed her, she went to her hideaway in a thicket of diamond willows where a crooked branch formed a natural seat. In the spring, when the pale green leaves had fulfilled the promise of the dormant buds, Kate had budded, too, into womanhood, absorbing scraps of knowledge and experience, putting them together and making them her own.

Like most farm girls, she had long since faced her moral and social problems; she knew what they were. Only material ones had remained. They couldn't afford a mattress for Robby's bed.

A myrtle warbler came to hang upside down from an alder branch. A red squirrel on a limb sat motionless, inconspicuous save for its white eye ring which Kate had learned to recognize. It chirped and flirted its tail, then scampered up the spruce. As she watched it, her eyes fell on the silvery-green, stringy moss hanging from the dry branches. She reached up and pulled some off, crushing it in her fingers, feeling the resilience. Here was Robby's mattress, hanging from the trees! She laughed to herself at this sudden and unrealized gift. It had been the solution of Indian women, too.

It was a tedious job, but the moss was dry and plentiful, and with potato sacks on the bottom and flour sacks on the top, she made a mattress to fit the bunk, hesitating only a moment before taking the oilcloth from the table to protect her handiwork. They could eat off a bare board surface for a while. After all, they did have plates.

Blueberries grew only on the poplar hills across the river. Now with Buck to ride, Kate didn't have to walk the two miles to pick them. He was not an ideal saddle horse, but then, she didn't have a saddle to put on him, anyway. With a rug thrown over his back, she could ride him across the river and up to the berry patch. Eric always rode him with only a halter, but he insisted Kate put one on top of a bridle from the harness. Buck could be headstrong at times. Eric tied in two short pieces of rope for reins, and so, with her rug and ropes, they ambled off to the berry patch.

On a short stretch of the main road, she saw a car in the distance. She pulled the horse aside into the thick brush until it had passed. She was embarrassed to be seen riding with a bridle with blinders, and ropes for reins. The braided rug kept working out from under her, and once when it hooked up on a branch she had to go back and get it. She stuffed it in the berry pail and went on.

As she jogged up the side road that led to the berry patch, she thought of the saying by which most homesteaders lived:

Use it up
Wear it out
Make it do
Or do without

The berry crop was patchy. She found a good place, knotted the rope reins together and tied Buck up with the halter shank. She picked eagerly; the first handful went into her mouth. The familiar smell of a stink bug sent her searching through the berries in her pail until she found the brown triangular-shaped insect and flipped it out onto the ground.

After three years of living close to nature, her senses had become keener. She had learned to interpret the first gusts of wind in the pine boughs, signs of an impending storm, and to welcome the gentler breeze from the river bars that would bring the heady scent of wolf willow in bloom. She knew the ominous voice of the river on the rise, the complaining sounds of mating porcupines. She adjusted her breathing to carrion laden air, or one that held the clean damp promise of rain. Her finger tips became sensitive and adept as she stripped the blueberry bushes of their ripe fruit.

The autumn silence was disturbed only by a noisy jay and the occasional stamping of the horse's feet as he warded off a botfly. Her pail was nearly full when she began to work her way back toward the horse. She caught the sound of a snapping twig and saw the fresh bear track in the path. Buck was snorting and blowing a frightened warning.

Kate made three fast decisions: to take her hard-earned berries with her, to ride the frightened horse with only a halter, and to mount him from the wrong side. She lost a few berries as she untied him, grasped his mane and scrambled aboard. "I could scream," she thought desperately, but held back; the horse was frightened enough. She ducked branches as Buck wheeled and started back down the trail.

When she reached the wire gate of the lease, she jumped down and opened it. Buck bounded through and swung close to her side, head held high and nostrils flaring. As she fumbled to fasten the stubborn wire loop, she heard a thumping sound and pictured the bear pounding its way along the path toward her. She pushed against the horse to gain working room and discovered the pounding was Buck's heart! There was no bear in sight.

Mounted again and jogging toward home, she reached down and patted Buck's shoulder to seal the pact. "Just a couple of fraidy cats," she laughed. "I won't tell if you don't."

Kate awoke the next morning to the faint smell of smoke in the air from the open window. Her bare feet on the cold floor hurried past Eric stacking kindling in the range. She opened the door. A blue haze hung above the trees.

"There's smoke out there."

"Probably from one of the mills. Somebody burning a slab pile."

"Burning them? What a waste!"

"Well, they pile up, and there isn't much sale for them, really. They have to pay stumpage on them if they sell them. They're not supposed to give them away either without paying. That's cheating the government! They can burn the whole damn pile if they want to, though." Eric filled the kettle and set it down noisily.

"Hm." Kate skimmed cream from an open pan of milk, stirred up the rest and poured it into a quart sealer for the porridge.

"Jess said he'd come down and help me put in the dead men for the cable. He may want to use it, too, in high water."

The smoke had grown more dense by the time Jess Durham arrived with his son, Chuck, now twelve years old. Kate had seen the boy before, though only briefly as he had slipped like a shadow through the trees, disappearing and appearing again behind a different tree. Now she saw under a shock of tan coloured hair, round, bright eyes like his grandmother's. He declined the milk Kate offered and took a cup of coffee with the men.

"Sure lots of smoke this morning." Eric tipped back in his chair and began to roll a cigarette.

"A big fire up on Moose Creek," Jess said. "They're asking for men. If the cable can wait a bit, I'd like to go. They're paying two-sixty a day and board."

Eric looked at Kate.

"You were right. That smoke was a little too thick for slash or a slab pile. I guess I better see if I can get on, too. We sure could use the money. They say some of those fires last spring were set just to make work."

"Guess you can't blame them none. A man's got to feed his family somehow." He paused. "They *all* may have work soon if they want it. Radio said this morning Britain just declared war on Germany."

"The hell!"

Eric let his chair down with a thump. For a moment he stared open-mouthed at Jess. Then he scratched a match on his pant leg and lit his cigarette. A few strings of tobacco flared and fell into his lap. He brushed at them absently and looked out the open door. "That means Canada, too."

Jess nodded again. "In time."

The dormant knot of fear was forming inside Kate again. She had managed to quiet it back when Chamberlain had made his "Peace with honour." Even now her anxiety tempered itself with random thoughts from childhood and another war, memories of the comic strips, the "funny papers," when Casey said to Jiggs, "I see you're back from the front" and Jiggs had replied, "I didn't know I was that thin." She and her brother had laughed together at that. Later on there was the forbidden *War Book* hidden in the back of the upstairs closet, the one Kate read in secret, a chronicle of the Great War with its pictures of tanks and cannons. In her tomboy days, she had been unimpressed with the photographs of bodies lying in the mud, but very interested in the full page plate of Big Bertha, the supercannon.

Kate's thoughts were brought back to the present as she heard Jess saying, "If we go over to the main road, they'll pick us up in a truck." Eric was going to the fire.

Jess and his boy left, saying he'd be back down right away and he and Eric could wait together for the truck. Kate turned to Eric. "What will you need? I better fix you some lunch."

"I won't need a lunch. They'll take us to the ranger station first and then back across the river with horses. Moose Creek is on this side."

"The fire's on this side of the river?"

"It won't come down this far, Kate. It must be over ten miles to Moose Creek. I'll need a bed roll of some kind. That Hudson Bay blanket should be enough. They'll have a tent set up at the main camp."

Kate held up a gray blanket. "It's pretty thin."

"It'll be all right. Robby, bring me my boots there by the door."

Robby ran to get them, eager to be included in the preparations. He stood by his father's side as Eric had another cup of coffee and the toast Kate insisted he eat. He put his hand on his son's shoulder. "You take care of Mom while I'm gone. Here's Jess now."

Kate and Robby walked as far as the log and waited until the men disappeared into the trees. On the way back, Kate lingered where the tall bushes hung heavy with orange-red rose hips. They reminded her of autumn on her father's farm, the warm feeling of the harvest, the cellar filling with vegetables and crocks of preserves, the snugness of preparing for winter. Eric's fire wages would help this year.

Kate couldn't keep Robby from wading in the cold backwaters of the spring where the minnows hid. That night he cried again with chapped and bleeding ankles. She bathed his feet in warm water, and when the vaseline jar was empty, she applied lard and put on his socks to protect his clean bed clothes.

Kate thought of her once, faraway dream of being a pharmacist. Her parents could not afford her education for that, but the dream had lingered. Boracic acid, iodine and plain lard were a far cry from the dispensary. She looked down at her son sleeping quietly now and felt a small sense of accomplishment.

The men fought fire for eleven days. Smoke hung thick and acrid in the air, fading the sun to an orange globe, lighting the night sky with wavering reflections of itself, billowing up at intervals as the night drafts fed the flames.

As Kate wrote in her diary the next morning, she remembered her mother telling her how as a little girl, she and her brother had huddled together, watching the rolling smoke and flames of a prairie fire. Only the ploughed fire guard around the buildings had saved their home.

Jess had said the fire was more than ten miles away, but Kate knew that with a wind it could travel fast. She watched the sky at night and slept lightly, starting up at even the familiar noises, the cow bell, Buck stamping close to the window, or rubbing his rump against the end log by the head of her bed.

The blue haze grew denser as clouds moved in. Kate was standing at the water hole scanning the sky. The big spruce lifted its skirts as a sudden breeze swept across the flat. Aspen leaves shivered and turned their pale backs to the wind. She smelled the freshness. It would rain soon and the fire fighting would be over.

The rain came that night, steady rain for three days. On Saturday Eric came home. She saw his tall, thin figure walking across the flat and ran to meet him. His clothes were black and his face looked darker than ever with its two-week growth of beard.

"Where's the tub? I sure need a bath."

"Full of rain water. I can empty it in the boiler. I'll heat soft water for you. You look like you could use some extra suds."

Kate put her arm around his waist as they walked back to the cabin, her feet skipping now and then to keep up with his long stride.

"Everything in camp was black. I sure would like a good cup of tea. The tea up there all tasted like burnt pine needles. How did you make out here?"

"All right. Martha sent Chuck down once to see if I needed any help. He's a funny little boy. He knocked on the door like a man, but not before he had sneaked up on the cabin a tree at a time. We fixed the east fence where a moose had run into it. He found hair on a broken wire—said it was evidence."

"He's a good kid," Eric said. "Jess would like to leave stringing the cable until after high water next June. He's got a lot of work to do before winter. I told him we could get by now we got the horse."

"We still have the log until then, anyway."

While Kate put on water for tea, Eric took down his banjo and began to play. Robby came running in to stand by Eric and put his hand on his father's bouncing knee, keeping time with a nod of his own head.

Eric seems more eager about the work here since coming home from fire fighting. Of course the money helps, nearly thirty dollars, but I think some of it is the change, the association with a different group of men, and finding we are not the only ones struggling. That time I went to Rocky with Eric, I talked to a woman in the grocery store and she said she always dried a few blueberries to put in cookies. I had begun to think I was the only one who ever did that.

I bought a few extra stamps yesterday, like reserve tickets between me and the outside world. I'll write to Eileen some day—tell her all the good things about living in the woods. Maybe I can convince myself. The end of September. The days are getting shorter. I've lit the lamp to finish this. Eric just called me outside. He may need some help—or maybe it's just to stand beside him and watch the moon coming up behind the trees. We need a lot of that.

In October the community held its annual harvest dance in Caroline, and Eric had a chance to earn three dollars with his banjo. After Kate had washed her own hair, she trimmed Eric's with a pair of clippers her father had passed on to them. The spring was broken and one handle had to be manipulated back and forth with a rubber sealer ring holding it to her thumb. She was efficient, slow, interrupted only by a few yelps from Eric when her tired thumb didn't quite complete a cutting stroke on the short hairs on the back of his neck.

With a shave and his shoes shined, Eric was ready. Kate took longer; her cosmetics were limited. Lipstick could only be applied from a spent tube of Tangee by digging it out with a toothpick and applying it with her finger. Rouge was going out of fashion and eye shadow coming in. Kate had tried some of Leah's once and liked the effect. With a smear of lard in the palm of her hand, she went to the stove, touched her finger to the under side of the lid and rubbed the soot into the lard. After a few tries with finger and wash cloth, she had the look she desired. Kate smiled at herself in the mirror and thought, *Pioneering sure had changed. In grandma's day this would have made her a scarlet woman.* The Jasmine box contained baking soda for deodorant. She and Eric both chewed a few grains of coffee to sweeten their breath.

They had to prime the truck before it would start, and they arrived at the dance after it had begun. Kate left Robby on a bench with two other children and joined the women around the gas-barrel stove. They moved over to make room for her. She revolved slowly until her legs were blotched red from the intense heat. She had got chilled at the river waiting for the truck to start. Even a fast polka had not warmed her when Rod-somebody and his wife, a couple Eric knew, invited them outside for dry throat remedy, guaranteed to cure chills and inhibitions.

He ushered them out behind the hall to his rig, groped around in the hay under the seat and came up with a bottle. He held it up to the bright moon. The water-clear contents splashed at half full. The men drank first, while the women stood hugging themselves and rubbing their legs together in the cold. Eric exhaled slowly through puckered lips, wiped his mouth with the back of his hand and held the bottle out to Kate.

"Watch that stuff. It's dynamite."

The liquid burned all the way down. When she had gasped back enough breath, she cautioned, "Don't anybody light a match."

By the time her throat had stopped burning, her head had begun applauding the tempo of the music and she felt as if it might detach itself and go bobbing off amongst the dancers.

Kate's father had taught her all the old standard dances, and she could manage a passable execution of the jitterbug.
It was a friendly crowd. She danced more with strangers than she did with men she knew, her popularity increasing after she and the drummer's girl friend sat on the stage with the orchestra at supper time.

The men talked music for awhile, then Eric turned to the

126

bass player. "I hear you're getting married."

"We'd like to. But if I get called up, that would mean Connie'd have to go to work or move in with her folks. Either way, it's a hell of a way to start a marriage."

"Same with Kate. She and the boy could never live over there on the homestead alone even with her allowance. I guess they'd not count the years in the army against us proving up, but all we've done so far would be wasted. We'd have to start all over."

Robby sat wide-eyed on a bench until supper time when he joined the other children sliding across the dance floor. When they turned to sailing paper plates, they were helped out by a few enthusiastic men who had forsaken their own sport of blowing up paper lunch bags and bursting them behind the women.

While the smaller children were being bedded down on the stage with quilts and overcoats, the floor was swept and scattered with corn meal. After a few swipes of the bow across violin strings, the dancing picked up again.

The festivities ended sometime after two o'clock. There was a scurry to find partners for the "home waltz" and a shifting stand at attention as the band played four bars of "God Save The King." Kate was laughing and exhausted.

The next morning, as Kate washed the dishes, her head still pulsed to "Bonapart's Retreat" and "The Johnson Rag." She hitched up a brassiere strap with a wet finger, executed a few quick shuffle steps, and went about her house work.

14

The first snow came early. Robby was happy on his sleigh. Unlike their first winter, Kate and Eric now welcomed the snow. The cold would prime up the squirrels, and they knew they could make it through the winter if fur prices held up. Sitting by the window, watching Robby and the dog romping through the fresh fall of snow, they discussed another winter move, up to a small cabin on Miles's place.

"What's the cabin like?"

"Small. But the roof is good, and there's an old cookstove in it and a few dishes. The people who used to own the place rented it out to fishermen in the summer. We'd have to take our own bedding and things. We'd take the cow, too. Miles said he'd feed it for some of the milk. Buck can range out. The snow's not deep under the trees."

"How far from Miles's place?"

"Right across the meadow from the house, on up that creek a little way."

"I suppose if we did move up there, you could trap on west as far as the forest reserve," said Kate.

"Maybe a few mink along the river, but it's that big stand of spruce I'm thinking about. The squirrels are eating spruce cones this year. Even if we only stay a few weeks, I can clean up on squirrels."

Kate hated to leave again. It seemed they'd just got settled down after the coal camp.

"What about the chickens?"

"Granny will take them until we get back. They're still laying good."

His remark confirmed what she suspected. He had planned

all this, even made arrangements for the chickens before asking her opinion! Her ego was ruffled at first. He had only been arming himself with answers in case she objected. She did that herself at times and wondered if Eric had seen through her as easily. He was the one who had to tramp through the snow and cold, and if he wanted her with him that much she would go. Robby was four now. She could manage for a few weeks in a smaller place, she told herself, and once again began packing.

Miles took them up in the sleigh, the cow tied behind. Even the necessities filled the cabin to cramped inconvenience. Kate arranged it as best she could so Robby had room to play and they could skin and care for hides.

After she had the room in order, she went to visit Leah at her place. It was less than a quarter mile up the winding creek. A short-cut path across the meadow took her right to Leah's back door.

"Come in, Kate. I just made a pot of tea. Where's Robby?"

"With Eric. He's making squirrel boards. I can't stay long. Eric wants to go hunting again before dark."

"I've got some milk and cream for you. It's good to have that again. Our cow isn't due until February."

They had their tea, sitting cross-legged in the spread of sunshine across the living room floor where Leah had been tying a quilt with bright coloured yarn. They looked at old copies of *The Ladies Home Journal* and listened to "September Song" on the radio.

The sun was slanting in the west window as Kate arose to go. "I'd better hurry. Eric will be ready to leave. From four o'clock on seems to be the best time to hunt squirrels."

"Bring Robby next time so you can stay longer," Leah called to Kate, already trotting away down the path to the cabin.

Eric hunted close to the cabin at first. When he went farther afield, he took his lunch and was gone all day. Kate read to Robby from the Sunday school papers her mother sent, finding it hard sometimes to explain a loving God when occasionally her own convictions had been shaken. Telling him, though, renewed her faith. Truly, a little child led her.

She delighted him with made up stories about Boots and Buck and the new calf. She wrote sing-song poetry for him. One morning, searching for a rhyming word for Robby's doggerel, she remembered a poem she had written in high school. Although the original poetry had long since been lost, phrases still lingered in her mind. She wrote them out and put the paper on the shelf above the table.

Eric came in at dusk with a dozen squirrels and a coyote he had shot. "It was poking around an old beaver house down on the river. It didn't even see me. I saw a few more tracks. Could have been all the same animal, though. The snow's not deep enough to stop them travelling a lot."

"It's big. Looks like a nice one, too. Are you going to skin it in here?" Kate looked around the crowded room.

"No. I'll just make a stretcher for it tonight and skin it outside in the morning."

He stepped back out the door and brought in an old, weathered snowshoe. "I found this down by the river. I thought Robby might like to play with it."

"Oh boy! A guitar!" Robby took the snowshoe and began strumming the webbing and humming a tune. Eric clapped his hands in rhythm. Kate savoured their pleasure. She set the pot of beans on the table.

"All right, you two. Concert's over. Supper's ready. Better wash up."

Eric averaged fifteen squirrels a day for over a week. He trapped another coyote at the pile of squirrel carcasses in the edge of the timber. With Leah close by, Kate didn't mind the crowded cabin so much at first. Kate spent most of the days outside with Robby, getting wood and building a snow slide for the both of them.

One afternoon Kate watched as Leah came across the open meadow. She hurried to clear the table and put on coffee. Leah kicked the snow from her boots and handed Kate a paper bag.

"A little gingerbread. I knew you couldn't bake in that oven. Hello Robby!"

"Hello, Aunt Leah."

Kate gave Robby a piece of gingerbread. "You can take it outside if you want. Just don't let the dog get it."

The boy, who usually wanted to stay and listen to grown-up talk, went outside to throw sticks for Leah's dog instead.

Kate put out cups. "How's your hand?" she asked.

Leah held up a finger, flexing it. "Getting better now, but I think I'll lose the nail."

"Bring your mending over. I have lots of time to do the hand work."

"That sure would help."

Kate reached for the paper on the shelf and handed it to Leah. "Do you want to read something?"

"Sure." Leah took the paper and read aloud.

What do they think of all day long, those men
Who walk behind the plow, or rest in shade,
And draw between their lips a fragile blade
Of some soft grass, or leaf, or now and then,
Glance westward at the sky, and wonder when
The life supporting rain so long delayed
Will turn the dusty grass to deeper jade;
Or to the robin's plea reply amen?

Do they in turning soil day after day,
Discover there deep in the earth's warm breast,
The secret of the seeds that lie at rest;
The bit of magic tightly hid away?
Do they by daylight shedding its first ray,
See nature wave her wand o'er yonder nest;
Or hear enchantment spoken softly, lest
The spell be broke, by man about his way?

"That's good, Kate. You should send it to some magazine."

"It should be typed. I can't print very neat."

"I'll do it for you. I have some plain writing paper at home.

Why not send it to Robby's Sunday School paper?" She picked up a copy of *Upward* and turned the pages. "They have poetry in here."

"I guess it's worth a try. Thanks, Leah."

Leah looked intently at Kate. "Did you get over your nausea?"

"Yes. Just lack of sleep and the stink of those coyote hides, I guess. I'm not pregnant, anyway. The odds are against that in this small place. One-room cabins are the best method of birth control I've heard about so far."

Leah laughed. "I know what you mean. Look, why don't I take Robby over with me for a few days?"

"Robby'd love that. So would Eric."

"How about you?"

"I'll pack his things. Thanks, Leah."

When Robby and Leah left, Kate put bread dressing in with the pot roast and soaked some dried apples to make a steamed pudding with raisins and cinnamon. With cream it was Eric's favorite. She smiled to herself as she made it, feeling slightly wicked.

Above the sound of the wind in the trees, Kate heard the crunch of snow in front of the cabin. She ran a comb through the back of her hair and brushed the curls toward her face before Eric opened the door. He stood there, framed in the doorway, smiling at her.

"Something sure smells good in here." He looked around. "Where's Robby?"

"Leah was over and took him home with her for a day or two. A change for him."

Eric put down the gun and took Kate in his arms. "I hope he enjoys his stay. I know I'm going to."

Squirrel hunting was good for awhile. A December storm dumped ten inches of snow in two days. Then the wind came up, blowing the last of the cloud debris from the sky. Kate stood at the small window watching the shifting snow. The wind, its greater force abated, still whipped the snow into piles, changed its mind and moved them at will. It unravelled a drift by the wood pile, strung it across the yard and knit it up on the other side. For two days they were confined to the cabin. Eric carried Robby to the outhouse in the timber. At the height of the storm, Kate learned the wisdom of a guide rail nailed to the trees.

When the storm was over, Eric hunted again with little success. He came in early and tossed the squirrel sack down by the door. Robby picked it up to look inside.

"Leave it alone! You'll get fleas."

He was rarely cross with Robby. Kate poured a cup of hot coffee and set it in front of him. "Let me take your wet things. I fixed a line above the stove. Robby, you go outside and play with Boots for a while." She saw the hurt look in her son's eyes, but she knew Eric was hurting more. "It must be hard walking in all that snow."

"Only in the open. There's hardly any in the timber. It's all on the trees. One shot up into that and you start an avalanche. I lost three squirrels because I couldn't see until it was too late. They drop out of a tree right down one of their holes." He sighed and drank his coffee. "We've done pretty good here, but I think I'd do as good back at the cabin now. The coyotes are moving again after the storm, and this deep snow will keep them on game and rabbit trails where I can set snares for them. I'll get some more wire and some locks."

"This is the twenty-first. Could we make it home for Christmas?" Kate thought of their first Christmas at the cabin, then the one at the coal camp. She wanted the next one to be in their own home.

"I think so. I'm getting a load of hay from Miles."

They left the next day, the two men ahead with a sleigh load of hay and Kate following in Miles's high-wheeled wagon with the household goods, and with Taffy, the brown cow, tied behind. Kate's farm experience extended only to cows, chickens and gardening. Fortunately the horses knew more than she did, for, in that well timbered land, where they built creek bridges no more than four inches wider than the wheel tracks, the horses plodded across while Kate shut her eyes and held her breath.

It had been above zero when they left. By the time they reached the heavy timber, where the trail took to an old creek bed, it was growing cold. The sleigh load of hay had tipped sideways many times in the ruts. With the three men hanging on the high side of the rack, they were able to get it upright again.

Kate kicked her feet against the front of the wagon box until a burning, itching feeling came back to her toes. The slip and grind of wheels on the snow measured out their progress. By six o'clock Robby was crying with cold and hunger.

"Don't cry, Robby. Your tears will freeze and only make you colder! Maybe we can stop and build a fire." The moon was coming up somewhere beyond the timber. Vertical shadows became trees again as Kate peered into them. A faint glow caught her eye and she pointed and called out. "What's that light over there?"

The sleigh ahead stopped and Miles shouted back, "It must be the squirrel hunter's camp. He's got a tent set up around here. I'll stop and see." He was gone only a few minutes. "Sure. You take the kid and go on in. We'll throw the stock a little feed first."

As the squeaking snow signalled their approach, a thin man with a plaid cap on the back of his head threw back the tent flap and invited them in. He dragged his cap off and tossed it on the pile of wood beside the small iron stove. He turned to stir the fire.

"Take off your jackets. The fire will soon give some heat. You're late on the road."

She told him how the rack kept tipping over. "And it was above zero when we left."

He stepped outside to consult a thermometer hanging from a branch. "Well, it's twenty below now. You'll be hungry, too."

Kate took off Robby's coat and held her warm palms on his cheeks until the white spots became red again. He leaned against her on the pole bunk and closed his eyes.

The man dumped the contents of various pots into a huge frying pan and put it on the stove. He made coffee for them and cocoa for the boy. The smell of the food soon overcame the musky odor of squirrel hides hanging from the ridge pole, the socks and gloves on the drying rack behind the stove, and the sweaty scent of the bed roll behind her.

Eric and Miles came in, and the men talked of hunting and fur prices while they ate. Robby had fallen asleep on the bunk.

In the warmth of the tent, Kate grew sleepy, too. She was loath to go out again into that frigid, uncertain world. That was the only time in her life she was tempted to crawl into a strange man's sleeping bag and go to sleep.

When at last they left the warm tent, she climbed up into the wagon and unwrapped the stiff lines. They had rolled a quilt around Robby and shaken him down into a big potato sack, tied the top around his neck and nestled him amongst the boxes where he fell asleep again. It was ten o'clock when they reached the trail that would lead to the river and the cabin.

"You take Robby and go on up to Pa's place," Eric said. "We'll tie the cow over there in the bushes and give her some feed and bedding. We'll unharness and bring the horses up later." He beat his mittened hands together and his breath smoked out of his mouth.

Kate unbundled Robby from his sack and quilt and stood him on the ground. It was less than a mile to the place on the hill. She picked up the boy and ran with him until her legs and lungs protested. Then she put him down to walk a short distance. At each turn of the uphill trail, she searched for a sight of the house, a lighted window, a waver of smoke. At last, through falling frost crystals, she saw the pale yellow glow of a coal oil lamp. Only the wise men would have understood.

Kate picked up her son and ran the last distance to the house. Granny met them at the door. Kate put Robby down, and in a few breathless words explained their plight. Her mother-in-law, who had been preparing for bed, left off braiding her hair and turned to the kitchen stove to open the damper and draft and push the kettle onto the front lid.

"Pa, you build up the fire in the heater. The men will be along soon. I'll heat the soup left from supper." She hurried, her slippered feet scuffing over the board floor, the half finished braid swinging across her thin shoulders. Kate, holding Robby close to the heater, was dumb with cold and exhaustion. She watched Granny's arthritic fingers pinch-measuring tea from the canister. She heard Miles and Eric outside.

After they had stabled and fed the horses, they came in and stood rubbing their cold hands over the heater. Granny served bowls of soup and hot tea. Talk dwindled to near silence as the fire drew the cold from them and their exhausted bodies demanded sleep.

In the morning they took the sleigh load of hay and the wagon to the river. The sudden cold had reinforced the ice below the ford, and they crossed to the cabin. After the household things had been carried inside and the hay unloaded near the barn, Eric and Miles drove the rigs back up to his father's place. It was late when Eric returned home. Kate had the cabin warm and a hot meal waiting.

The next morning, Eric shoveled the snow away from the door and cleared the paths to the outbuildings. They had brought the chickens home. With fresh eggs Christmas morning and the venison roast Kate had been saving, the day passed happily. There were even gifts. Robby was delighted with the set of blocks Eric had made for him, and Eric had pretended not to see as Kate knit a pair of mitts from raw wool. On Christmas Eve, Eric built a set of shelves for their few books and the catalogues, with a special shelf for Kate's Bible and dictionary. He tied a new red wool scarf in a big bow to the spruce branch nailed above it.

Kate hoped they could get a battery radio sometime. She remembered the carols last Christmas at the coal camp. She began to hum "Silent Night" as she worked. Eric took down his banjo and joined in softly. Robby sang along, too; even at his age he could carry a tune. Eric smiled at his son's wordless chanting, encouraging him with a slow beat of his foot. Eric's dark head bent forward, contrasted with Robby's red curls. They were so different, yet so much alike with their love of music.

Remembering their first Christmas and their bare little tree, Kate was thankful for the progress they had made in three years. She wrapped the red scarf around her neck, feeling nearly elegant, nearly pretty, and nearly without worries. Still, they had only two years left. Time was slipping away.

The cold spell lasted into January. One night, Eric nudged Kate awake.

"What is it?"

"Coyote. Listen."

A frenzied yelping broke into the silence.

"He's chasing rabbits."

"Near your snares?"

"I think so. I put a string of them right down that cut line."

Eric swung the bedroom window wide, and they crouched on their knees on the bed and listened, the cold air rushing in around them. The coyote barked again and was silent. In the moonlight, they watched a weasel, only the black tip of its tail marking its progress against the snow, as it hunted mice in the wood pile.

"I'm getting cold."

They shut the window, but sleep had abandoned them both.

"Let's make some coffee."

Eric built up the fire and they sat with their coats around their shoulders and their feet on the open oven door and talked about the coyote, wondering what the sudden silence meant. Had the coyote caught its quarry, or had they snared the coyote? They were hopeful as children as they huddled together with their coffee.

Eric left at daylight the next morning to check the sets. The pebbly frost had cleared from the window, and Robby, kneeling on a box, watched for his father's return.

"He's got one! He's got a coyote! I can see it." Robby was ecstatic.

Kate hurried to the window. Sure enough, Eric was striding along with the animal balanced over his shoulder. It was frozen stiff. He came in and put it on the floor. "Looks like a good one, well furred and silvery. How's the coffee pot? Sure is cold out there." He brushed the frost from his eyebrows and rubbed his ears with the palms of his hands. "One of the other snares was sprung. That willow brush is full of rabbit trails!"

Robby was on his knees examining the animal's teeth and making snarling noises.

"We'll have to leave it in here until it thaws out, I'm afraid. We better hang it up."

"Where?"

"Not over the table, I guess. How about in there?"

"Over the bed!"

"We can't have it too near the stove. There won't be any blood, honey," Eric explained quickly. "It wasn't shot. You better put some papers down, though."

He hung it from a beam, and Kate put a sheet of brown paper from an Eaton's parcel across the bed.

"There may be a few fleas drop off when the heat hits it."

"Ugh! How much do you think we'll get for it, Eric?"

"Should bring ten dollars."

"Oh well, that's worth a few fleas!"

A February thaw settled the deep snow, so Eric took the rifle and went up to the slough on the top land. He knew the coyotes liked to hunt mice there in the long dry grass. It was dark when Kate heard a single shot. She waited impatiently for his return. He must have shot something to be gone this long, unless....She pushed the nagging thought from her mind and checked the waiting supper. Eric sauntered in empty handed. She met him at the door.

"Where's the gun, Eric?"

"Anybody here?" he asked, looking around.

"No." She looked him over anxiously. He had taken off his mitts. There was dried blood on his hands.

"I left the gun back at the big tree. I got a moose on the edge of the slough. We better go up and dress it out. I cut its throat. It bled out good."

Kate laughed with relief. "We better eat first."

They ate a hurried supper. Eric sharpened his knife and found one for Kate he had made out of a saw blade, while she got Robby into boots and warm clothing. With the sleigh, a hand saw and the lantern, the three of them returned to the slough. The moose lay half buried, the deep snow crimson around its head. Kate circled the beast in primitive inspection.

"It's a cow."

"Yeah, a dry cow, in pretty good shape, too. I'll build a fire to warm our hands."

Robby sat on the sleigh, breaking small sticks, feeding the blaze, happy to be part of such a grown-up expedition. The melting snow where the animal had lain kept their feet cold. Bare to the elbows, Kate helped pull out the mass of entrails. Although her stomach rebelled at the stench, she paused to let her cold, aching hands absorb the animal heat. It was midnight before they were finished.

"We'll take home what meat we can on the sleigh," said Eric. "We better bury the rest in the snow for tonight. You gather up the things, Kate, and I'll take the head and hide back into the brush. The coyotes will find it there."

They covered the carcass with snow and laid some poplar branches across it to discourage scavengers. Kate pulled her aching hands, crusty with blood, inside her ragged coat sleeves. The sleigh dragged heavily in the deep snow, but their hearts were light. One shot and they had enough meat to feed them for weeks. They could share with Pa and Granny and take some up to Miles, too.

They soon had the cabin warm again. Kate washed the blood from her hands and heated up the soup left from supper. Eric hung the meat outside to cool and put the heart and liver in a pan of salt water. When he came in, he picked up the lantern and shook it.

"It's almost dry. Want me to light the lamp so you can see?"

"I put the last of the oil in the lantern. There's a little in the lamp, but we better save it for an emergency. Open the front of the stove. We can eat by firelight."

When they went back the next day they found that rabbits had come to eat the fresh poplar bark and had fouled the snow and some of the meat beneath it. Kate was anguished. She could justify illegal killing for food, but waste was breaking a law.

Supper was over and they were listening to the grama-phone, a whining Hawaiian band, and a male vocalist singing "Yacka Hula Hickey Dula," a phrase Robby liked to chant when his blocks finally teetered in a pile higher than his head. Robby seemed to have a wonderful musical language of his own.

Eric glanced out the window, into the gathering dusk. It was snowing lightly.

"I better get that pail of water before it gets too dark."

He returned with the water, set the still dripping pail on the shelf and turned to Kate, smiling.

"Come outside," he said, with an air of mystery.

Twenty feet from the house he stopped.

"Look at these tracks."

"A lynx?"

"Lynx don't have bare pads. That was a cougar!"

Kate began to retreat. "They look awful fresh to me."

"They are. It just left. There's no snow in them. Look, it stood here a while, the tracks are melted into the path." Eric paused, thoughtful. "I bet it heard the music. Cats are curious." Eric seemed delighted, but Kate was apprehensive.

"I wish I'd seen it," she lied as she backed in the door. Inside, she pointed up to the 32.20 rifle hanging on a pole beam. "Is that thing loaded?"

"The magazine is full. There's none in the barrel. You have to lever one in."

Kate felt relief, knowing she could handle the rifle if she needed it. Still, it was some time before she stopped looking for more tracks close to the cabin. On dark nights, she wished the lantern was a little brighter or the outhouse a little closer.

It was the first of March and the squirrel season officially over. They could take a few more. It would be two weeks before their hides would start turning blue again. Kate wondered how wise they had been to buy the horse. Although they had meat, and vegetables her folks had grown, they had to buy feed for the animals until they could get another horse, harness and machinery to break the ground and raise a crop. She hated being dependent on Eric's father for a wagon all the time. They needed wire to fence off a small pasture for the cow, or some spikes so they could use rails.

Kate was looking out the window at a gray jay sitting on the chopping block, its head cocked sideways. She, too, was speculating. What was Eileen Rathdorf doing this dull spring day? Probably teaching in a bright, warm school room and then going home to her clean and roomy house. Kate's toes pushed the rag rug over to cover the grease spot left by a beaver hide on the warped shiplap. She could not imagine Eileen's high heels tapping across a floor like that.

Her angry, envious thoughts persisted as she removed the boxes on the trunk and opened the lid. What had once been her hope chest was now a veritable Baucis and Philemon pitcher. As quickly as she used the articles from her meager holdings, the trunk was filled again by contributions from the family, especially Aunt Clara, who every spring sent a box of clothing which always contained some bright ornament or a household gadget of some kind.

At times like these, when the weather kept them both in the house, Kate would put a chair beside the trunk for Robby and they would go through the contents together. The pot holders in the shape of Dutch girls kept Robby amused. He was fascinated by the electric knife sharpener. Kate was, too. The only electricity they saw were jagged strokes of lightning behind the rain clouds.

Most of her wedding gifts had been practical, except for some crocheted wool cushion tops, very popular at the time. There was still one multicoloured one in the trunk. She had already ripped up two and knit a sweater for Robby in all seven colours. Joseph had nothing on her son. For a child who liked to climb trees, a hand knit sweater was a hazard. Occasionally he hung up on a limb and spun down like a spider on a thread of coloured yarn. Once after she had rescued him, one of his sleeves fell off. She put aside the remaining cushion top. She could knit some mitts for Robby. The ones she had made from a worn-out sweater were getting thin.

Winter lingered and so did Kate's unrest. It was growing hard again to be hopeful, to be satisfied with so little. Had it been like this for her mother and grandmother starting out? There had been schools even on the prairies. There was no municipal assistance with roads or bridges here. Lying on the south side of the river, the homestead was in an Improvement District. Eric laughingly called it an "improve-it-yourself district." But there was so little they could do to help themselves. Sometimes she felt like giving up, simply letting go of all their dreams.

She swept down the dusty cobwebs clinging to the rough boards and developed a weepy cold. When Eric, who had taken Robby with him to cut posts, was out of sight she flung herself across the bed and finally sobbed out her frustration. Then, exhausted and quiet, she arose and made some tea.

She was calmly folding the clothes that had been drying on a line above the stove when Eric and the boy returned.

"Is your cold worse? You look rough. You should lie down for a while."

Kate looked at the bed, wondering if there were tear stains on the pillow. "I'll be all right. I've just been rubbing my eyes. Do you want some lunch?" *We've lived through worse times,* she told herself.

Kate finished knitting the mitts for Robby. She sat patting them out on her knee. It was a good feeling to have them ready before the old ones wore out. She got up, put the mitts away and began to shape the bread dough into loaves. Eric had gone across the log bridge on the river to work on the truck. When he came back he threw down a greasy part.

"That wheel bearing is shot." One long finger rotated the bearing slowly. "I was lucky to get all the way home last time."

"What now?"

"I'll have to go to Rocky, I guess." He stared distractedly out the window.

"You mean walk?"

"Guess so. I'll catch a ride some of the way, maybe."

"It's thirty miles!"

"I know, Kate."

"We could get a storm. You know what March is like!"

"I'm afraid I do, but we have to have the truck. I'll be all right." He returned to a grim contemplation of the bearing.

Eric left the next morning before daylight. Kate gave him a sanhe had barely enough money to buy the repair.

It was still snowing the next day when he came limping in, pulled a box from his pocket and put it on the table.

"I got it."

"It looks like you've had it, too. Here, sit by the fire and I'll fix you something to eat."

"Wait, wait. I'm not cold and not very hungry. What happened was, I caught a few rides into town and was ready to come back by noon, but I only got one short ride coming back. It was bad enough in daylight in those slippery ruts with the fresh snow, but then it was dark before I got half way home."

"Where did you sleep?"

"I got as far as old man Taylor's place."

"That's twenty miles!"

"I know. I know every mile."

He had his boots off and was holding his ankle, rotating his foot. "You couldn't find better people. The old man said he'd been on the road like that lots of times and knew all about it. Mrs. Taylor had a big moose stew and they gave me a cot to sleep on. They said never to pass their place if we needed help. When I said something about it being so late at night, he said, 'The later the hour, the greater the need'."

Kate's throat tightened with gratitude for those who had gone before them. Without those first settlers, the way would have been hard, indeed, and somehow she felt, even beyond her own low spirits, and even with war threatening out in the larger world, that the understanding and generosity of everyday people would carry them through.

15

A thaw the second week in March dropped the shelf of ice along the river bank, and Fred Hanover rode over and talked to Eric. He came to say there was a week or two of work cutting railroad ties in a camp out of Rocky Mountain House.

He's going up," Eric told Kate. "I said I'd go, too. I hate to leave you here alone, but we need more hay for the stock."

So her husband was off to find paying work again—the regular rhythm of their lives on the homestead. "We'll be all right. There's lots of that moose left. If it turns warm I'll have to can the rest."

"I could take up the few traps, I guess." He looked out the window, musing. "But if we get another wet snow the mink will run again. Their fur is usually good until the end of March."

"Leave them, then, Eric. We can manage."

The morning Eric left, Kate and Robby hauled wood to fill the big wood box, piling it high against the wall, for March had not had its final tantrum, the equinox storm. They hunted a few squirrels, but the hides were already turning blue. Mink, living in and out of the cold water, stayed prime longer.

One afternoon Kate and Robby took the dog and walked up to see Granny. From the bridge on the river it was less than two miles to Eric's parents' place on the hill. Once on the main road, Robby ran ahead, kicking lumps of frozen horse manure ahead of him. They turned off on the hill road and crossed a little creek, still ice bound, except under the pole bridge. There were fresh mink tracks on both sides of the open water. Mink! If only she could catch one of those while Eric was away! She had watched him set traps for mink, and there was still some of that mink-scent bait he had concocted, the stuff he said worked good in springtime. Tomorrow she would set a trap here and hide it, for she had no license to trap other than on their own land.

Robby skipped ahead, stopped and called back, "'Member the night we ran up here to Granny's when it was so cold?"

"Sure do. Remember how good the fire in that old airtight felt when we got there?"

Granny met them at the door. "Come in. Where's Eric? I wish he'd come. I wanted to talk to him."

"Eric got a job cutting ties up at Rocky. He won't be home for a couple weeks. We thought we'd walk up and see how you folks were doing."

"We're all right. Leastways Pa is. He's off cutting wood somewhere. I've not been very well with my constipation and all."

"I'm sorry. Maybe when the weather gets nicer and you can get out more. It might help."

"It won't help none. Here, Robby, you take off those boots and dry your socks."

"They're not wet, Granny."

"They're bound to be. You shouldn't have dragged the child out in all this snow. He'll catch a cold more than likely. I'll make some hot tea before you start back."

Kate sighed. She watched Robby pull off his boots and lay his socks on the wood box. She imagined setting a trap, catching a mink all by herself, to shake off Granny's ill humour. She made cheerful conversation as they drank their tea, and then she and Robby started for home.

The next morning, Kate took up two squirrel traps and made sets on both sides of the creek under the pole bridge. She built one house of sticks and rocks from the creek bed and set the other trap under a willow root. She dipped sticks into the jar of potent bait and tossed them into the back of each set.

"Whew! That's some love potion. Don't touch that bottle, Robby, or you'll have to have a bath before you go to bed."

Two days passed with no sign of mink. The third morning Robby shook Kate awake. "Look, Mom! It's snowing those great big flakes! Dad calls this a mink snow."

A spring storm swept down on the cabin. It had already piled up eight inches of soft wet flakes. They had a bowl of porridge and Kate milked the cow before they set out for the creek. At the logs across the river they stopped. Slush had formed a jam above, and two inches of water was running over the bridge. Eric had strung a rope for them to hang onto as they crossed, but she could not risk taking the boy over that.

They went back to the house. Kate fixed up the fire in the cookstove and shut the drafts. She could not put a fire in the heater now. It had burned so thin on one side, there was a small hole near the bottom edge. She brought out her button box, and cut some brass wire in short lengths.

"Robby, you sit here at the table. You can sort out the buttons and string them on these wires. Try to find the ones that are all alike. There's bread and butter on this plate, and I'm putting the clock on the table. When the big hand gets all around to here, I'll be home. If you get cold put on your coat. Stay in the house and don't touch the fire."

Disappointment flickered in his eyes.

"You bring home a mink."

"Well, I sure will if there's one there."

Without Robby along, Kate could travel faster. She wouldn't need her sweater under her jacket. If she ran part of the way even the jacket would be too warm, for it was made from a man's overcoat and had a chamois lining across the shoulders. She took a paper bag from her sweater pocket and put it in the jacket with the bottle of mink bait. She checked the fire again, hugged Robby and left.

The water across the logs had gone down a little. Once across, Kate hurried along, her feet slipping in the fresh snow as it packed on the trail. When she reached the pole bridge on the creek, she stopped to look for the trap across the stream. A sudden squall startled her. There was a mink in the set at her feet!

She stepped away and searched for a smooth stick. Eric had told her the most humane way to kill a mink was to stun it and then stand on it, so she stood a long time with her foot across it before she put it in the brown paper bag, reset the trap and started back. She had done it! She had caught a mink. It wasn't so hard. Skinning and stretching the hide would be the worst, for Eric had taken his jackknife, and all she had was the knife Eric had made for her.

On the short stretch of main road, a man on horseback was fast catching up to her. He was riding bareback, probably another homesteader. She looked down and saw that a little blood from the mink's nose had stained the paper sack. She couldn't let the man know she had been poaching, and so she tucked the bag under her coat and held it down with her left arm.

When the rider came alongside Kate, he got off and walked with her. She slowed her pace, turning toward him and taking a few steps backward to maneuver herself to the left side of the road. She'd be turning off that direction soon. It also kept the slight bulge under her jacket away from him.

"You walking far?" he asked.

"No. I go south on the trail up there ahead. We live across the river."

"Oh, the Morgans. I met Eric in town one day. I'm Jason Barnes from up on the old Argall place."

They walked along slowly. The horse led grudgingly with outstretched neck. She saw the man's patched coat and mismatched gloves, another recent settler, it seemed. Halfway through a casual remark, Kate's body stiffened as she felt the "dead" animal under her arm begin to squirm. What if it bit her? She squeezed tighter on the bag and searched frantically along the road for the path to the river. Her speech faltered, and the man looked enquiringly at her.

"Just don't want to miss my turn-off," she said, forcing a smile.

The mink squirmed again. She pressed tighter. Only a few more steps now. Seeing the well marked trail, the man slowed as if to continue the conversation, but Kate, still smiling, said, "It was nice meeting you. I have to hurry."

She turned quickly onto the river road. Behind a bush, she removed the little critter and killed it some more.

When Kate reached the river, the slush jam had piled higher, and now four inches of water ran over the logs. She had to get home! Robby, alone, would be waiting and watching the clock. She found a driftwood pole and tried to push at the obstruction, but the swift water beneath it tore the pole from her hands and sucked it down and out of sight. She had been a fool to take a chance crossing in the first place! Kate tried to quell her mounting panic as she dug frantically at a few rocks that showed up through the snow. She kicked them loose and carried them over to the log. Aiming at the middle of the piled up slush, she threw one of them. It disappeared. Slowly the mass began breaking up. She heaved two more into it and stood watching the water recede until she could cross safely. She ran to the cabin to find Robby still stringing buttons.

He had put on his coat. Thank God he was all right! Kate hugged him. "You were a good boy, Robby, to do as I told you. I just want you always to be safe. Do you want to look in that paper bag?"

The boy opened it eagerly. "A mink! You caught a mink!" He pulled it out and patted the soft rich fur. "Daddy'll be surprised. Are you going to skin it?"

"I'm going to try."

I did it. I caught a mink all by myself. My triumph is tempered with guilt, my thoughtlessness in leaving Robby alone and trusting the river. There were fresh tracks today. Maybe we can get another mink before Eric comes home. But I'll always take Robby with me, and if the river comes up while we're gone, at least we'll be together. I seem to be keeping God busy these days. Maybe sometime I will learn to think before I do things.

They caught three more mink before Eric returned. Robby met his father at the door.

"Do you know how much two and two is?" Robby asked. "Do you?"

"Sure, it's four." He took his father's hand. "Come and see."

At the other end of the room hung four mink skins, two on each side of his bunk.

"Hey, where'd you get all those?"

"Mom caught 'em. Mom and me."

Eric turned to Kate. "All at the river?"

"Well, no. I poached three of them on Alfred Creek."

"Little crook." He kissed her warmly. "You sure make a good homesteader's wife."

The warm April wind took the remaining snow, and grew to heavy gusts by nightfall. Eric locked the stock in the little barn and brought in extra wood and water. Kate let the dog in the house. There was no sign of rain. The tattered clouds strung across a moonlit sky, and still the wind blew, steady now, swaying the tall spruce and flattening the willows by the spring. The door shuddered against its latch. Kate shoved the butcher knife behind the casing to stop the rattling. They heard the wash boiler leave the side of the cabin and roll over and over into the underbrush.

"It's going to blow the house away!" Robby's arm was curled around the dog's neck, and Boots was whining uneasily.

"No, Robby. It can't blow this house away," said Kate. "You finsih your bread and milk and get ready for bed. I'll tell you a story."

"'Bout a dinosaur?"

"Sure!"

He went to sleep on their bed and Eric let him stay, tucking him in next to the wall. Eric and Kate lay with their arms around each other, listening to the big trees cracking and crashing down in the timber, trees they had counted on for lumber.

By daybreak the gale had abated as quickly as it had come. They went outside to a yard swept clean of last autumn's pine needles and scattered with branches of spruce. Kate retrieved the boiler, with only a dent along the seam. Eric could solder that. The milk strainer hung limp and ragged high in a pine.

They left Robby sleeping and went out the path into the timber. It was mostly the tallest trees that had fallen, criss-crossing in a tangled barricade. Many still standing were stripped of their branches as the bigger ones had swept down them. Some were bent half over to hold a leaning tree.

"It's not as bad as it sounded last night," Eric said. "You and Rob be careful out here until all those hung-up ones come down."

Eric brought in the mail and tossed a thick catalogue on the table. Kate always waited eagerly for the new Eaton's catalogue, especially the Spring and Summer one, showing new merchandise, new fashions. She picked it up, wondering if they would have some of those new nylon stockings she had heard about. She flipped through the pages eagerly.

Eric was still standing beside her holding an envelope in his hand. "It's for you, Kate. Looks like a cheque."

"Let me see!" She reached for the letter, slipped her thumb under the flap and ripped it open. "It *is* a cheque. A dollar and a half." She held it by both ends and read it over again.

Eric picked up the envelope and read the address in the corner. "Southern Baptist Convention. Kate, you been preaching on the side?"

"No, silly. I sent them a poem a long time ago and they've bought it. They're going to publish it in *Upward,* a Sunday school paper."

"Great, honey. That'll buy a whole bag of flour."

Kate looked up. Eric was smiling at her. The money would buy flour, but he had missed the point. She had sold a poem! The seed had borne fruit. Maybe she would write more. Her diary that night was long and detailed, and the last two lines rhymed.

By the end of May the first spring run-off had come and gone. The river settled temporarily. Eric borrowed his father's walking plough to break up the small patch they had cleared on the top land for a garden. It was slow work. He stopped often to rest the horse, pulling the plough back to chop away a hidden root. Eric's lean body was dragged this way and that by the plough.

Kate watched as Eric picked up a handful of tan soil and kicked at a rock, faintly orange and blotched with black. The whole area had burned off at one time. It took many years to build up the dark soil again. He rubbed his hands over Buck's head and shoulders where the black flies had gathered, leaving red streaks across the horse's buckskin hide. He built a smudge fire and tied the horse in the smoke while he and Kate sat in the shade and had coffee. It was hard going for one horse.

"I wish I had some oats to give him," Eric sighed.

Dear old Buck: Kate remembered their bear-scare together. He was pulling faithfully and hard, as they all were.

This was their first garden, and Kate was eager to plant the seeds she had so carefully selected from the brightly coloured pages of the Dominion Seed Catalogue. After ploughing, Kate raked and planted, and when the carrots and turnips appeared, she hoed the weeds which were only wild plants, spindly regrowth, more adapted to the soil and weather than the vegetables that came up grudgingly. The garden needed manure. They wouldn't have much of that until they could grow enough forage to keep animals. It was a slow round of progress, one thing tied to another, a deeply interdependent spiral of life.

Kate had heard about people living in the dust bowl in Saskatchewan, whole fields blown away, leaving them with nothing. She had also seen pictures in magazines of produce markets in big cities with row upon row of fresh vegetables. She and Eric and their homestead fell somewhere in between, she thought. She pulled vigorously at the clover and goldenrod, and was thankful they would have vegetables for winter. She leaned back on her heels and watched two white cabbage butterflies dance across the garden, and, finding no cabbages, spiral off together.

It had been four years since Kate had seen the mosquitoes as bad as this. They came in waves, big ones that buzzed a menacing symphony, and small, silent ones that arrived in clouds and flew directly to their target.

She went to the trunk for help. Her mother had passed along two large lace curtains. Kate had dreamed about the day she would have a real picture window for them. But that was The Future. The mosquitoes were Now. She cut one panel and hung it across the opening to Robby's bunk and stitched the rest together to stretch over the wire strung from the head to the foot rails of their own bed.

That night, after they had smudged out the cabin, they lay listening to the few insects trapped inside the netting, waiting for them to land.

"Hold on. Wait a minute," Eric said. He listened and slapped, listened and slapped again. "Got the little discord! There, hear that? A perfect E flat!"

"I'll flatten some more if I get a chance."

They slept better that night but were awakened by Robby muttering to himself. Kate crawled out to investigate. She found him on his hands and knees, his nose close to the mesh, his eyes crossed as he watched the mosquitoes swarming on the other side of the screening. His childish voice gloated.

"Buzz, you devils!"

Kate never opened an old can without asking Eric about it first, not out of deference to him but for her own sake. He was always mixing up animal bait and putting it in cans. For coyote he used beaver castors, because coyotes liked to explore beaver dams. Lynx bait was a mixture of beaver, anise oil, valerian, bergamot, catnip and a vile smelling gum of asofetida. To Kate, the whole thing came out smelling like valerian, a rather pleasant odor which lingered for days. Mink bait smelled like mink.

One hot day, when Eric was away, she detected a new stench, something like that dead deer they had found on the river bar. She circled the house a few times, sniffing the air. All seemed fresh enough. When she entered the cabin again, she found it was coming from inside the house. She knew that would happen someday. One of those bait cans had rotted through!

She took them down from the top log under the eaves. They were all tightly sealed and odorless. She turned to the food shelves, but there was never anything left over to spoil. The cellar then?

She took up enough floor boards to hang her head down through the hole and look around. Maybe they hadn't eaten that last turnip! She inhaled gingerly. There was only a damp earthy smell.

As she raised her head, she saw it, on the floor—a two quart sealer behind the stove. Scales shone and bones made tiny white lines against the glass. So that was what he had done with that big sucker! She reached for the jar. The first movement set the contents to bubbling. It could explode! She rushed the thing outside, deposited it under a pine and went for the shovel.

When Eric came home she confronted him.

"What was that awful stuff behind the stove?"

"Mink bait. They live on fish along the river. I forgot it. Is it still there?"

"No."

"Where is it?"

"I buried it."

"Is it all right?"

"Yes and no. It hadn't blown up the last I saw it."

When they went out to the tree, they saw the long scratch marks on the ground. The dog had shared her opinion and helped bury it.

"I'm sorry," Eric laughed. "I forgot it was still in the house."

They went back inside and Kate, now feeling safe from the exploding mink bait, began to put away the groceries he had brought. Eric took down the banjo and played a few chords, his mind somewhere else for a few minutes. Then he hung it back up.

"You know, there's a couple of guys in town selling barbwire real cheap, a dollar for a big roll of it. They're getting it in from Saskatchewan from those abandoned farms, stealing it, I guess. But those farmers aren't going back to that land, do you think? In some places they dig it out of a foot of sand."

Kate felt a chill. Was it that bad out there? Eric went on. "Some of it's pretty brittle and some's rusty, but we could patch up some more fence with it."

"Maybe you better see if you can get some," Kate agreed. "The cow needs more pasture and a shady place to fight those damned bulldog flies." She put away the baking powder and salt. "We'd better take what's offered, I guess. But I sure feel sorry for those people."

16

With the cooler than seasonal days, the snow in the mountains prolonged the second high water until well into July. The foot bridge was damaged, barely passable. Once the river had settled, Eric and Jess Durham finally began to put in the cable.

They strung it across the river with Jess's team, hoisted it onto the log A-frames high above the water and fastened the ends to "dead men"—heavy cottonwood logs buried in the gravel, well back from the high water mark. Kate watched with happy anticipation.

Eric made a cart for crossing, a pole hung from the cable by a stout wire at both ends, each fastened to a pulley. He built a ladder and a platform to mount the trolley. They had to sit sideways on the hanging pole, unhook it and coast down to the middle of the sagging cable, then propel themselves hand over hand up the other side.

Eric crossed first. Then it was Kate's turn to try. She hesitated a moment before letting go and coasting to the middle of the river. Although the pole seat cleared the surface by several feet, she held her legs straight out as the cart rolled closer to the fast water. Would she have the strength to get herself up the incline to the platform on the other side? She felt the strain of muscles in the back of her upper arms as her fingers tightened on the cable and she progressed slowly, a few inches at a time, toward the far shore. With one final pull, her feet touched the platform and she reached for the wire hook to secure the cart. She looked back at the swift water. At least this didn't test her balance, too, like walking the log did. Her trip back was easier.

Five-year-old Robby was worried. "I can't do that, Dad!"

"You don't have to. I'll tie you on and you hold on tight to the wire. Mom will catch you on the other side."

"All right, but you push real hard."

Kate saw the relief in her son's eyes and wished she could be as easily convinced.

She crossed again and shot the cart back to Eric. He sat Robby on the pole and tied a suitcase strap around under his arms and up to the top of the framework. He placed the boy's hands on the wire support and told him to hang on. Then he gave the cart a hard shove. Kate knew Eric tied him securely, but the child looked so small from across the river. The wire in his hands was invisible as if he grasped only air. Her son's outline grew larger as he came toward her, his red curls blown back from his face, his brown eyes fixed on her outstretched arms. She pried loose his gripping fingers, lifted him down, and sent the cart back for Eric to cross.

It was safe enough, although when they crossed after dark, Kate always suffered a few seconds of anxiety from the time she heard the cable zinging until the boy emerged from out of the dusk into her waiting hands. But Robby had a certain sturdy fearlessness: it was one thing the homestead had given him that would last the rest of his life.

As much as Kate enjoyed the added access the cable gave them to community life across the river, it was the quiet, closeness to the woods and its creatures that gave her the strength to carry on at times.

The wild animals accepted the human invasion. Each day a squirrel came to sit in the window and eat bread crusts. Kate demanded her territory back when it decided to build a nest in her wash tub. Porcupines came to chew on the cardboard boxes she had stored in the outhouse, eating away at the glued seams. One baby porky made his home there. At first Kate never turned her back on him, but after a while they learned to tolerate each other, and he stayed around until half grown and all the boxes were riddled beyond use. Eric called him Little John.

In spring time, when the white throat sparrows were calling and the air was laden with the scent of wolf willow, Kate liked to sit on a log at the river and wait for a beaver to cut a poplar tree and float it down river around the bend. Sometimes a deer came to drink or to fight flies on the bar, its long ears flapping, tail flagging. It was the animal's world then.

Kate took Robby to the river one morning and told him about Holland and how the people built dikes to hold back the sea water. She sat on her favorite rock by a backwater while Robby built dikes and planted the polder land with weeds and flowers stuck in the mud.

I have to do this right. Our son is going to have the best education I can give him, and when I can no longer teach him, I'll let him go. By then we will find a way. I'm not sure Eric sees how important this is to Robby. A child's mind is so elastic. It can reach out and accept things so easily.

From those small yellowed pictures in my mother's album, I have tried to piece together a life for my grandparents. I can see in their stance and in their eyes a determination like our own: bareness and pride and hope. History books will tell of the hunger marches and strikes, but how will our descendants find out about our everyday lives? I wish I had film for the camera. I'd like a picture of Robby in his bare feet and patches learning about a distant land....

It was a hot July day, and Kate looked out the cabin door to see a buck deer standing broadside less than sixty feet away. She blinked away the possibility of hallucination, and backed slowly inside. She thought of the empty smokehouse and compassion gave way to their need. She motioned Robby to the bench behind the door and held up a finger to silence him.

The 32.20 rifle was on the beam above. With shaking hands, she took it down and slipped in a half dozen shells. The deer was still there, looking up toward the sound of Eric cutting brush on the hill. The front sight bobbed with every heartbeat, until she eased over and steadied the barrel against the door jamb. "Please don't miss it!" she pleaded with herself.

She fired. The deer stiffened, raised itself until its front feet were off the ground, then lowered and remained standing. She levered in another shell and aimed her second shot to the left. The buck flinched and stood there. She pulled to the right and shot again. The deer collapsed. Kate smiled triumphantly.

She was sawing away on its throat with the dull butcher knife when Eric appeared, out of breath, running hard.

"What happened, Kate? Where's Robby? I heard three shots. Are you all right? Where's Robby?"

At his father's voice, Robby ran out, calling, "Mommy shot a deer! Mommy shot a deer!"

Eric looked at his son, then at Kate and the deer lying at her feet. He stared at it and shook his head.

"She sure did! Those three shots had me worried, though. Kate, you know that's a distress signal."

"But Eric, it took three shots to get him to fall down!"

When they skinned the deer, Eric examined the carcass. All three bullets had hit the animal. The first one had nicked its heart. The second one got him in the throat, another lethal hit. The last was a superfluous gut shot.

"You sure put a lot of holes in him, honey."

"Well, I didn't know where the first one hit, so I tried to bracket my shots. I knew if I killed one end the other end would die for sure."

Eric laughed and hugged her.

"At least you didn't spoil any meat. Do you want to save the horns from your first trophy?"

The two spikes were still in velvet.

"People will know it was shot out of season, won't they?"

"Yeah, maybe."

They peeled off the velvet, leaving stark white antlers. She put them away for a month, and later she painted them red.

Eric made a shield for them and hung them above the door. Whenever he saw someone looking at them, he always said, "Oh them, they're off Kate's first husband. He was a real devil."

Eric took a hind quarter of the deer up to his folks. He was gone all afternoon. Kate took the tub and scrub board to the shady side of the cabin and started the wash. The white clothes had been soaked, boiled, washed, rinsed and hung on the line. She rubbed lard on the black greasy spot on Eric's work pants and rolled them up. Coal oil would take out both later. When she pushed his shirt down into the cooling wash water a familiar odor arose, more than the sweat of long hours in the sun—his own man smell, Eric. Her thoughts drifted back to warm summer nights when his lean body lay close to hers.

When Eric came back, he stopped at the corner of the house and stood with shoulders slumped tiredly.

"Guess we walk from now on. The rear end's gone on the truck. I only got a hundred yards from the river when it started to go. I got it back to the river bar, but that's it. I had to walk up to Pa's with the meat. A good thing you didn't shoot a moose."

Kate stared at him. "What will it cost to fix it?"

"More than it's worth." Eric shook his head.

Another expense or another loss. She had hoped they could soon afford a hand powered washing machine. It looked like the old washboard for a while yet.

"Go on in. There's some coffee to heat up. I'll rinse the tub first." She wiped the tub and washboard and hung them up. *Like ants,* she thought. *We're like ants in a sand trap.* As a child she would dig a hole in the sand and put an ant in it and watch it try to climb the sides until it had pulled down enough grains of sand to make its escape. How many more grains of sand for them? Their log bridge had finally washed away when the far bank caved in. They had put up the cable. Now the truck was useless. What next?

When she went in, Eric was sitting at the table, leaning on his arms, his lips moving slowly, unaware of the bubbling coffee pot. Kate pushed it back and poured in a little more water before serving it. She waited for him to speak.

"If I get Pa's team to haul the truck across the river, do you think you could steer it? The river's low now. I can rig up the motor for sawing wood."

"I could try."

Eric hitched the harnessed horses to the front of the truck and Kate took Robby in the cab with her. They started out, horses and truck, the nineteenth century pulling the twentieth along behind it. With Kate steering and Eric walking alongside the team, the truck rolled smoothly to the river's edge.

"Now you fix your eyes on the other shore and hold the wheel steady. If you watch the water you'll want to steer upstream against it. So *don't* watch the water."

Eric urged the horses into the river. Kate looked past him sitting on the hood of the truck and found a tree for her mark. The small tires rode easily over the rocks until midstream. The left front one, wedged by a boulder, whipped the wheel in her hands, and as the team lurched to free its burden, Eric was jerked off the hood and down in front of the truck. The horses were lunging now, the singletrees churning the water.

Robby was crying and calling to his father. Kate yelled at Eric. "Pull the pin! Let them go! Leave the damned thing here!"

If Eric heard, he did not heed. He struggled to his feet and wrapped the lines around the submerged bumper. He fought his way alongside the down stream horse and grasped its bridle. His presence and voice quieted them. He backed them up to free the wheel and waded on, leading the team the rest of the way across the river.

The worst was over, but Kate's fear was swept over by anger. Why couldn't something go right for them? Four years of this struggle, their accomplishments so meager they were a mockery.

Their timber had blown down, leaving enough to be salvaged if they worked hard at it. The garden had helped feed them, *and* the rabbits *and* the woodchucks. They had shared their chickens with hawks and their eggs with skunks—just as the Hanovers had shared their moose meat that first fall.

Kate felt a flash of guilt for her fury.

When at last the truck was safely out of the river, she lifted Robby down and ran to Eric, hugging his lean, dripping body.

"I was so scared when you fell!"

He held her close.

"So was I, partner." He reached into his shirt pocket. "Look there. I got my tobacco wet."

She looked up and saw his serious face, the laughter in his eyes.

"You're safe. That's all that matters."

Robby refused to ride in the truck as the horses pulled it across the flat toward the house. The next morning they began to dismantle it. Kate thought again of ants as they carried off the parts. Eric rigged up the engine for sawing wood and traded off some posts for a buzzsaw. With the chassis made into a Bennett buggy, they drove Buck for short trips. Eric put the cracked windshield in the barn door so they didn't have to leave it open or carry a lantern to see inside. The seat, set into a wooden frame in the cabin, became their chesterfield. Robby claimed the one good headlamp and left-over parts for his play house behind the cabin.

Although little of the truck had been wasted, they were again without a means of travelling very far. Dances were out.

Kate could have wept with frustration, but she didn't. She promised herself a good cry sometime soon and simply went on brushing down the cobwebs, jabbing the broom into the high corners. The sun, finding a break in the clouds, formed a rectangle of light across the floor, its beam turning the dust motes to silver. She stopped to watch them sparkling, realizing the rest of the air was as filled with dust, needing only a little sunshine to make it come alive.

In front of the clothes closet she stopped, suddenly remembering the jelly beans she had hidden for good luck so long ago. She climbed on a chair and found the dust covered jar. Moisture had crept in and the colours ran together when she shook the dust from the glass. The failed car sure wasn't very good luck, but after that terrifying moment in the river, having Eric beside her was all the good fortune she needed. She studied the candy.

"As mixed up as the Morgans," she said aloud, and picked out a sticky black one and put it in her mouth.

17

As the end of September drew near, mice invaded the cabin. They moved in under the house, built nests and multiplied faster than Kate's one trap could catch them.

"We need a cat," Kate said, after some thought. "I wonder if Durhams have a kitten we could get?"

Eric looked up from his coffee, his dark hair dangling in his eyes. "Pa said there's a stray cat hanging around their place, a big old tom, real friendly. They'd take it in, but you know how cats make Granny sneeze."

Kate went up to see about it, but Granny said the cat hadn't been around for a few days.

"Pa saw it one day down by the bridge," she said, gesturing toward the creek. "It'll likely come back. You come up sometime and pick cranberries out back. We've had a few frosts, so they should be good now." Granny's bad moods seemed to be mollified by the glowing fall weather.

"I will. I'll pick some for you, too. I know it's hard for you to get up and down."

As Kate walked back, she scuffed her feet along through the yellow poplar leaves. A few blue daisies contrasted softly against the red-orange rose hips. Her wandering gaze was arrested suddenly by two green eyes staring at her from the underbrush. A lynx? No, that cat! Its yellow and white stripes blended into the background. It certainly was a big one. She squatted down and called to it. It came slowly toward her, let her touch it and stroke its back. Before long, it was purring and stropping itself on her legs.

"Well, Tiger. You want to come home with me?" She picked it up. "You're a heavy brute. Boots shouldn't give you a rough time. You could whip him first round."

Kate wished she had brought something to feed it, but by carrying and coaxing she got it as far as the river. Then she saw there was no way it would sit on her lap as she pulled herself across on the cable. Well, if Robby could cross, it could too.

She took the strap off the trolley, and cinched it up behind the cat's front legs. Then she tied the strap to the bottom pole, suspending the cat from it. After two attempts, she managed to hitch herself onto the pole without coming in contact with the furious cat.

Although the water was low, the cable had stretched some since it was put up and the cat, revolving and clawing air, cleared the fast water by a few inches. Kate held her feet out of the way. Once across, she had to get the frightened, yowling cat down to the ground.

"You're a tiger, all right," she said, making several attempts to untie the leather strap. She pulled off her sweater, and as the cat swung away from her, she flung it quickly around the cat and tied the arms in a snug knot. When she got the cat on the ground, she untied the arms of the sweater and the cat took off across the river bar, stopping once to claw the restraining leather strap from its neck.

It climbed up the nearest tree, and no amount of coaxing would bring it down, so Kate went on to the house. Eric laughed when she told him. "Don't worry. It'll find its way down here. It sure won't go back across the river."

The next morning it was at the cabin, aloof and suspicious. When it had eaten its fill of mice, it killed them and brought them to Robby in exchange for praise and petting. With her small, yellow soldier Kate won the mouse war.

The winter of 1941 was coming on them. The real war had not touched them yet. They were going to make it through their fourth winter. Kate's low spirits over their poverty and isolation hung on like a chronic cold, but she was too busy to think about it, or if she did, she told herself they would win out eventually.

In early November, Eric and his father got a job shingling a roof east of Caroline. They might have driven to the job, but they couldn't expect the farmer to feed the horses while they worked on his roof. So they walked the fifteen miles to the job, counting on catching a few rides along the way.

The squirrels were getting prime again, and while Eric was gone Kate hunted close to the cabin, taking Robby with her. She found the brass wire in Eric's pack and set some snares for them. On a pole between two trees, she set six small loops.

The next day she had two squirrels hanging from the pole. By not having to use a shell on them she had saved two cents. With the short-barrel .22 it was hard to be accurate. Some men claimed they could hit a squirrel in the head every shot. Kate admired their skill and doubted their veracity.

She expected Eric home Saturday night, but there was no sign of him. She gave up looking toward the river when it grew too dark to see. It was nearly midnight when she blew out the light and went to bed.

Kate and Robby were having breakfast. The dog barked a loud warning and they hurried to the door. A black object was moving across the flat.

"What's that?" Robby pressed close to her side.

Kate stared. She saw a familiar hat on top and two long legs below. She put her hand on Robby's shoulder and laughed. "It's Daddy carrying something."

They met him on the path. He put his burden down, a new air tight heater.

"We sure need that!" Kate said, happily. "The old one is burned clear through, now. I've been putting the dish pan under it at night in case some ashes fell out."

"I know. I was worried about it all the time I was gone. I knew you wouldn't take any chances, though."

"That must have taken a lot of your wages." Kate touched the shiny, blued top of the heater.

"Not really. We got into Caroline before noon and could have come on home, but Pa insisted on staking me to a few games of pool. It was pay day for a lot of mill hands and most of them saw wood better than they play pool. I made enough off them to buy the heater."

They walked to the cabin, and Eric put the stove inside. Lifting the lid, he took out a bag of groceries. "Here, Robby, I got an apple in here somewhere."

With the December cold the river began to freeze over in places, not yet solid enough for crossing, while the open stretches of water were flanked with shelves of ice, crowding the stream to greater depth and making crossing with Buck too hazardous. Eric had walked to the Post Office. Kate heard the crunch and squeak of snow and went to unlatch the door for him. A roll of white, frosty air swept along the floor as he came in. She greeted him, took the mail he handed her, and turned back to the oven to take out a pan of molasses cookies.

"Those smell good. Any coffee in the pot? It sure is cold out there."

"In a minute," Kate said. "Robby, you go out and get me three sticks of kindling. Put on your blue coat."

Eric objected. "He's big enough to bring in an armful."

"I know." She showed him a piece of wrapping paper where she had written a large number three. "He's learning his numbers and I want him to relate them to something practical. And that's why I baked these cookies in squares and triangles."

"You've got a big job ahead of you."

"He's five. It's time."

Eric tossed the mail on the table, a fur price list from Sidney I. Robinson and a report on sales at the first Edmonton Fur Auction. Long haired fur was coming back in style. Lynx and coyote were up again this year. A folded political flyer was full of problems and promises. There was a letter from Kate's mother. She tore it open eagerly. She hated the way Eric always took a knife and carefully slit the envelope, leaving no rough edges to grasp. From her mother's small writing, she read aloud to Eric.

Dear Kate and Eric,
We hoped we could spend Christmas out there with you,

but Maggie, our best milk cow, cut herself in the wire
gate. Although the vet said she was healing good, we can't
expect someone else to do the chores and look after her,
too. She still needs to be tended twice a day. I didn't want
you to be expecting us. Dad is going to town now so I will
mail this today. I'll write again soon.
                    Love,
                    Mom and Dad

Kate was disappointed and silent, holding the letter in her hand. When she looked up at Eric he was smiling.

"How would you like to go out to your folks for Christmas?"

"How? Walk?"

"No. I saw Fred at the Post Office and he's going out that way to see his girl friend. He'd take us out the day before Christmas and bring us back the day after. The chickens would be all right for three days. I could give them extra feed and put some hot rocks under their water pan. It won't freeze up that way. And the calf can milk the cow for a couple days, or maybe young Chuck would come down. He milks their two cows all the time." He smiled down at her.

"I'd love that, Eric!"

As Kate went about her housework the next few days, she found herself humming carols and thinking of her childhood Christmases. She could almost smell those twisted, colored, wax candles. She had been allowed to help move the holders around on the branches until the colours were distributed evenly. They were always lighted on Christmas Eve as her family sat around the tree and sang "Silent Night," or "O Tannenbaum" when a German neighbour was invited to share their evening.

Her father would take the team and sleigh and gather up the relatives for the big dinner in the farm house, and Kate would stand on a chair and wait by the window for the sound of the tiny Swiss bells on the harness and the jangle of trace chains. She wanted that noisy, happy kind of Christmas again.

On the 24th of December, Fred drove to the river to pick

them up. He put a cardboard in front of the radiator, and soon the noisy heater had melted half circles in the frosty windshield.

A team pulling a jumper crowded the snow-filled ditch to let them pass. Fred slowed as much as he dared so he wouldn't frighten the anxious horses. The little house built on the front half of a bob sleigh was constructed from scrap boards. A stove pipe issuing a stream of smoke poked up from the roof, and the faces of two children peered out a small window in the back.

As they reached more open country, white smoke columns stood tall above the scattered farm houses. Kate pictured the kitchens, warm and fragrant with the smell of baking, front rooms with cards standing on sideboards.

A plume of smoke billowed on the horizon. Eric shifted Robby onto his knee.

"Listen. You'll hear the whistle."

It came, echoing mournfully in the crisp air, plunging Kate back into her memories of growing up beside a railroad track. She remembered the year Uncle Max and Aunt Doris had come all the way from Winnipeg—the boisterous greetings, smuggled packages, and most of all, the lingering train smell on their clothes.

Aunt Clara's clothing box that spring contained half a roll of wallpaper. Kate took the three inch border strip, turned the purple flowers to the wall, and printed the upper and lower case letters on the white back. She strung it out along the top log above the table, and the three of them played games at mealtime while Robby learned his letters.

The Frazers, who ran the little store at the bend of the river, helped, too. They saved strips of cardboard from boxes of bulk cookies, and Kate made flash cards from them. After making that small concession to sight reading, she taught Robby as she had been taught, by phonics. She explained that both the letters C and G made two sounds when they talked to us, just like a dog is still a dog whether it barks or growls.

Kate helped Robby with a colour chart. They made crayoned circles in the three primary colours, and Robby scribbled one on top of the other to see the secondary colours emerge.

"What if I mix red and green?"

"Try it."

"Ugh, it's just brown."

"Brown's a pretty colour when it's on a baby rabbit."

"Yeah!" Robby nodded.

With that Robby had escaped into his own world, imagining baby rabbits, and Kate knew that to bring him back now would erase much of what he had learned. She let him find and make his own comparisons, and so throughout the winter they worked each day at his lessons.

Kate was putting a cake of yeast in a cup of water to soak when Eric came in from the barn, brushed the snow away and put down the milk pail and lantern. He said, "Come outside."

Kate went out to stand in the frosty darkness.

"Listen."

The sound began like a rush of wind, increased to a low moan and broke into a howl. She drew in her breath.

"A wolf?"

"Yes. Spooky, isn't it?"

She agreed and pressed closer to his side.

"He's farther away than he sounds."

"I hope so!"

A few days later, they went out to the river to see if the ice was strong enough to cross. There was still twenty feet of open water in the middle. They stood looking at the blue ice channel and the swift water.

"Look at these." Eric pointed to tracks in the snow. "Wolves. Two of them." He edged as close as he dared to the water. "They've crossed the river. Swam almost straight across."

Kate was looking down at the splash marks in the snow. "They stopped and shook themselves here, didn't they? That means they're on our side of the river, now."

Eric ran a finger through a track. The snow was crusted. "Don't worry. They're long gone by now."

They walked back to the house, Kate thinking how strong and determined wolves must be.

She had once seen a painting of a Russian family in a sleigh being pursued closely by a pack of slavering wolves. There had been printed stories, too, of desperate parents throwing out one of the children to delay the raiders and save the rest of the family. She had asked her father which child he would toss out, her or her brother?

He had laughed and said, "There are no wolves around here, Kate. Don't worry."

Well, there were wolves around the homestead now, Kate thought, more than that mythical one that had haunted their doorstep a few times in the past. They were following the elk herd that had moved down from the north onto the Idlewylde flats. A few wolves had come in closer to the settlements, but so far the only kills reported had been game.

For the first time, Kate felt a real uneasiness with the wild animals. Except for the one bear that had come into the yard, they had seen bears only at a distance across the flat, and once there had been tracks at the slop hole behind the outhouse. For a while after that Kate had taken a quick peek behind it before entering. But bears in the wild minded their own business and stayed out of the way of human beings if they could. Wolves were a different matter. Kate glanced up at the rifle on the beam and took down the box of shells from the top log and counted them.

Squirrel hunting was their bread and butter income now. Kate only trapped at the chip piles near the cabin, not taking more than two from each den. It was the females which fed on the buried cones. The dog squirrels sat in the upper branches where they could be shot.

When squirrel hides went up to fifteen cents Kate began to hunt in earnest. That year they were living in the pines and she could hear them eating the hard cones fifty yards away. She would walk toward the sound until she found a den, then stand motionless until the animal's curiosity overcame it. It would make a few experimental chirps, giving away its position.

Towards spring, when they were reckless with their mating antics, it was easy to call them down from the highest tree. A noise like a quick succession of old-fashioned kisses and a drawn out one like the end of an ice cream soda drove them frantic.

Kate and Eric admired the hides lined up along the gable end of the cabin, the tails a sweep of rusty brown. Eric said, "What have we got now, two hundred?"

"And four. I got four today. At fifteen cents, it only takes five to get ten pounds of sugar. Ten for fifty pounds of flour." Kate laughed to herself. "We're back to the fur-trade days."

When the vernal equinox storm came a few days early, they welcomed it. Kate and Eric and even Robby watched in silence as the big soft flakes dipped and floated down to settle on the ground like a benediction of peace, a hushing of the agonies of winter. They knew, too, that the mink would run again.

By April, the mallards returned to the backwaters on the river. Eric sat with the double barreled 12 gauge shotgun across his knees and stared out the window, dreaming, thinking. After a while he picked up the cleaning cord and began to run it through the barrels, still musing about ducks. Kate went on punching down the bread dough. Fred had promised to come over with the tractor and plough before the first spring run-off to break up the small piece of land they had cleared on the flat. For the first time it would be ploughed with a tractor. This was progress! Kate, remembering this, turned to ask if the river was coming up.

Eric was loading the gun, still caught up in his reverie. She saw him snap it shut, cock one hammer and pull the trigger. The deafening blast was followed by another as the gun recoiled and the butt struck the wall behind him. The end of the barrel lay in his hand and blood dripped slowly onto his lap. Kate ran to him, pushed the gun onto the floor and held his arm up. A ragged piece of flesh between his thumb and forefinger was bleeding freely now.

"My God, Eric! Move your fingers!"

A slight response assured her no bones were broken. She looked into his upturned face and saw the dazed look of a newly awakened child.

"Where's Robby?" he asked.

"Outside. He's all right."

The boy burst in crying. He stared at the blood on his father's hands and sobbed louder.

"It's all right. Daddy's all right. Just a cut on his hand. You sit here. Eric, you have to have some help with that. No, don't move around. Lie down and hold your hand up."

"What a fool thing to do!" Eric shook his head slowly.

Kate wrapped a clean dish towel snugly around his hand, binding the fingers together, and propped his arm up against the wall.

"Stay still now, and hold your wrist with the other hand. It will slow the bleeding. I'll get Fred or someone to come for you. The Stoleys are out here now in their summer cottage. She's a nurse. She'll know what to do. Robby, bring Daddy a drink, and stay with him until I get back."

Kate's heart was pounding as she ran up the trail to the cable. She never noticed that a few broken strands of steel had torn her palms until she was down and running up the river bar. She wiped them across her hips as she ran on. Up the river and through the woods, the mile and a half slipped by steadily.

There was no car in the Hanover's yard, no one in sight. She pounded on the door. No answer. There had to be someone home! She pounded again. Young Tim came around the corner.

"Mrs. Morgan. Fred took the folks up to Rocky. Something wrong?"

"It's Eric. He shot his hand. It's bleeding bad. Can you come over with a horse or something and take him down to Mrs. Stoley?"

"Sure. Help me saddle up."

One horse was in the barn and Tim caught up another from the small pasture behind. They rode back as fast as the rocky trail would allow. Kate kept telling herself that Eric could lose a lot of blood and still be all right. The Stoleys had a car, and they could take him to a doctor if need be. She was thankful no bones were broken; he would still be able to play his banjo. His hand would heal, but to take away Eric's music would leave a scar nothing could heal.

The horses, sensing the urgency, splashed into the river, stumbling over the slippery rocks, and raced on down the flat to the cabin. Eric met them at the door, relief in his eyes. Kate put a hand on Robby's shoulder and reached for the curtain on the kitchen shelves to make a sling. She tied Eric's arm up under his chin, and watched as Tim helped him into the saddle.

When the men were mounted and on their way, she turned back to the house, assuring Robby his daddy was coming back.

"Mrs. Stoley will fix his hand, Robby. Don't cry."

Kate had helped skin and gut a moose and deer, but she felt nauseated scrubbing up her husband's blood from the kitchen floor, especially when she found a piece of flesh hanging from the log wall. One charge had blown a hole through her ironing board and a stray shot had shattered the glass on Robby's favorite picture of Strongheart.

Kate knew Eric's pain was not all physical. Caught up in one of his day dreams, it had been a careless accident and he was ashamed and angry with himself. How dreamy they both were, Robby and Eric! They had escaped this time from serious injury, but the incident left Kate wondering what they would do if one of them were really hurt. Well, they would do just as she had done now—use their heads, and fast. She washed her hands and jammed the bread dough back down into the dishpan where it belonged.

18

By the time the Hanover boys were ready to come over to plough the flat for them, a sudden spring storm and local run-off had swollen the river. They built an apron of boards across the back of the tractor for fording. When angling down stream, the current helped push it across. The small front wheels reared and plunged over the big rocks as the water piled up behind it.

As she washed the coffee cups Kate listened for the sound of the tractor. At last it came, throbbing into the warm May morning. She hurried out to the flat. The plough had already made one round in the opening, an irregular furrow embracing all their hard work in clearing the land, with each round squeezing their frustrations into memory. Now they could raise some feed, maybe get another horse! There'd be fertilizer for the garden. She could can vegetables for the winter.

The men's voices, raised high above the sound of the tractor and river, came clearly as they stopped to dig out a boulder or to chop away at a hidden drift log. The flat had been built up years before by flood waters from the wayward river.

Robby followed the plough. Kate slipped off her shoes and followed, too, her toes curling into the cool earth, her fingers cradling the scooped-up soil, some sandy, some black where willow growth had enriched it. This must be how the prairie settlers felt when they saw their straight, black furrows claiming their future from the earth. A real sense of accomplishment, a warm, joyous feeling swept through her. This was another milestone, like the day they had filed on their land. A few crows came to inspect the newly turned sod and settled in the trees by the spring, cawing their approval.

That night Kate's scribbler diary had no more room to write, so she took the label from a can of tomatoes, turned it over and recorded their victory.

By the time the river was again low enough to cross with Pa's team and disk, it was too late for planting green feed that year. They worked up the ground and left it fallow. That night Eric spoke aloud what had been on his mind for some time.

"Our five years are up this fall. Even if we could get another six acres broke up, we're supposed to have eight in crop and then we're still seven animals short for the ten we need to prove up."

Five years. In one way they had been an eternity, but they had gone by so fast. Kate's usual well of resourcefulness went dry, leaving only a dull fear inside her. Her mind rummaged for an answer, nosing like a rat in a maze for a possible way out. There seemed only one thing to do.

"I'll write to Edmonton. Maybe they'll give us an extension."

She wrote that night, explaining how they had no horses or machinery those first years, and that it was often necessary to work away from home to support themselves. She read the letter over several times. It sounded convincing; she had to admit she had a way with words.

She offered the letter to Eric. "Want to read it over?"

Eric, sitting by the window sharpening the axe, glanced up. "No. You're better at that than I am."

Kate read it again, hesitated, then added a quick postscript. She leaned the sealed and stamped envelope up beside the clock. Eric was going to the Post Office the next day.

They waited. The answer came in two weeks. They were granted an extension, another year to make the necessary improvements. The letter also listed the address of the nearest Relief Office. Eric put the letter on the table, smiling.

"That's sure good news! Now if I can get a little work so we can keep going, we may make it." He picked up the letter, read it again, then tossed it back on the table. "We don't need relief money. All we need is a little more time."

Kate put a hand on his arm.

"That was my fault. I don't want us to go on relief, either. I just ended my letter by asking about the nearest office, a hint of the alternative if they wouldn't give us the extension."

"That was sneaky."

"It worked." She put her arms around him and kissed him on the chin. "You need a shave."

The extension renewed Kate's hope, but it was still hard sometimes to overcome the feeling of impending defeat that had grown in her these last months. She got up and tossed a pair of worn out socks back into the mending box. Eric was sitting on the corner bench patching his rubber boot with the tube patching kit from the car. She could smell the glue as he squeezed the tube and smeared it on the rubber, then pressed on the patch and held it down with his thumb. He looked up.

"Anything wrong?"

"Not really. Why don't we go over to Hanovers tonight? There's a moon and we can take the shortcut up the river."

"This is Friday. They'll all be going to that dance in Caroline, the young folks, that is."

"I wish we could go."

"Fred asked us to go with them. When we sell a few of those posts, maybe we can go to a few dances."

Work was Kate's only therapy for depression. She started to clean the bedroom end of the house. Eric had given her a wooden cigar box which she had lined with flowered wall paper for a trinket box. Most times when her avid cleaning got that far, she would sit down and look through the box and her gray mood would disappear.

She opened the lid and picked up her lapel pin, a funny little dog made of coloured pipe cleaners. Her mother's Homefront Group had made them to raise money for the war effort. She moved her compact, and there, underneath it, was a dollar bill. She called Eric.

"Look what I found. Did you put this dollar in here?"

"Not me. You must have."

"If I'd had one I'd remember it. Wait a minute. Mom was looking at that box the last time they were here. I bet she slipped it in."

Kate stood looking at the bill. When she looked up, Eric was smiling.

"Come on," he said. "Let's go. It's only fifty cents, ladies free, and I can give Fred the rest for gas."

"You know he'll never take it."

"Then I'll buy a package of cigarettes and be a real sport for our night out on the town."

So much has happened I have not had time to keep up with my diary. I enjoy all the birds and animals near the cabin—but I did not count on the wolves. Eric says they are the wariest of all. I sure hope he's right....Eric's hand is healing well, thanks to friends and neighbours....Five years have gone by so fast. I wonder if we would have tried homesteading if we had known it would be this hard and slow. Still, what else was there? Thank God we do have a home for now, and they've given us another year to prove up....I feel like a truant school girl this morning. The dance last night was the break we both needed. That dollar might have bought food for our stomachs, but the dance was a feast for our spirits. I haven't heard Eric whistle at work for a long time. I remember the time my mother brought out the egg money she had been saving to buy new curtains and took us all to the chautauqua in the big tent on the ball diamond. At ten years old, I lived in another world for a week. I think Mom did it again!

In late July, Kate's father wrote and said the government was building huts in Red Deer and they were looking for men. Eric put down the letter.

"I better go. Maybe we can rent some kind of a shack at

Sylvan Lake for a while."

"The cow and chickens again? I don't want to part with Taffy."

"We don't need to. Jess said any time we wanted to go away just let him know, and we could turn her loose with his stock. He'd want to milk her anyway, now. And the chickens, well, maybe we could kill them and you could can them for winter."

"How long before you'd go?"

"A week, maybe, if I can get somebody to haul our stuff out. Let's get a furnished place so we only need a few things."

"I could stay here."

"No. You and Robby are coming if I go."

"Guess I'd better. That's where you met me. There might be better pickin's in the summer, the beach and all."

"Would you be worried?"

"Yes."

"Good. Start packing."

Kate knew one reason she and Eric had so few arguments: she simply didn't argue. She couldn't see the point in it since their goal was the same—to keep the homestead.

Kate had helped can chicken on the farm. She didn't mind the job after the first stink of scalding them. They were mature birds and well feathered after moulting, so there were not all those annoying pin feathers to pick. Since there was no need to draw them, fingers searching for the last scrap of lungs between the ribs, she soon had a pile of parts to boil and put into sealers and boil again for hours in the hot cabin. A delicious pot of soup was always left over from the first boiling. She lined up the finished jars to cool and to be admired before they were stored under the bed.

Jess was glad to have the cow to milk. Granny said she'd take Boots if she could keep him this time, because he didn't bark all night like her last dog did.

Before they left, they sowed the flat to clover, Kate walking ahead, broadcasting the seed by hand, and Eric following dragging a big hand made wooden rake to cover the seeds.

She looked back at the furrowed earth, knowing that at least they would have some early summer pasture.

Eric traded his shot gun to a man with a light truck to take them out to Kate's folks while they looked for a place to live, handing it over with a look of "good riddance."

They stayed at her parents' farm at Sylvan Lake for two days. Up in her old room, Kate lay for a long time after Eric was asleep, listening to the familiar night noises of cow bells and a dog barking in the distance. This room always had the magic to unwind time. She was sixteen again. She wanted to hear the robins caroling outside her window at daybreak. Tonight she wanted to hear the soaring cries of the night hawk, the zooming dives, but she knew that was only their mating display. That time for them was over. Eric's breathing became a gentle snore. She nudged him in the ribs and he turned over to face the wall. Kate closed her eyes. At least there were no mosquitoes.

The tourist season was at its peak, and everyone with an empty garage put in a bed, a stove and a few pots and rented it out. Eric found a ten by fourteen two-room shack across from the tennis court. The rent was ten dollars a week, and the woman wanted a month in advance. When she found Kate was Jim Wilson's daughter she settled for a two-week advance and said she'd have her son fix the clothes line.

Eric was hired on the construction job the following Monday and commuted the eighteen miles to work on the bus. Kate took Robby to the beach at Sylvan Lake every day the first while. She took off her shoes and waded out with him. When he began to feel the lift of the water, he suddenly wanted to go back. All summer he had played in the shallow spring, but had been warned away from the swift river so often that the large expanse of the lake frightened him. With encouragement from Kate, he began splashing about in the shallow water at the edge. Shy at first, from his years of playing alone, he was soon digging in the sand with other children, glancing up often to make sure his mother was still there.

Kate saw Eileen Rathdorf at the beach, slim and tanned in a

two-piece bathing suit. Kate was tanned, too, a painful process of burn and peel until she had attained a deep golden shade, but only on her face and the V of her throat—a farmer's tan.

"Are you vacationing?" Eileen asked brightly, waving and smiling.

"No. Eric's working in Red Deer. We're only here for a few weeks."

"Where are you living?"

"Across from the tennis court."

"Oh, that big white house?"

"No. There's a little place across the alley."

Eileen paused, trying to think of the place. "Jack and I are going to Toronto when he gets his holidays, so we'll have to get together for a visit before you go back. Nice seeing you again!"

Kate felt a strange sense of dismissal as she watched Eileen get into the big, black Chrysler Royal, its ornate bumper gleaming in the sun, its visored windshield frowning above the long tapered hood. A tall aerial, with a coyote tail dangling from its tip, whipped as the car lurched and rolled away. She watched it turn the corner and disappear. Imagine having a radio in your car. Imagine having a radio.

She called Robby, bought him an ice cream cone at the stand by the boat house and walked slowly back up town, stopping at the butcher shop to buy hamburger for supper. After so many years of wild meat, Kate had almost forgotten how good beef tasted.

With his first pay cheque, Eric bought a second-hand Star, a blue sedan. In place of those popular hood ornaments, it had a round heat guage on the radiator. The roof didn't leak and the upholstery was good. This time they would be able to move back to the homestead in style.

For Kate, the enchantment of the thriving summer resort soon wore thin. She had been born and raised here and knew much of the gaiety of the vacationers from as far away as Edmonton and Calgary was only a week or two snatched from more sober living, a time for cramming enjoyment, dispelling frustrations. The three thronging dance halls were a Mecca where dreams were born and many of them died.

Sometimes Kate and Eric went to a dance on Saturday night, taking Robby with them. The jitney dances were ten cents now. Eric didn't dance much. He hadn't learned the latest steps, since he played for most of the dances they went to, instead of dancing. He liked to listen to the music and often went down to the halls alone on Sunday afternoons to hear the bands practice.

Kate grew tired of sitting in the doorway watching the tennis players in the courts across the road, the women's tanned bodies in flashing white, the men's bandy-legged stance. She needed to work, something to do.

Most of the permanent cottagers carried on with their own household chores, except for the more mundane cleaning and weekly wash. Kate began doing washing on the scrub board for a family with two teenage girls, no ironing, just the weekly wash, for which they gave her a dollar. Eric protested.

"You don't have to work, Kate. I don't like it."

"I know, but I'm tired of doing nothing all day. We can't spend all our time at the farm or the beach. It isn't hard. Their clothes aren't very dirty."

"They shouldn't be. By the pile they bring they must change them twice a day."

He was still protesting when she quit washing and went to work with her mother, cleaning summer cottages for thirty cents an hour. The cottages bore carved or painted signs—Hart's-acres, Sheila's Shack, and The Dales—Hal and Betty.

Most were equipped with left-over furniture from the owner's city homes, wobbly tables, leather covered chesterfields, old-fashioned wooden rockers and faded brocade drapes. Kate wondered what their homes looked like. A few cottages were occupied all summer by the owners, and they, too, hired help through the rental agency.

One cottage had a huge porch with a dozen windows and

as many panes in each. Kate's fingers were bruised from polishing into all those corners, and it was four-thirty by the time they finished. The lady brought out her purse.

"Let me see. That's two and a half hours."

"We started at twelve-thirty," Lila Wilson reminded her.

"Oh yes, so you did. Father and I finished lunch a little early today."

Kate's mother went on in a controlled voice. "And it is now four-thirty. That's four hours."

The lady looked at the clock on the wall and shook her head. "It only says three-thirty, my dear."

"Like it has for the last hour," said Lila sharply. "I believe it stopped while we were doing the back shed."

The matron consulted her watch.

"Well, so it is. I'll have to have Father look at that clock!"

She paid them and they left. As they went down the steps, Lila muttered, "Old bitch! I'd like to fix her clock."

Another lady, whose house seemed quite clean to start with, suggested they take time off to have coffee, and before they left, insisted they share a drink of gin with her. Kate and her mother were still giggling when Kate stopped to pick up Robby at the farm. Jim Wilson eyed them suspiciously.

"I didn't realize doing housework was so much fun," he commented.

The man from the agency, Mr. Larkin, didn't always inspect the cottages before he assigned them, leaving it up to Lila to decide the work to be done and the hours they put in. He warned her that Hangover House might need some extra cleaning, but even Lila was not prepared for the shambles. They both recoiled from the liquor-laden air that assaulted them. One glance took in the circle of assorted bottles and overflowing ashtrays in the center of the living room floor, the broken window and the overturned furniture. Lila shook her head in disgust.

"You stay here, Kate. I'll run back into town and get Mr. Larkin. He'd better have a look at this before we start. It'll take us hours to clean up this mess. Maybe you can open the windows and start heating some water. I'll be right back."

Kate, taking shallow breaths, walked through the sprawling cottage, opening windows and doors. She closed one bedroom door again, quickly. Someone's drink had not agreed with them. She'd save that room especially for Mr. Larkin. When she had a fire going in the kitchen stove, she went outside and sat on the top step of the long stair leading down to the lake.

Would she want a life like these wealthy people who could afford two houses, one for summer? Yes and no. She wanted more comforts, life a little easier, but not the society. If this was social status, it was petty and hollow compared to the sincerity of her own neighbours, the challenges of the wilderness, the mission she and Eric shared.

They'd had it all, anyway, really, those things that stand for the better life—mink and orchids, steak by candle light, soft music. The mink were wild. The orchids were placed gently in her lap as she sat in the rocking chair sewing for the baby. The moose, gutted and skinned in the deep wet snow left them warm and grateful. When the last of the coal oil was gone they had eaten their steaks by candle light while the kettle hummed soft music on the back of the kitchen range.

Kate had learned in times like those to take life as it comes, for unless you woo despair, it goes away by itself. A gray spring day could be made shining again by the haunting call of the chickadee telling them it was only winter that had come apart at the seams.

The sound of waves slapping gently at the row boat tied to the pier, an early autumn leaf fluttering down, the fresh sweet breeze from the lake was all she wanted now.

By the first of September the cottagers with children had returned home. The Labour Day dances wound up the season. Only the gulls patrolling the empty beaches broke the silence as the village returned to its winter apathy.

Robby was six that August. Kate enrolled him in school in Sylvan Lake. Eric was hesitant. "You know we'll be going home again in a few weeks. We have to start cutting the timber that big wind blew down, the beetles will be at it already."

"I know, but I wanted him to see what a real school was like, to be with other children. I want him to learn to share."

"That shouldn't take long," Eric said. "He's never had very much."

Robby attended school for six weeks before Eric's job was over, and they began packing to go home. Besides salvaging the blown-down trees for saw logs, Eric wanted to enlarge the barn before winter. They needed another horse for logging.

They had talked some of staying out where Eric might get more work, where Robby could go to school. But finally, it was Kate who said no. They had sacrificed too much to give up the land now, she said. When the land was theirs, when they had a place to come home to, they could think of going away to work. She was ready to go back now. She did want a more comfortable life, but on *her* terms.

Eric's work would be finished the middle of October. Kate began preparing for their return to the homestead.

She never sang much when Eric was around. His accurate ear would have been offended by her off-key warbling. Alone now, in the small house, she hummed randomly as she packed. She had put away a can of strawberry jam, and one of tobacco for Eric. After some deliberation, she had bought a cake of fragrant soap to put in the cardboard box with her underthings. It would help through the long winter to have this small luxury.

It was Sunday, and Kate's folks had asked her and Eric to the farm for lunch. While the eggs for the salad were boiling, they sat on the porch and watched a man coming down the railroad track. From a distance they could see the hump of a sack over his shoulder.

As his slow steps, measured to the spacing of the ties, brought him closer, they saw his uneven gait was partly a limp. Beneath a battered hat, he had dark hair and whiskers. He stopped and took a pail from his pack to scoop water from the deep ditch.

"I hope he's not going to drink that," Lila said, as the man disappeared across the track and down the other side out of sight. "I guess it won't hurt for coffee if he boils it."

"There's not nearly as many men go by or stop in now," Jim Wilson said. "A few years ago there'd be five or six bail off the rods out here when the train slowed for the main crossing. There's some that are pretty desperate for work. They can't all join the army. Looks like he's started a fire. There's a little smoke coming up over there."

They were eating lunch when the dog barked and they looked out to see the man crawling through the railway fence. He put his sack down and limped toward the house. He had shaved and combed his hair. He carried his hat in his hand.

Jim went to the door and quieted the dog. It growled without threat and went to lay in the shade. Before the man could speak, Jim called to his wife, "Mother, have we got a bite to eat for this man?"

"Of course."

Lila cut two thick slices of home made bread and made a sandwich with three boiled eggs left from salad making. She turned to Kate. "You go down to the milk house and fill this pickle jar with milk. He can take it with him."

As Kate passed the man sitting on the steps, he glanced up. She saw the gray in his dark hair and the defeat in his eyes. Through all the hard times she and Eric had known, they had always had each other; this man's aloneness struck her to the heart. She felt tears sting her eyes, and knew that she was richer than he—not so much in money but in hope and laughter. In the milk house, she poured the jar nearly to the top with milk and finished filling it from the cream pitcher in the cooler.

On Eric's last day he was later than usual coming home. He drove up, unloaded his tools and then carried in a big box and set it on the table.

"A radio. I thought we could use some connection with the outside world when we go back. I know you like baseball games, and the series starts next week. Here's the batteries.

The six volt is second hand, but I can charge it up with the car if it goes down."

They hooked up the radio and turned it on. Someone was singing "Fools Rush In."

Eric nodded slowly. "Ain't it the truth!"

19

The leaves had gone from the trees by the time they drove back to the homestead. Only white waxberries and red rose hips still clinging to the low bushes gave colour to the roadsides. At last Kate spied the evergreens. The ones planted in rows along a fence did not count with Kate; she had had enough of straight lines and restrictive fences.

Small spruce had sprung up along the ditches. The trail across the river bar looked unused, but at the river there was evidence of campers having stopped there, charcoal remains of a fire, paper scattered and caught in the dry brush.

Kate stood at the river's edge looking at the cable trolley hanging useless in midstream. Someone had unhooked it and let it go.

"Damn city people!" Eric said. "It looks like I'll have to pull a Tarzan and go after it."

"No! Remember you hurt your shoulder on the job. You almost had to quit work with that."

"Well, I can't walk on water, not yet. I guess I'll have to wade. It's all right. The water's lower than that time we pulled the truck across. I'll catch Buck and bring the Bennett buggy back."

She watched him wade into the water and walk down stream, taking long steps as the water carried him along. Robby played along the bank, throwing rocks and drawing letters and numbers in a sandy spot. Kate sat in the car out of the cool October breeze. She'd have to continue his lessons now. She wondered if she could handle it? She had been so confident before the time came. She thought uneasily of the responsibility of the years ahead, the training of a young mind.

Eric was coming along the flat, the buggy rolling smoothly across the ploughed and seeded land. She wondered if the clover had come up, if it had a good enough start to survive the winter. When Eric reached the river bank across from the car, he stopped, unhitched Buck, fastened up the traces and rode the horse up stream to the trolley.

"Catch it, Kate. Then send it across to me."

He shoved it over to her and she held it while he rode back across the river. She pushed it hard and he caught it and fastened it securely on the home side of the stream. He hitched the horse again and drove over to the car to pick up their things. And then they were across the Clearwater and home.

The long view across the flat showed faint green. Eric stopped the horse and jumped down to examine the ground.

"It's coming! The clover's coming! It's pretty small yet. I hope it doesn't winter kill."

Kate checked it, too, and saw tiny three-leafed plants tight to the ground. Here was positive results of their long hours of work, an added pleasure to the way she always felt when coming back to the homestead. She caught Robby's hand and the two of them raced each other across the field to the cabin.

For Kate, the radio brought the excitement of the baseball play-offs into the cabin, but more than the entertainment itself was the sound of new voices. She cheered with the crowd when DeMaggio set his record of fifty-six games of safe hits. But all this could not make the war news less disturbing. The voices that came from the little brown box on the shelf brought the world situation home to them more forcibly than the week-old passed-on news they had relied on before.

The Atlantic Charter, the billion dollar lend-lease to Russia and the conference with Japanese envoys on the invasion of Thailand had more significance when coupled with the daily reports of the fighting. In November they listened as the newscaster summed up the Pan-American conference. *The United States has met with Latin-American republics to consolidate economic and military co-operation for the defence of the Western Hemisphere.*

Kate felt a measure of relief. They had lived their lives by reprieves.

Before long, Kate knew she would need some help, some direction, with Robby's school work. She wrote to the Correspondence School Branch in Edmonton, asking if she could buy the course and teach him on her own, since there would be times they could not complete a lesson in the required two weeks. The Branch was helpful. The boy would have to write an examination by Grade IV. They also offered help boarding out children who were too far from a school. But Kate did not have her child to let someone else raise him. She sent for the course.

Eric worked at the fallen timber, cutting and skidding logs onto a rollway. The beetles were only under the bark as yet. It would be another year before they would begin their destruction. A light snowfall early in December made skidding easier for Buck, and made sawing and trimming more difficult for Eric. He came in early, wet and cold, and stood turning and drying his soaked pant legs before the air tight wood stove.

They had recharged the wet battery for the radio and it was playing softly—"Beer Barrel Polka." Eric drummed his cold fingers on his hips. The announcer's voice cut in: "We interrupt this program....Japanese war planes have bombed the port of Pearl Harbour....battleships sunk....warships damaged....bomber command in the Philippines destroyed." There were more details, lost to them in the shock.

On December 8, they learned that the United States had declared war on Japan and that Germany and Italy had retaliated; the whole world was being drawn into the conflict. By April of 1942 food was rationed. Kate needed coupons for tea and coffee, sugar and butter. Each person was issued a book with sets of coloured, numbered coupons, each valid on consecutive dates. The war had, in this small way, come to the homestead.

By the first of June, the clover on the flat was green, thin in spots, and thicker where the seed had rain-washed into the hollows. They bought another horse that was broken to ride. Robby named it Scruffy for its patchy winter coat, although when it shed, the horse was sleek and trim. Its dark colour and tall frame contrasted with Buck when they were driven as a team.

One morning at the peak of high water, Kate was awakened by an intermittent churning sound at the river. She and Eric jumped out of bed and ran down the path. The current had cut into their side and directed its force against the opposite bank. The supporting A-frame was gone and the cable hung down in the water. The current would stretch it to the limit. Then it would leap out of the water and snap back to start over. They stood helpless, watching the bouncing cable slowly beating out their renewed isolation. Kate shivered in the early morning chill. Eric put his arm around her.

"You're cold. Let's go back. There's nothing we can do."

By the time the water had gone down in July, the cable had been torn from the dead men and strung down river, half buried in the rocks and debris. They left it there.

Eric found a tree farther down stream for a foot bridge so they could cross to the car. So much for progress. They were back where they had started. Kate still feared the river's strength, and she hated it for its wanton willfulness to destroy. She stood watching the water, clear now, and gentle in its newly formed bed. She knew those deeper pools promised food when the whitefish began to school up in the fall. The river would make up for its destruction.

After that crowded place at Sylvan Lake, the cabin seemed big for awhile. I saw some progress. The clover, however patchy, is the beginning of a cycle of independence for us....And then we stood at the river, watching its angry hands tearing out the cable. I saw all that work wasted. It is so hard to be hopeful. But we have to go on—we have no other choice we can live with.

Kate was delving into the trunk in search of some dark material to patch the elbow of Eric's shirt when, in the very bottom, she uncovered her tennis racquet. She took it out and knelt beside the trunk, bouncing the worn ball with the racquet still in the press. Eric came up behind her.

"You should leave that out and play with it. You could bounce it off the back of the house. There's no window there."

"I suppose I could. You know, I won the doubles one year in high school, me and what's-his-name."

"Yes, you told me," Eric said in a bored tone. He turned to walk out the door.

Kate frowned. Surely he wasn't upset about her one athletic victory so long ago. More than likely it was because Roger, her tennis partner, was a blonde Adonis whose father was the manager of the local bank. She was about to put the racquet and ball back into the trunk when Eric appeared with Robby's snowshoe guitar and challenged her to a game.

"With that?"

"Sure, come on." He laughed. "You'll have to keep score. I don't know about all that love stuff."

"We don't have a net!"

"Don't need one. I'll string up something we can use."

He snapped the lines of the harness together and tied them between two trees, while Kate scratched out a singles court in the pine needles. Robby watched their game, laughing, running, following each stroke.

They played three games and Eric won them all. At first she thought it was uneven ground that made the ball bounce off in unexpected directions. Then she remembered. As a youth, Eric had been an inveterate pool player. He was putting English on the darned thing. Kate's tennis career was over, and the ghost of Roger what's-his-name was laid to rest.

By August Eric had several rollways piled with logs. The Homestead Act allowed them to saw only enough lumber for their own use before they had the title to the land. For them to do even that meant hauling logs across the river to a private mill. Rough lumber sold for ten dollars a thousand and local small mills charged four dollars for sawing, or would saw for half the lumber.

The patched up tires on the Bennett buggy would not carry even a small load of logs, so they borrowed Pa's wagon to haul some across to Levy's mill, enough to begin an addition on the barn. They had it started. The stringers were set on big rocks dug into the ground and they needed a few more spikes to finish putting up the studding.

Eric lingered at the table after lunch, more quiet than usual. At last he spoke.

"I think I'll enlist, Kate."

"No!"

Kate dropped the mixing spoon and let it lay. She went to his side and put a hand on his shoulder, a persuasive touch.

"No, Eric. You don't need to go. The war will be over soon. The States is in it now, and even if it does go on, you may be called up soon enough."

He didn't answer. He sat there looking at the floor. Kate knew the pressure he was under, the responsibility of a family, never enough money for the things they needed. Tim Hanover had joined up. She had heard the brave talk of other men who had volunteered. Being patriotic covered many contingencies.

Kate spoke first. "I know it's hard, always doing without material and tools to work with. But we'll get by somehow. You buy the spikes you need for the barn. I'll can the blueberries without sugar. We can add it when we open the jars this winter. There'll be trapping money again." She paused. "Unless—unless you *want* to go."

Eric, still silent, shook his head slowly. He put his arm around her and drew her down onto his lap. Kate continued. "You said Sam Levy, over across the river, wanted to sell that old mill of his. Maybe he'd take some logs to saw in his new mill in exchange."

"We're not supposed to sell or trade off logs until we get

the patent."

"Oh, to hell with their laws. I'd rather see you in jail than in the army. We could run a small mill by ourselves, maybe get Jess to help sometimes."

When she got up, Eric still held her hand and said he'd think about it.

They got the mill. It took most of the skidded logs to pay for it and the McCormack Deering tractor to run it. The river was low in August, and Eric drove the tractor across to the homestead. Since most of the heavy timbers on the mill had to be replaced, he was able to bring the rest of it across with the team and Pa's wagon. Eric spent a week replacing the rotted timbers and lining up the carriage.

When they operated the mill alone, Eric rolled the logs onto the carriage and ran the saw, too. Kate kept the slabs and lumber pulled away at the other end. Whenever Jess helped, he did the tailsawing and piled the lumber and Kate canted the logs onto the carriage. Robby shovelled the sawdust away from the conveyer. The whole family worked—they would save the homestead together.

Kate hated to see the tall proud trees come down. She soon became expert, however, at judging the board feet in a log, converting it to dollars and mentally spending the money. They needed equipment for logging and clearing land. The new house seemed always to be last on the list.

When they stopped the mill at noon, Eric would gas up the tractor, file the saw, or put more dressing on the belt while Kate went to the house and made lunch.

After they had eaten, she sat Robby down to his workbook and reader. She had bought coloured stars and small prizes. It may have been bribery, but it worked.

It was evening, a day's work finished and supper over. Kate watched Eric drumming his fingers on the table and staring out the window. She tore out a sheet of lined scribbler paper, filled her fountain pen and began to write. Eric turned away from the window.

"Tell your folks the cable's out and we have another log."

"I'm not writing to them. I'm writing to the Department of Lands and Mines for another extension. We may not get it, but at least we'll know where we stand. If they kick us off the place, they can damn well feed us."

Her pen went racing across the page. Eric got up and moved over to stand behind her, his hands on her shoulders. He leaned down and laid his cheek against her hair.

"Remind them never to tangle with a red-head."

I hope the mill works out. At least Eric hasn't mentioned enlisting again. I don't think he really wanted to go. It has its advantages, the money, the experience, the comradeship, even a little glamour. But it all comes down to killing. I know we could never fight tanks and bombs from here, but if the enemy came as equals to take our home, he'd fight fiercely, and I'd be right beside him. Oh, I don't know. I don't understand it all. I guess there is more than one way to die.

I don't know which is harder on my pride, admitting we can't make it here, or begging the government for more time....But if that is what it takes.

They cut down the Star sedan, too, putting on a truck back to haul gas for the mill; as a truck they could get more gas coupons. The west country had survived the spring road break-up where mudholes could only be crossed by taking a run at them, hoping for the best, a kind of mud skiing. The worst was having the gas tank gored by a pry pole buried in the mud. For a few days, when "the big mud hole" was impassable for all vehicles, a man from Caroline left his car on the town side to taxi people to the store. When they reached the mud hole again, they carried their boxes and bags through the brush to their own vehicles.

The heat of July dried most of the roads, but two weeks of steady rain in August made them difficult again. Detours were often worse than the holes they were avoiding. Kate and Eric drove to town one rainy Saturday for tractor gas. On the way home that night, they had gone only a half mile on one detour when the truck sputtered and stopped.

"That vacuum tank again! I thought I had it fixed. Must be leaking air somewhere."

Eric lifted the hood and peered under it. Shading his lighter from the raindrops, he searched for the trouble. Robby was sniffing the air.

"I smell gas."

Kate looked over at her small son; his tone of voice was so mature and responsible it startled her. Eric put out his lighter.

"It can't be flooded." He walked around the truck and kicked at the gas tank. It responded with a hollow sound. "We can't be out of gas, either. I filled up in town."

He got down on his knees and looked under the tank.

"Christ! The bung's gone, tore right off! It must have been that big rock in that last mudhole."

"What do we do now?" Kate was thinking of the five miles back to town. They were still seven miles from home.

"Any old rags behind the seat?"

"I don't see any. What good would they do?"

"If we could plug up the hole, we got ten gallons of purple gas in that can."

After a few seconds of silence, in which Kate weighed some values, she said, "You can have my underskirt. It's only one I made from a flour sack. I'm sure not going to undress in this rain, but if you want to cut the straps with your jackknife, I'll slip out of it."

"Sure you don't mind?"

"I don't want to sit here all night."

Eric opened his jackknife, groped in the darkness down the neck of Kate's blouse, and slipped the blade under the straps. Kate bent her head away as he cut through each one. Eric stood waiting while she squirmed the garment down and off over her feet.

"That should do it," he said.

He went around the truck, and she could hear the empty tank resounding hollowly as he jammed the cloth into the

196

ragged hole.

Eric, wet, covered with mud and smelling of gas, climbed back into the truck and drove like a demon down the muddy ruts. The gas leaked out faster than it burned, but they made the next seven miles on the ten gallons and had to walk only a hundred yards to the river.

Kate kindled the fire in the range and put the kettle on to heat. Now they'd have to sell more lumber to buy a new gas tank and some more gas to saw more lumber. She mumbled out her frustration to Eric who only shook his head and smiled wanly at her. But when Robby was in bed and Kate and Eric were sitting beside the stove, their clothes drying on a line above them, Eric reached out and drew Kate's head down on his shoulder.

"We'll make out all right, Kate. I can get a second hand tank somewhere and put it on myself. It doesn't have to be for a Star car as long as I can fasten it up."

His quiet response always calmed her fears, just as her quick bursts of energy and determination lifted his depressions. Kate sighed and pressed her damp, red head closer to him.

Eric began to make a pile of lumber for the new house. It never got very big. There were always needs—a new gas tank or more oats for the skid horse. Kate was sitting by the window mending socks when she heard a snuffing sound outside along the cabin wall. As she raised up to look out, a bear raised up and looked in. Kate froze. The bear, seeing her face emerge from his own image in the glass, swung away and loped off toward the sidehill. When Eric and Robby came in from the mill, she asked again for another dog.

"What kind?"

"I don't care. Just one that will warn me of bears and things."

Eric brought home a lop-eared hound. He was trained to chase cougar, but a rabbit or deer would do, so they had to keep him tied. Kate called him Sport, and hoped he didn't like bears.

The letter from Edmonton came at last. Kate's hand shook as she tore the envelope. Another reprieve! The letter laid out the requirements: *Ten acres broken, eight in crop. Ten head of stock and the place fenced.*

Eric read the letter again and put it down. Kate could see his lips moving slowly as he calculated. He turned to her.

"We may make it yet, partner."

20

The three of them went down to Kate's favorite fishing hole at the mouth of the spring creek. Robby walked a short way into the tangled underbrush and then cried out in pain. Kate, picturing a bear or cougar, burst through the brush after him, but when she reached him, he waved her away.

"I want my daddy!"

Eric threw down his fishing pole and came running.

"It's all right," Kate said. "He just got caught in his zipper."

"Just!"

It was Robby's first grown-up pair of pants, with a zipper instead of buttons. From afar, she gave advice. "You can't undo it again. You'll have to cut the zipper at the bottom. It'll come apart."

The boy's sobbing became hysterical when he saw his father open the blade of his jackknife. The next few minutes created a new bond between father and son, and relegated Kate from then on to minor roles like fixing a broken shoe lace or tying the rubber bands on a sling shot.

Eric went into Caroline the next day for rivets to repair the tractor belt. By late afternoon he still hadn't returned, even though Kate expected him home long before dark. There was only one log across the river now. Her uneasiness grew as dusk approached. When she could no longer see the dog house in the dark, she took the lantern and Robby and the dog and went to the river.

She stood on the bank and thought of all the sane things first—a flat tire, or an empty gas tank. Then came the thought of a car accident; those brakes were not very good. She knew he would never take a chance with the river, so she waited there with her hound dog, her seven-year-old, and a feeble coal oil light.

She shook the lantern. The contents barely splashed. She put her mouth to the hole in the tubing and blew out the flame. Robby crowded close to her side as darkness rushed in. The sound of the swift water was intensified as her senses became alert. She felt the movement of damp air on her face, and caught the drift of pungent smoke from the extinguished flame. Her staring eyes tried to pierce the darkness.

This was where those two wolves had crossed! Imagination had already created wolves behind her, tongues lolling, eyes gleaming, when the hound stuck his cold wet nose in the palm of her hand.

She screamed.

"Damn you! Go lay down! No. Come back here. Come on, Sport, nice dog."

She lit the lantern again and waited.

The dog's deep-throated growl startled her. He was looking across the river. Then came a bark of greeting as Eric, seeing the light, called out. She set the lantern on the end of the log and shaded its glow from his eyes as he came toward her out of the darkness.

"Thank God! I was so worried."

He put an arm around her. "I know. I'm sorry, but I stayed to play pool. There was a bunch of hunters in there celebrating getting their game. Great rifle shots, maybe, but they were no good at pool. I took eight dollars off them. Here, Robby, take my hand. We'll go first. The light won't be in our eyes that way."

At the cabin, Eric put the small box of groceries on the table. He reached into his pocket and pulled out a handful of crumpled bills, smiling.

"You take this and get something you need."

Kate smoothed the bills into neat piles before she put them away. The next morning she got out the Army and Navy catalogue and sent for underwear for all of them. Eric looked over her shoulder.

"Save enough to buy a pair of those new nylon stockings for yourself."

Eight dollars for a day's work—a day's play! Maybe Eric missed his calling. I can picture him, thumbs hooked in the pockets of his fancy vest, a rakish black hat. How dashing! But my Eric's not the dashing kind—at least not without a haircut. And I'm no Klondike Kate. But there's no bigger gamble than homesteading. We've tossed our chips in together. Fate, it's your deal.

Fall had always been a time for Kate to reflect, to take stock of their supplies and of herself. She had grown and changed. She was more self-reliant than the young woman who had stood in the yard of her mother-in-law's house with a grubby baby, wondering where the next dollar was coming from. Robby had grown, too, far beyond his seven years in maturity and independence. Eric and she had submerged their differences in their common goal, more often too tired to waste energy in an argument that could be settled by compromise.

They had a home and two horses, and although Clarabelle had ended up in the stew pot, they had another cow. Their timber had blown down, but for a time, they'd had the cable across the river. There were gains and there were losses, but Kate felt she could meet whatever came. It was a fragile resolution, and needed the support of good neighbours and a little good luck.

They lived that winter by trapping when the snow was deep and by sawing lumber on warmer days. Kate, busy with Robby's school work, wished sometimes that the old tractor would refuse to start, but it was only a mass of cold iron and practicality; it had no heart. Whenever she heard it chug a few times and gather itself into its powerful rhythm, she would pull on wool socks and rubbers and go out to the mill.

After the New Year, she sent for Rob's Grade III lessons. He had kept up well for his age; he would be eight in the summer. She had stressed only the basics and disregarded some of the simple projects like snow angels, and doll's furniture from construction paper. He was already building his own tree house, and definitely did not need doll furniture.

She tried to keep her teaching practical. He learned the principles of the lever from the wheelbarrow, the tweezers and the pry pole.

Fractions baffled him. One half an apple plus one half was still two halves of an apple until Kate took two tomato cans, each half full of water, and poured them into one. In turn, she was stymied by his question, *How come a fluffy little chicken hatches from a sloppy old egg?*

Once when it seemed he would never remember a simple multiplication, she shouted, "Look! You can remember that Jack and Jill went up the hill. Why can't you remember three times eight is twenty-four?"

She was ashamed of having yelled at him until she saw his brown eyes bright with amusement. He sidled out the door chanting, "Jack and Jill went up the hill. Three times eight is twenty-four." He never forgot it.

In June he finished the required work for Grade III and Kate declared a summer holiday. She took two cups of coffee out behind the house where Eric was building a boat. Robby, who tagged his father everywhere now, was there eager to help.

"There's cracks in it." The boy pointed. "It'll leak."

"We're going to fill the cracks."

"With moss?"

Eric laughed. "No, I'm afraid that wouldn't do. We'll use oakum."

"What's oakum?"

"It's unravelled rope. Hand me that paper bag over there. I'll need you to help me."

Robby picked up the package and held it to his nose. "It smells like tar. Here you are, Dad." He said the last word tentatively.

"Thanks, Rob," Eric replied, his tone casual.

Kate, sitting on the block of wood, sipped her coffee and witnessed another milestone in her son's childhood.

It took two days to finish the boat. It was fourteen feet long, the bow high and pointed, the bottom wide and rounded. For all its size it rode like a chip on the water. From dry poles, Eric shaped oars with wide paddle ends. A half buried log jutting out into the water formed a backwater on the home side of the river. They tied the boat up there. Eric became skillful at judging the right angle to hold in the water, using the swift current to help take them across. Once over, they floated it upstream and pulled it onto the bank so the return trip landed them back at the log.

They bought a flashlight and when they crossed after dark, Kate sat in the stern with Rob and held the beam on the landing place.

One dark night at the end of June, coming home from Hanovers, Kate was glad to see the water had gone down a little. Still the current seemed to be taking them down stream faster than usual. The beam on the log was angling fast, almost striking Eric as he rowed hard. The log slipped by. Not far below, the river struck directly into a log jam. She tried to hold the light steady, frightened, shaking. Would they make it? Or would they end up against those logs and be sucked under? She tried not to convey her fear to the boy leaning sleepily against her, but her body stiffened and the light bobbed against the bank.

Then the boat touched the shore. Eric leaped out with the rope held fast, bound over his knee, his feet skidding in the gravel until the swift water pressed the boat against the bank. Kate and Rob scrambled out. Only then did she speak.

"What happened? We're way below the log! I tried to hold the light on it."

"You were doing all right. Look at the oar."

The paddle end was gone. He had brought them home with only one oar, pulling and braking to make the best of the current. Kate flashed the light on the log jam only a few feet away.

They struggled up the bank with the sleepy child.

21

In July Fred Hanover married Grace Tower from Red Deer. The ceremony was performed quietly in the city, and the local people, cheated of a wedding to celebrate, chivareed the couple when they returned home. Fred had built a log house on the corner of his father's quarter. The neighbours came at twilight, dark shadows gathering at the far end of the lane. At a signal, they marched up shouting, banging pans and ringing bells. They circled the house a few times and then pounded on the door, calling, "Open up!"

Fred had warned Grace about the possibility of a chivaree. She had grown up in a city and had never seen this form of rural welcome. Shy at first, she was soon caught up in the boisterous round of good wishes and wisecracks. The revellers brought sandwiches and cake, and they made coffee in Grace's new wash boiler. Someone had borrowed cups from the community hall, thick white cups with strings tied around the handles to identify them. Fred passed out chocolates.

Most people brought a small gift to help the couple starting out, giving according to their circumstance. Eric brought his banjo, and with Tim on the guitar, he led a singsong. They sat Fred and his bride down in the middle of the living room floor and grouped around them while the others sneaked off, one or two at a time, to prepare the bridal chamber.

The women snuggled a Shirley Temple doll, complete with diaper and bottle, between the pillows and remade the bed carefully. The men tied a cow bell to the springs under the bed. They put a large box of home-made pickles and preserves beside it, and as they left, Kate hoped Grace would appreciate the humour. She also hoped Grace would have as steady a life partner as she herself had.

In late August, Eric made a deal with Miles. Eric would graze a dozen of his brother's yearling calves on the open range south of the homestead while Miles fenced off part of his own wild pasture to be sown to timothy. In return Eric was to get a load of hay.

As Kate watched the young stock fighting flies in the brush shelter, her hope of getting the title to the homestead rose again.

All the final decisions concerning eligibility were at the discretion of the Homestead Inspector. Kate and Eric were now two years over the five year limit. Eric counted out fifty dollars.

"Well, there it is. You put this away for the final fee and we'll apply for the patent."

"Do you think we have enough land broken up?"

"No, but if this won't do we'll never make it, Kate. This may be the only time we have fifty dollars we can let go of."

They filled out the final paper and sent it to Edmonton.

Kate was late starting the wash. She had soaked the towels and underwear and had the water heating in the boiler when Eric called for her to help him fix the fence behind the house. A moose had blundered into it, breaking the top wire. He stretched it while she attempted to drive the bent staples into the bone-dry tamarack post. The staple caromed off into the grass, and she couldn't find it. She used a nail, pounded it in and bent it over the wire.

By the time she returned to the house and her washboard, she was hot and frustrated. She winced as the soap suds stung her raw knuckle. She put a spoonful of Gillet's Lye in the boiler and waited until the gray foam on the top had broken the water's hardness. She skimmed it off and picked up a bar of P&G soap. Shaving flakes from the new bar always calmed her. The soft resiliency was a mild sensual challenge, like biting into an art gum eraser at school, or squeezing a fresh puff ball until it burst and surprised her with its bright textures. She was lost in her thoughts when Eric came to the door.

"There's a horse coming across the flat. Looks like that tall bay of Hanovers, but the rider's not Fred or the old man."

Kate put the lid on the boiler, brushed back the hair from her forehead and looked outside. The horse came into view, a stout man in the saddle, bare headed in the hot sun, one hand holding knotted reins and the other gripping the saddle horn. He rode to the door, looking hot and flustered.

"This the Morgan place?"

"Yes."

The man dismounted slowly.

"I'm Cal Motts, the Homestead Inspector. I had to borrow this horse to get over here." His voice was edged with annoyance.

"I'm Eric Morgan and this is my wife, Kate. Come in."

The horse, relieved of its burden, stepped sideways and enriched the soil. The man looked embarrassed.

"I'll put that on my flower bed," Kate told him.

Eric tied the horse to a tree. "Maybe we'd better sit out here where it's cool. The wife's washing and the cabin's pretty hot."

They sat on the bench beside the door. Rob stood beside his father, looking at the stranger. Kate tried not to look anxious. She watched Eric's hands methodically rolling a cigarette and caught his glance as he raised his head to run his tongue along the paper. They would both be glad when this was over. Very glad. They would either be home free or completely desperate.

The inspector smiled faintly. "What were you folks hiding from over here? Seems to me there's better land across the river."

"We didn't have the equipment to work it. At least there's some timber on the place. A little, anyway," Eric added, for there were rules about homesteading land with too much timber.

"Let's see, you filed in thirty-six. That's seven years ago!"

"We've had two extensions. We couldn't make it any sooner. You came across one piece of breaking. The rest is on the top land. We can go up and see it."

The man shook his head. Did that mean he didn't want to see it or he couldn't accept it? Kate swallowed noisily. To hide her anxiety she went into the cabin and busied herself stirring the fire and pushing the kettle around to find the hottest spot. She heard Eric say, "We didn't know you were coming or I would have run the stock in. They're ranging out south of here."

She didn't hear the answer. Rob came into the cabin and asked her, "Can we take Uncle Miles's calves back now?"

Dear Robby! In his own way he had shared their concern, but at eight years his knowledge exceeded his wisdom. She bent down quickly and whispered urgently to the boy.

"Don't say another *word* until that man leaves."

She listened for the fateful words of rejection, but Eric was telling Motts they had a pretty good root house in the sidehill.

"Yes, I can see it."

He couldn't see it from where he stood and had no intention of moving very far. He stepped aside and looked down the length of the cabin, then back toward the barn. He turned to Robby, standing in the doorway. "Where do you go to school?"

Rob, afraid to speak, looked at his mother. Kate put a hand on his shoulder. "He's shy," she said. "I teach him. It's fifteen miles to a school."

She went back in to wring out the white clothes and put them in the boiler. There was a long silence, then the inspector's firm voice. "If you folks have lived over here for seven years, you deserve the place! There'll be no problem."

Kate almost laughed aloud.

Eric offered his hand. "Thank you. This is a pretty important day for us."

Kate reached for the towel and wiped away the dampness

from her forehead and the moisture from the corners of her eyes. She stepped outside and invited the inspector to share the noonday pot of stew. He looked at Rob, from his bare feet and patched clothes to his thin face and eyes peering out through tumbled hair, eyes too serious for a child.

"Thank you, but I've got to get on back."

Eric led the horse over and handed the reins to Kate while he gave the inspector a leg up into the saddle. The man turned and held up a hand in farewell, having just handed them their land and their hopes, released them and enabled them to go on. The three of them watched as the horse jogged off across the flat and disappeared into the trees. Eric and Kate hugged each other and bent down to include Rob in the embrace.

"It's over! The worst is over! We won! Now we can plan on something permanent," Eric looked around. "It isn't much, but it's ours."

Rob was smiling, though his eyes were troubled.

"Did I say something wrong, Mom?"

"No. No, everything is all right." She kissed him to reassure. "Let's eat that stew."

In ten days the long brown envelope arrived from Edmonton with the title. Although the final word was an anti-climax, Kate put out her Quaker Oats cups and set a bouquet of blue daisies on the table. They had a festive celebration, a feast, a saved-for-company can of corned beef for the entree. After the fresh baked bread and a quart of wild strawberries, they were sated and quiet and happy. Except for the occasional sigh of relief, they were busy with their own thoughts, almost afraid to display their great joy lest it be snatched from them.

The driving force eased, they could look forward more calmly toward making a living from their acres. There were logs to be cut for the new house. Still they faced the fact they would have to sell most of the lumber to keep going for another year. They would have to scrap some of their long term dreams and put the rest on hold, getting their second wind. Kate and Eric looked across the table at each other, and lifted their flowered cups in a silent toast.

22

When the first September rains had exhausted themselves and the wind had blown for two days across a rain-washed sky, the season collapsed into Indian summer. Kate and Rob took a sealer of coffee to Eric who was putting a rail on the west fence. The myopic moose was still running into the wire and ripping it off the posts.

They took the skid trail through the timber on the way back. Rob stopped at an old creek bed where the dewberries were ripening, each one a mound of dark red bubbles of sweetness. Kate picked a few, walked on into the timber and sat down on a fallen log. It was cool there and quiet, save for the scolding chatter of a red squirrel. It sat motionless on a higher branch, its bushy tail curved over its hunched back.

A few tight-fisted fronds poked up through the leaf mold, reminding her of the potted fern in her parents' crowded living room, and how she had watched it send up its pale shoots to uncurl into lacy foliage. She remembered that her grandmother had had a dress of that same muted green with sprigs of feathery leaves.

Kate wondered what vivid memories she was laying up for her son, and remembered her words about someday telling her story. It would be for him and his children. She called Rob to see the miniature forest of moss and liverworts growing on a rotted stump.

Rob had enjoyed three weeks away from school work. When his Grade IV books arrived, he literally buried his head in his lessons, opening the texts and inhaling the new smell of them. She took advantage of his enthusiasm, covering as much as they could in the first few weeks in anticipation of the time his interest would lag and she could declare another holiday.

In late November they studied only by daylight, for the coal oil supply was low and Kate refused to let Rob read by candle light. She thought again of Eileen Rathdorf, not Eileen herself so much as her well-lighted, well-equipped school, and she wondered again how long she could teach her son. Enough to prepare him for today's world? This was not the early pioneering era of the past where a man was considered educated if he could decipher a newspaper and "figure."

Her own father had only managed Grade VI before he began to haul coal across the prairies to the settlers in the Crossfield area, and then to work at the coke ovens at Michelle in B.C. By the time he was eighteen he had his own quarter of land at Dog Pound. Kate still had a few years before they would have to send Robby away to school. She kept on, inventing new teaching techniques, using whatever she could find around her.

The winter of 1944 crept up on them. Eric came in with an armful of wood. "It doesn't look like this cold spell is going to let up. I'll have to start that truck and go into town."

"We need lard," said Kate. "This wild meat doesn't have much fat on it." They had fallen into the ancient problem of "fat hunger," faced by the Indians in the centuries before them.

Eric shoveled coals from the heater into a pail to put under the oil pan, and took a blanket to throw over the hood. But these offerings were insufficient against the extreme cold which had sucked the life from the old battery. It ground out its death rattle and was silent. He came back for the six-volt from the radio and managed to get the motor going.

Kate mended socks until it was too dusky in the cabin to see the dark yarn. She was cutting potatoes into the simmering broth on the stove when she heard Eric call. She hurried to the door to see him pushing a blanket-covered object on the toboggan. At the door he whipped off the blanket and there was a treadle sewing machine.

"Oh, Eric! Where did you get that? Does it work?"

"I think so. Some bachelor south of town brought it in for scrap metal."

"What a waste!"

"I gave him three dollars for it. His sister died and he didn't want it. That scrap sure is piling up. I don't think they collect it much any more, but it does let people get rid of their junk and feel they're helping the war effort, you know, like collecting lead paper and toothpaste tubes."

She didn't want to hear about the war effort. She wanted to see if the machine would run. They brought it inside. Eric filled the lamp and the lantern and lit them both to examine the machine. They worked on it all evening, cleaning, oiling and adjusting. At last with a gentle pull to help the worn feed dogs along, it sewed an even seam. Kate was ecstatic. She rummaged through the drawers which revealed thread and assorted treasures the man had not bothered to remove. She wanted to hem up a curtain from a piece of flowered chintz, but Eric objected.

"Put your toys away now and come to bed."

"In a minute." Her head was full of plans.

She caught up on the mending and making over. The shoulder of her winter coat was beyond patching again, and she had been wearing the short one from her navy suit, though it wasn't meant for December weather. There was a heavy blue coat in Aunt Clara's box. It was almost new, but was badly faded across the shoulders and down one sleeve. She ripped the seams, picked all the loose threads and brushed away the lint that had gathered. After pressing each piece carefully, she sewed the coat back up inside out. It was bright and unfaded, but the buttonholes were then on the wrong side, so she made new ones, stitched up the old ones and sewed big buttons over them.

When Kate sewed in the evening, the lamp on the table was too high to shine in a pant leg or sleeve so she could see inside it. Kate fastened a piece of broken mirror onto an elastic around her head, and by bowing her neck she could direct the reflected and intensified light on the moving needle. She restitched the patchwork quilt she had so labouriously sewn by hand. It made a colourful bedspread.

"It looks like a real pioneer cabin, now," Eric said.

Yet the constant whirr of her machine could not obliterate the news of the fierece fighting in the Aleutians. The war was suddenly very close to home.

Sometimes in the winter when the snow was dry, Kate wore moccasins with slip-on rubbers. They were light on the feet. Most of the time, though, she wore those stiff, ankle-high, laced rubber boots commonly called "Ankle Burners." While hunting squirrels, Eric had come across an old game hunter's camp, and hanging from a limb was a pair of smooth horse hide shoe-pacs, made like a moccasin, with extra soles rounding up on the toes like miniature skis. Except for a few teeth marks around the top, they were still good. With a pair of heavy socks they fit Kate.

After a short walk on the icy path to the spring, she suspected the footwear had been abandoned, not forgotten. They were so glassy smooth on the bottom that she fell three times. She stomped into the house, unlaced them and flung them across the room.

"I can't stand up in these damned things." She pushed up her sleeve and examined a red, swollen elbow.

Eric retrieved the offending shoes and ran a hand along the sole. "Guess not. They're slick as a hen's tit. Maybe I can fix them, put some cleats on the bottom or something."

"I don't ever want to see them again. Give them to the dog to chew on!"

He accepted her proposal of such waste in his exasperatingly calm manner. When her anger had paid the debt of a bruised elbow, she agreed to let him try to fix them. He walked across the river up to his father's place and came back with an iron shoe last, a few strips of old car tire and a piece of felt from a discarded sweat pad. He riveted rubber cleats on the soles, and then split the felt and shaped it into insoles to cover the rivet heads inside the boots. She wore her "new" shoe-pacs for three winters. Sometimes she looked at them and realized that what we throw aside in anger may well stay with us for some time to come, like thoughts and experiences.

The shrinking snow drifts and the chickadee's promise of spring did little to relieve Kate's usual winter depression. The pile of lumber they were putting aside for the house had grown so slowly. She was sitting by the table sorting buttons, trying to find a white one big enough for the flap of Eric's underwear. He complained he couldn't manage those little ones when his hands were cold.

Hoofbeats grew louder on the path. Eric must have decided to do some skidding after all, she thought, and looked out to see a gray horse, and Leah dismounting. Kate flung open the door, and Leah called out, "I'm on my way to the Post Office. I thought I'd stop by for a cup of coffee."

Rob came running from the barn.

"Aunt Leah! Can I take your horse? Can I? Dad's at the barn." Rob was just learning to lead horses.

She handed him the reins and he led the mare away, looking over his shoulder with cautious pride.

"Come on in! I'm glad you came. I was sitting here feeling sorry for myself. How was the ford?"

"Not bad. Eric must have chopped down some of the ice along the shore."

"Yes. We have to ford now. You can't trust the ice bridges since the thaw."

"I can't stay long," Leah said. "I wanted to come, though. You must get lonely over here. I brought you some magazines."

"Good! I'll pass them on to Martha Durham. Her mother likes them, too."

Leah put several dog-eared *Good Housekeeping* books on the table as Kate turned to add another stick to the fire and measure water into the coffee pot.

"Do you feel all right?" Leah asked.

"Oh yes, just a little tired. We sawed up some lumber yesterday, the first we've had the mill going this spring."

"I thought you looked a little pale."

"Nothing time won't cure. I'm all for nature when it comes to flowers and animals, but I don't think it's fair for a woman to have to be grateful for a belly ache."

Leah laughed with her.

"How's Rob's lessons coming?"

"All right, I guess. I don't push him too hard. There's so much said nowadays about kids not achieving their potential. Well, who does? If I did I'd have had those dishes done a long time ago. Kids are human, too, most of the time."

Leah flipped through one of the magazines. "I wanted to show you something. There's a piece in here about making a dress form. I'm going to try it myself."

"That sure would help in making over. Here, have a little more tea before you go."

Leah left, and Kate walked along beside her horse as far as the spring. "Come again soon," she called and waved.

Eric and Rob had gone up to the top land to search for a birch big enough to make a shovel handle, so Kate decided to make the dress form. She got out the magazine, found the detailed instructions, gathered the materials: strips of cloth, water, flour and salt. As she started to mix the flour and water, she thought maybe she should fix the base first. She stripped to the waist and would herself up mummy-like with the strips of cloth. *Spread paste in a thick, even layer,* the instructions said. She used a kindling stick to reach between her shoulders.

It was supposed to harden into a firm shape, be cut up one side, slipped off, and there you had it—a perfect dress form to fit your patterns on.

She sat down to read the magazine while the form dried. It was a slow process, and when the warm, wet mixture started to cool off, she began to shiver. She built up the fire in the heater and squatted beside it, turning round and round. The

216

paste steamed encouragingly while her skin turned from blue to red. Some hot tea might help, she thought. She walked woodenly to the table, and she saw it. The cup of salt—still sitting there. No wonder the darned thing didn't harden!

While she was trying to get the messy, sticky plaster off, she heard voices and caught a glimpse through the side window —Rob, Eric, and a stranger with a rifle and a pack on his back. Another lost hunter? What if they come in!

She didn't own a dressing gown and she couldn't put her coat on over the gluey mess. Crouching low, she scuttled to the door and jammed it shut with a table knife shoved behind the casing. Eric was pointing toward the river and the log bridge. She stood in the darkest corner until the voices receded. A quick look revealed Rob walking along with the man toward the river.

She was still struggling with the sticky mess when Eric tried the door and then tapped four times—his signal that meant the visitor was gone and could *he* come in? She removed the knife and slunk back to her corner.

Eric stood in the doorway, staring at her, fascinated.

"You mixing up biscuits or what?"

She didn't turn around; she could tell by his voice he was laughing.

"Shut up and help me out of this!"

When he finally stopped laughing, he helped to extricate her.

"It was supposed to be a dress form. It didn't work," she admitted.

"I gathered that."

23

They had talked of it before, of raising a few pigs. If they could get one sow, or maybe two, and a small chop mill—they had the gas engine—they would be able to turn off the pigs in November at the latest.

"Select bacon hogs are over seventeen dollars a hundred weight now and we should be able to get feed oats for fifty cents a bushel. I'd like to give it a try. What do you say, Kate?"

"Why not? If we try enough things something's bound to work out for us. The law of averages must be swinging our way by now. We can always butcher and have our own ham and bacon."

They bought a Yorkshire sow due to farrow in three weeks, and a chop mill that needed a little fixing up. The river was low before the first run-off, and Eric brought everything across in the Bennett buggy.

In true pig fashion, Polly decided to have her litter the last day of April during a rain storm, one that ended up with two inches of wet snow. Eric came back from the barn, turned the lantern down and set it by the door.

"There's time for another cup of coffee before I go back. She'll be a while yet. It's cold out there. We may have to bring the little ones in the house at first. She's pretty restless, her first litter. She could lay on one."

"Can I go back with you, Dad?"

"I guess so. Put on your boots and a warm coat."

Kate emptied the wood box and arranged an armful of hay in the bottom ready for the piglets. Rob came in alone and announced happily, "She's got six little ones. Dad says there's going to be more. I think I'll stay in the house and help you."

"Are you cold?"

"No, I just don't feel so good. My stomach feels funny."

She saw the paleness around his nose and mouth and the wonder in his eyes. Live births were different from baby robins.

"Maybe you're too tired. Better have something to eat, some bread and milk, and get into bed." Kate tried to keep from smiling.

"I'm not hungry."

The sow had twelve lively pigs. Even the snub-nosed runt was active. They kept them in the house until daylight, until the mother was ready to accept her young and suckle them.

When high water came, they hauled Polly's oats across in the boat. Then the feed ran short and there was no money for more, so they traded a couple of weaner pigs for oats to chop. They continued this Peter and Paul economics until by late September they had only four pigs left. They butchered one and sold the rest. They knew by then they couldn't make a go of pigs until they could raise their own grain.

"I guess it's back to squirrel hunting," Eric said. He paused, thinking. Kate waited. "What would you think of going on a trap line for the winter? I hear they're leasing out the lines of trappers who are in the services. We might get one with a few marten or lynx as well as squirrels."

"It would get us through the winter," Kate admitted.

They applied and got a line up on the head of the Tay. The map in the forestry office had shown a cabin on the creek, and Eric rode up to check it out, to see if it was habitable. Kate waited anxiously. It would mean Durhams taking the cow again. This time they could give him the calf for feeding the cow all winter. The horses could range out in the forest reserve; a permit was only a few dollars. She had adapted to these shifts, plans sacrificed to the needs of the hour. How did other people get ahead? She knew many of them didn't. So far she and Eric had been spared the indignity of having to apply for relief.

When Eric returned she could tell by the brightness of his

eyes that he was excited. "There's a good cabin. It's small, but it doesn't look like the roof leaks. It's built against a bank and dug down a couple feet into the ground, so it should be warm. There's lots of wood up back of the cabin."

"How do we get in to it?"

"I rode across country, but we'd have to drive to the Ram River oil well on Prairie Creek and walk in from there on the Baseline Trail. It's the long way around, but we can get almost to the cabin that way."

"How far do we have to walk?"

"Not over six miles."

Eric paused, and when she seemed to accept the prospect of the long walk, he went on to describe the country and the thrill of seeing a herd of elk on the Idlewylde Flats. Kate wanted to ask more questions, but remained silent, drifting in the wake of Eric's enthusiasm.

Eric made one more trip with both horses, piling bedding and traps on Buck. When he got back, he made a canvas canopy on the back of the truck. They would have to leave it at the oil well and make several trips to pack everything up to the cabin. Eric watched Kate sort clothes.

"Remember, we have to pack all that stuff in from the truck."

"I know, but we have to have one change of clothes so I can wash." Eric's idea of a move was a frying pan and a change of socks. "And there's Rob's school things. I'll still have to teach him up there. I wish we could take the blackboard."

"Yeah, I forgot about that." Eric thought for a moment. "There's some of that slating left out in the woodshed, I think. I'll make another little board that'll fit in a pack." He stood looking at his banjo hanging on the wall. "I'd sure like to take that along."

Kate reached around his long legs and added a bundle of her personal things to the growing pile on the bed.

"I'll sing to you."

Eric had brought home another hound pup they called Coon. The morning they left for the trap line, Coon rode in the back of the truck, while Sport was coaxed into the crowded cab where they could listen to his familiar hicupping. He always got car sick. The road southwest from Rocky Mountain House to the Ram River site was well travelled. At last, in a clearing in the trees, they saw the derrick. They parked the truck on the fringe of the noisy activity, voices pitched above the pounding motors and the clanging of pipes. Men moved about the cluster of shacks in the edge of the woods.

Eric began arranging their packs. His pack board was heavily loaded. Kate slipped into her pack sack and helped Rob with the straps of his smaller one filled with bread and dried fruit.

It was still daylight when they reached the Baseline Trail and an old abandoned forestry cabin. Rob went in to explore it, but a quick look at the pack rat's nest of sticks and rubbish in the corner was enough.

"Whew. It stinks in there," he said, hurrying out.

The trail from there on was unused except for short stretches where moose or deer had walked along. Kate's eyes adjusted to the growing dusk until Eric, in the lead, had to use the flashlight to find the path along the side hill. He went first, then Rob and the dogs. Kate followed. They plodded on in the darkness, up and down hill, the steady motion of Coon's hind legs adding to Kate's illusion that they had been walking like this forever.

Her pack straps dug into her shoulders and her knees ached from trying to keep her balance. The crusted snow on the path was slippery, and going down hill was the hardest. They had stopped to rest when the faint howl of a wolf invaded the silence. Before its voice had faded, the pack ahead answered, a loud chorus of hoarse cries. Sport gave a deep-throated growl and Coon cowered beside Eric. Rob sidled up to his mother.

"What was that?"

"Wolves," Eric told him. He turned out the light. "Don't they sound nice?"

Kate put her hand on Rob's shoulder. Even a small boy was some comfort. The wolves howled again.

"Let's go on," she urged. "How far is it now?"

"We follow this ridge a while, then go down onto the Tay."

He turned on the light and Kate trudged on, shoved by the wall of darkness behind her, her ears straining for the sound that thrilled her but that she didn't want to hear.

At last they reached the Tay. Eric flashed the light across the narrow ice-bound stream.

"How far now?"

"Only a short way up the creek."

The wolves howled again.

"I think we're up the creek already," Kate mumbled.

The stream had flooded and frozen, leaving ripples of slippery ice. They found the game trail along the top of the bank. Eric pointed with the light and located the half-cabin, half-dugout in the side hill, the face of it revealing a small window and a door of split logs.

"There it is, Kate!"

They climbed the short steep bank and stood before the cabin.

Kate eased her pack to the ground and helped Rob out of his while Eric unlocked the heavy door and swung it inward. He shone the flashlight inside, and she was startled when he dropped down off the threshold.

"Watch your step. It's a two foot drop to the floor. Here, take my hand. I'll have to build a step there. And watch your head!"

Rob went first and Kate followed him, sliding down to the packed earth floor strewn with chips and pine needles. A sweep of light around the small room showed a stove fashioned from a car gas tank and a high double bunk of poles mattressed with hay. Eric had made a lower bunk across the foot for Rob. When they had lit the coal oil lamp and put it on the table of flattened poles, Kate saw how compact the room was. The stove sat high on a bracket, giving space underneath for wood. Traps and stretchers were stored under the bunk, and Rob's bed was a place to sit and cook from a shelf along the wall.

"I'll tie Sport and get some wood for the fire."

Eric had suspended the roll of bedding by a wire from the roof to keep the mice from building a nest in it. It was after midnight before they had it opened up and the claminess dispelled by the roaring fire. With the pipe nearly half as big as the stove, it was more noisy than efficient. The mice had found the candles and sculptured them with tooth marks. Eric lit one to save their oil. By then the pot of strong coffee could not ward off sleep, and the three of them surrendered.

Kate awoke to the sound of the dogs barking urgently. She raised up and bumped her head on the log roof. She lay there, rubbing her scalp, watching the dirt trickle through from above, and she thought, *We really haven't come very far.*

The dogs had stopped barking. It didn't seem to be anything important. She watched a tiny shrew make its way through the mountain of quilt over her drawn-up knees, and she raised a hand to brush it away. It stopped and lifted its long, inquisitive nose to test the air, boldly. It was a stand-off. At last it retreated. She stretched her aching legs and raised cautiously on one elbow. Rob's head appeared over the foot of the bunk.

"Can we get up now? I'll start the fire."

"Yes, but be quiet," she whispered. "Don't wake Dad. And don't walk on this dirt floor in your sock feet. Put your boots on."

After a breakfast of porridge, toast, and coffee made with snow water, Kate took a can and followed Eric down to the creek. He cut a hole in the ice, and the water boiled up, pale amber and tasting of dry grass. It quenched her thirst better than the snow water and made somewhat better coffee, though tea was barely drinkable, resembling some of those herbal concoctions touted along with rose hips and dandelion greens. They didn't drink much tea, anyway, and Rob had cocoa.

They turned Sport loose and watched as he bounded down the opening in front of the dugout and stopped short, his wide lips flaring as he picked up a scent. Eric shook his head, called the hound back and tied him again. They had never been able to break him of chasing game as well as cougar.

They examined tracks behind the cabin. "A moose all right," Eric said. "It went right down the creek. I better see if I can get us some meat. The season will soon be closed."

Eric spent the next few days cutting trail and setting traps while Kate settled in, getting Rob started on his school work. On the third day it was growing dark when Eric came in. He had set some traps, shot a few squirrels and seen some marten tracks. Best of all he brought home the hind quarter of a big mule deer.

"I brought what I could carry and left the rest hanging in a tree. I'll go back in the morning with the packboard."

"Can I go with you, Dad? Please." Rob was eager to share in his father's work; school work came a poor second.

"You can both go if you bring your pack sacks," said Eric. "It's only about two miles upstream, but we have to cross a swampy place that's tough walking."

Rob looked at Kate.

"O.K. We'll both go." Kate motioned toward Sport and Coon. "Let's take the dogs. They can have a good feed on the scraps."

The next morning Kate put Rob's pack on him while Eric fastened a short chain between the collars of the two dogs to keep them from running off on rabbit trails. It worked well whenever they left the path, for they usually chose opposite sides of a tree. Although age often increased a hound's stubborness, it had brought a certain amount of wisdom to old Sport, and he was always the first to retreat and disentangle them. The result was more disastrous when they ran one on each side of Kate's legs as she walked up the slippery creek ice.

The hummocks and the willows in the swampy opening made footing hazardous. When Eric staggered and fell to his knees with his load, Rob and Kate lifted the packboard to steady him as he regained his feet.

"You should have let us carry more of that," she said.

"It isn't heavy, it's this rough terrain." Eric beat the snow from his knees. "Sometimes I wish my mother had been frightened by a moose."

When I was young I thought log cabins were romantic. They're not. They're dark, dusty and crowded, and as long as we're trapping for a living, they stink. The squirrels are not too bad, but that weasel Eric got the first day is sickening. Maybe it had been living in the cabin before we came. I'm glad it wasn't a pack rat....I must put some prunes to soak for tomorrow.

Although the stove was flattened on the top for cooking, there was no oven. Sometimes Kate made bannock in the frying pan. After three weeks their bread was gone and they went into Rocky for supplies.

"Have all the bears hibernated now?" Kate asked.

"I expect so. That last storm would drive the last of them in. We'll have the dogs with us."

"It wasn't that. I wondered if we could take those bars off the window?"

Eric had driven spikes through two poles and nailed them across the window, points outward, to discourage raiding bears.

"Sure. They do stop a lot of light."

With their empty packs, they started down the trail. There had been a new fall of snow and walking was slow, so Kate took note of all the things she had missed coming up in the dark. The hillside they followed dropped away to a deep ravine filled with spruce. Rabbit trails criss-crossed in the patches of willow. She saw the long measured tracks of moose, the scuffing marks of deer as they dragged their feet through the snow. A few poplars were still draped with ribbons of dry bark where deer had rubbed the velvet from their antlers in the fall. Eric showed them marten tracks that looked like tiny rabbit tracks.

"I'm glad you told me," Kate confessed. I was beginning to think rabbits could climb trees."

Rob stopped. "What's that awful smell?"

"Sulphur."

"From the oil well?"

"I don't think so," said Eric. "There's supposed to be a moose lick along here somewhere."

They came upon game tracks crossing the trail, going down the bank to where a small spring oozed out of the ground. Bubbles rose to the surface, bursting and filling the air with a strange sulphur-like smell. Eric knelt down, lit his lighter and held it where the gas was coming up. The bubbles broke, exploding in a tiny burst of flame. He let Rob hold the lighter and ignite them.

"Do you mean the wild animals actually drink that stuff?" Rob asked, amazed.

"Sure. There's something in it they like."

The six miles to the oil well seemed shorter in daylight. The noise of the rig grew louder until at last they were there. While Kate was shifting some things around in the cab of their old truck, Eric stood talking to one of the workmen. He came back with the news: the Siegfried Line had been broken. News of the war tore at Kate's heart. She had a feeling of being trapped between two worlds. She hated the killing of animals that they had to do to survive in her world, and yet in the other they were killing men, thousands of them. She could not understand the reasons, and suddenly she loved her clean wilderness with a fierce love.

They called to Rob where he stood watching the men on the derrick, and at the sound of their voices, the dogs came from the direction of the cook house, waddling, their legs stiff like Tinker-Toy animals. It looked like they would have extra unscheduled stops before reaching Rocky Mountain House.

They got a room at the lower hotel. Kate had left a box of better clothes in the truck. Even after a bath in the big tub at the end of the hall, shivers still plagued her as she changed from long-johns to rayon stockings and a skirt.

Eric tied the dogs in a shed at the back of the hotel and gave them some water. Rob was concerned. He stroked old Sport. "What are they going to eat?"

"They've had enough grub to last them a week. I saved a couple squirrel carcasses from those we shot on the way out. I'll give them those before we go to bed. They're sure as hell going to be riding on an empty stomach going back."

"Where are *we* going to eat?"

"The restaurant, I guess."

"And can we go to a show? You said if we get five squirrels on the way out we could go to a show. We got eight, remember?"

"I think we can afford a show," Eric laughed.

A meal in a restaurant was a treat for Kate, too. For dessert, Rob had chocolate pudding, his favorite. It was a generous serving, but when the firm mixture resisted his spoon, he announced loudly, "Gee, Mom, you can make better puddin' than this." Kate was embarrassed and flattered at the same time.

They went to see *Random Harvest* with Ronald Coleman and Greer Garson, and Rob fell asleep before the end. Back at the hotel the three of them slept in the double bed, crowded but more comfortable than the pole and hay bunk, and once again they found themselves in the strange contrast between a pioneer life and twentieth century conveniences.

When the stores opened the next morning, they bought their groceries and started back, leaving behind all the small luxuries of town. Along a straight stretch of road, Rob pointed into the trees, where a large group of men were working.

"Look at those men, Dad! They're all dressed alike."

"They're men from the internment camp, prisoners of war," Eric said.

"Our men?"

"No. German prisoners."

The men, who had looked up as the truck passed, turned back to cutting wood.

"Look, Dad. They've all got red patches on the back of their shirts."

"Those are targets."

"Targets?"

Kate touched Eric's arm lightly. Their glances met.

"So they can find them easy if they get lost in the woods," Eric said, quickly.

"Are all those guys Germans?"

"Yes."

"But they look just like us."

"Yes, I know."

24

They settled down to trapline living. Line holders were issued extra sugar rations, and with those Kate bought brown sugar and maple flavouring and made syrup for their hotcakes. Eric enjoyed them for supper after a hard day hunting, until he began to complain of a toothache. He stuffed the hollow molar with aspirin and finally cotton soaked in oil of cloves, with only temporary relief. The nagging pain grew to an unbearable throbbing, until at one point he had not slept for two nights. From exhaustion he dozed between mouthfuls of cold water, which seemed to kill the pain.

"You can't keep this up, Eric." Kate stroked his forehead. "You'll be too weak to walk down to the truck. We're going into Rocky."

During the six mile walk, Eric scooped up snow and held it against the abscessed tooth. At the oil well they found a discarded beer bottle, filled it with cold water, and in the old truck headed for the nearest dentist thirty miles away. Eric, imbibing from the brown bottle, pressed his foot to the floor boards, less in pain now, but desperate to reach town before the dentist's office closed.

When they drove into Rocky Mountain House, it was too late, but there was still a light in the upstairs window of the dentist's office. As Kate opened the car door, the light dimmed. She bounded up the stairs and pounded on the locked door. The dentist came, drying his hands and protesting.

"Office hours are over. Come back Monday."

"My husband hasn't slept for three nights. We walked six miles and drove thirty to get here. Please see him."

Eric came up the stairs, holding his jaw. The dentist eyed him briefly.

"Sit here. I'll have a look at it."

He looked suspiciously at the bottle in Eric's hand.

"It's only cold water," Kate said.

"Hmmm. Well, I couldn't pull it now while it's aching. I couldn't be responsible for the results."

Eric didn't say anything, but he had a wild glare in his eyes, and his silence and stance implied he might not be responsible either. The dentist gave in, and after some prodding and speculating, the tooth came out.

Kate paid the dentist, and they went down to the truck where Rob was waiting with the dogs. Eric was holding his jaw. "We better go have something to eat before we start out. It will be midnight before we get back to the cabin."

"We're not going back up there tonight. We've got enough money to stay at the hotel for one night. Better yet, let's go down to your folks tomorrow. It's the same distance in the car and we wouldn't have that six mile walk in the dark. You can't trap until that swelling goes down, anyway."

Eric was running his tongue along his lip. "It doesn't hurt much now. The throbbing is gone."

"It will as soon as the freezing comes out. Come on, Eric. You can have some soup if it's not too hot."

The night man at the hotel recognized them from their last stay and put a cot in the room for Rob. Eric, who had taken three aspirin, slept restlessly. In the morning, Kate saw the blood spots on his pillow case. Before they left, she put it to soak in cold water in the wash basin.

They reached Pa's place before noon. Granny was delighted. "It's only three days before Christmas. You stay right here with us. Your cabin will be cold and damp. Miles and Leah are coming down, too. Pa, you'll have to get a little tree, now that Robby is going to be here. He can help you trim it."

Kate didn't need any coaxing. She was tired. She had wanted to check on the cabin before they went back, but Eric could do that when he went over to pick up the toboggan. It was nice to see Granny in such good spirits, and Kate enjoyed helping her bake cookies and prepare the big venison roast.

Kate and Eric had not planned for Christmas on the trap line. There were no gifts except the red truck Pa and Granny bought for Rob. Eric went out to the wood shed and sawed lengths from an old broom handle for pretend saw logs. Rob spent the day hauling them from one spot to another on the floor.

Kate was glad to see Leah again. When dinner was over, they sent Granny into the bedroom to rest while they cleared the table, washed the dishes and talked.

They returned to the line the day after Christmas, taking the toboggan back with them. It eliminated the heavy back-packs. There had been a deep snow which almost obliterated the trail, and the toboggan kept sliding sideways. Eric sorted through the .22 shells and brass wire in his pocket and came up with a length of lace leather which he tied to the back of the load.

"Here, you hold onto this and maybe you can keep it from slipping off the path."

He whittled a long forked stick for Kate to push with on the steeper hills. This way they reached a point along the Baseline Trail before dark. They stopped, built a fire and dug into the grub sack for something to eat. They cut bread in thick slices with a hunting knife, dabbed them with chunks of cold butter and topped them with sardines. Kate ate standing up, leaning against a tree to rest her back. Rob ran over to investigate a teepee-like structure of logs. Then they heard his desperate voice.

"Dad!" he called. "I'm in a trap!"

He had stepped into a lynx set, the jaws catching the heel of his rubber boot. Eric laughingly released him and reset the trap, putting dry moss under the pan so it wouldn't freeze down. He kicked a layer of snow over the top.

"There, that won't be much good until the next snowfall gets rid of the man scent. Now don't go running off the trail after this, Rob. You know what those houses are for! You even helped me set a few."

"I know, but I thought the trail was the dividing line between our line and that other guy, and if it is, he's got his trap on our side," Rob replied, logically.

"Maybe you're right," Eric conceded, "but hardly enough to start a range war. How's your foot?"

"It doesn't hurt. I guess my boot was frozen up."

"We better get going, then. It sure has been slow so far."

Kate was tired, and glad of the times Eric stopped to examine tracks crossing the trail. When he stopped, she could stop. It was well into the night when they reached the cabin. She looked at the mound of snow with only the door and window discernable. *Oh well,* she thought, *all I want is a hot cup of coffee and to crawl into that bunk.*

Kate kicked away the snow while Eric unlocked the door and opened it to find the cabin inside as white as it was outside. The roof and walls were covered with an inch of frost.

"Don't it look pretty, Mom!" Rob seemed delighted.

Kate didn't trust herself to answer; she was too tired. But by the time Eric had lit the lamp she had to agree with the boy. The whole cabin glittered tinsel-bright. Kate smiled, thinking that it had had its own Christmas while they were away, all by itself.

Eric picked up the wood shavings he had left on the stove. The tips of the curled wood were festooned with sparkling feathers of frost.

"They're pretty, but they're too damp to start a fire. I'll get some dry spruce twigs outside. Maybe you two can brush off some of that frost into the dishpan before it melts all over everything."

With a hot fire the room did not drip as they had feared. It filled slowly with steam, so that they had to open the door and let it escape to find another host, like a ghost seeking an imagination to live on. By repeating the process, they managed to clear the logs of moisture. Rob was nodding on his bunk. Kate persuaded him to go to bed with a warmed rock tucked in beside him. Eric and Kate drank coffee to keep awake and stoke the greedy little stove until almost daylight, tired as they were. She realized how deeply weary she was, how this life was wearing her down. She was young and strong, but even youth and strength has its limits. Would she even survive to tell the story of their lives, much less figure out how? But this was giving in. She shook the thought away.

They slept late the next morning and spent the day shovelling snow, clearing a path to the water hole and the wood pile. All the traps had to be dug out from under the deep snow and reset.

Kate was awakened that night by a thumping on the roof. A bear? No, the bears had gone to bed. A succession of thumps like something running across the roof. Those wolves! She jabbed Eric in the ribs.

"Eric, wake up. There's something on the roof!"

He mumbled and sat up.

"You mean that noise? It's only snow falling off the trees. The wind was coming up when we went to bed."

She lay for a while listening to the night noises. A dry branch rasped along a leaning tree like some monster breathing slowly. The rising wind whipped dead pine needles against the window pane. By morning the trees were freed of their burden, and quiet had come again.

Eric was putting traps into a pack sack.

"Do you think you and Rob could make it up to that lynx set we made on the ridge and pick up that trap? I found a good place up the valley for coyotes and I need a bigger trap."

"Sure. We can take our time."

Rob was anxious to go. Besides adventure, it meant getting out of some lessons.

"You take the 32.20," Eric told her. "I'll take the .22 for squirrels. Sport is the best squirrel dog, so I'll take him and Coon can go with you. He doesn't know much yet, but he'll be good company." Eric, as usual had everything planned.

It was a steep climb to the top of the ridge. They found a fallen log, brushed off some of the snow and sat resting. Coon ran haphazardly, poking his nose into the depressions. Then suddenly Kate heard him give a few quick yelps.

"He's found something," said Rob. "He's found a track. Coon! Come back here!"

The dog obeyed, for he had not yet experienced the excitement of the chase. They examined the tracks, deep puncture marks in the snow.

"Dad would say it's a lynx." Rob pointed. "There's no pad marks."

From a straight line of prints they couldn't tell which way the animal had gone. The pup sniffed both ways, then took the trail toward the trap. They followed hastily, floundering in the deeper drifts. The tent-like house was still intact.

They searched the underbrush nearby. When the dog stopped stiff-legged, Kate levered a shell into the rifle barrel and moved ahead. Breeding triumphed over puppy fear as a deep baying broke the silence. They saw the lynx then, only its head above the log, its yellow eyes staring.

"Hold the dog!"

Kate raised the rifle and shot the cat before the hound could wrest free of Rob's grip. Then he leaped ahead and dove at the quarry, nosing its limp body.

The lynx never moved. Rob was the first to approach it. Kate's hesitation was not fear; she knew the animal was dead. She was remembering the two round, yellow eyes staring at her as she aimed the gun. Rob's enthusiasm washed over her sudden sadness. The animal had been caught by only two toes, verifying what Eric had said, that lynx seldom fight a trap. A bolder animal would have escaped.

"Look at the long, silvery fur, Mom. I'll bet you get a lot of money for this. Can I carry it back? It's not heavy."

"Yes, of course, if you want to."

Kate's legs ached from tramping through the deep snow. Going back down the hill was easier. They followed their own tracks, their prize an encouragement. It would take a lot of squirrels to match the price they would get for the lynx.

Kate's anticipation matched Rob's as they waited for Eric to return that evening. She had agreed to hide the animal under the bunk at first. They wanted to extract as much drama from the situation as they could. At last they heard the crunching of the snow. Their moment had come.

Eric flung open the door and stood smiling at them. Did he know, she wondered? Then he reached behind him and dragged in his catch, a cougar.

"That's why I was so late. Sport must have run him three miles before he treed in a little pine."

"What a cat! Look at those claws!" Kate lifted a paw in her hands.

"It's an old Tom. He sure was heavy to pack."

"I'll heat up the beans. Rob and I got hungry so we ate."

"Did you pick up that trap?"

Kate looked at Rob, who dove under the bunk and brought out the lynx, displaying it wordlessly.

"Well, I'll be damned. I didn't think that set was any good."

"It was alive and Mom shot it."

Lying beside the cougar, their catch seemed to shrink in size and significance, but Eric reassured them. "That sure is a fine skin." He fluffed the long soft fur.

"Your cat's bigger," Rob said.

"Maybe, but that lynx will bring a lot more money. The cougar will only be bounty money and a few extra dollars for the hide. Lynx are a darned good price. Good work, you guys." He put his arm around Kate and extended a hand to Rob who shook it proudly.

When they skinned the cougar they found pieces of porcupine quill embedded in gristle that moved freely under the skin of its front legs. Eric skinned it open, flat for a rug mount. The lynx had to be cased and even its furred feet skinned out.

That night Sport slipped out of his collar. Both dogs came waddling back at daylight.

"They've been out to the cougar carcass. It looks like they've had a good feed. Better not let them in the cabin for a while."

Eric nailed the cougar skull on the outside of the door. Its open jaws made a handy place to stuff their mitts when they had to unlock the cabin.

Rob added shrews to his menagerie of pets. He caught two of them and put them in a pail.

"You can't keep them like that. They'll starve!" said Kate.

"I'll feed them meat and flies."

There were plenty of flies, big blue ones which had hidden away in the moss chinking in the fall, and appeared every day to bumble against the window pane. The boy fed his pets faithfully for several days, amused at their activity, burrowing in the grass nest he made for them, until one morning one of them disappeared.

"It must have got out." He searched the grass carefully and found bits of fur.

"The little cannibal," Kate said. "I heard they do that but I didn't believe it. It's probably a good thing. There's getting to be too darned many of them around here, so there's one less."

When she saw her son's face she was sorry she had let her irritation include his pets. "Why don't you put the other one outside in the woods? Maybe it will go away."

She had always coped well enough with pests, but lately she had been more impatient, more irritated than usual with with the crowded cabin, the constant stale, animal smell of drying hides. It hadn't been as good a season as they had hoped. The snow hadn't been deep enough to confine the game to trails, and the fur animals followed the game. She was relieved when the dogs barked and Eric leaned in the door and said, "Put on the coffee pot. Someone's coming up the trail. It looks like Rolly from the line down the creek."

Kate looked out the window and recognized the small man in the red plaid mackinaw. She had seen him in Rocky once at Finbergs with a bale of furs. He stopped to talk to Eric before they came in. His voice was deep and his laugh an infectious chuckle, a welcome addition to the conversation.

The small coffee pot was replenished several times as they talked long into the night. Rob, so fascinated by Rolly's stories, was the first to nod. He relinquished his bed to their guest and climbed up to the back of the big bunk where he fell asleep.

When Kate began to shift on the hard block of wood, Eric said, "Why don't you get into bed? We can still sit up and talk."

Rolly agreed. "You do that. I'll just go into the kitchen." He swung around and faced the stove while Kate slipped off her outer garments. She crawled in beside Rob and let the droning voices lull her into a deeper sleep.

Her protesting stomach woke her. The air was hot and full of cigarette smoke. She pulled on her jeans and slid to the floor. As she reached the door the candle light dimmed and she turned to see the two men in a wavering outline. As the nail in the door raked her back, she slumped to the floor and darkness closed in.

"She's coming round," she heard someone say. Against the starlit sky she saw the tree tops in relief as she lay head down across Eric's knees. They must have carried her outside. Eric was wiping the snow from her face.

"I'm all right. I want to go back in now."

"All that damned heat and smoke up there," Eric said. He steadied her down into the cabin. When she was back in bed, he stood beside the bunk and gave her a quizzical look. "Do you want a cup of coffee?"

"Ugh!"

As she pulled the blanket over her head, she heard him confide to their guest: "I half expected that."

Kate had, too. Now it seemed certain. She was pregnant again. She lay for a long time thinking, her mind drifting back to her childhood and that other book in the upstairs closet, the *Baby Book*. It, too, she had read in secret. On the first page was a picture of a half-clad woman with a big belly. Before she could read, the picture had frightened her. When she had learned there was a baby inside, she was fascinated. The picture was called "The Pride of Pregnancy."

She would be proud, of course, but she would need extra strength to dispel the nagging thoughts of four of them crowded into their own cabin on the homestead. She reached out to touch Rob on the bunk beside her and let the men's lowered voices urge her back to sleep.

On the next trip out for supplies, they cut across country to the truck at the oil rig, climbing to a high ridge where they could see the valley below. Old tracks had melted out and crusted, leaving shadowy evidence of where a deer had scuffed through the deeper snow on the edge of some poplars, where a cat had walked a fallen log, only icy remnants of its measured steps remaining.

Eric pointed. "See those five tracks down there coming out of the timber and all coming together there in the opening?"

"Yes."

"That's wolf tracks. They're hunting. They do that—they fan out and then come back together, sometimes all walking in the same track. You'd think only one animal had gone along."

Eric stood behind and above Kate on the slope. He put a hand on her shoulder. There was a moment of quiet, then his feet slipped and he slid down, kicking her feet from under her. She landed on his lap and they went tobogganing down the hill. She knew before they stopped that they would live their lives this way, sudden decisions, plunging headlong into the future together.

25

In March they returned to the homestead. Eric brought in the few furs they had not sold.

"I had hoped to do better than this. But we did eat good up there." After a pause he added, "Maybe better than if we'd stayed here."

Kate wondered if he had been sharing some of her thoughts. After nine years, they had resigned themselves to the possibility of having no more children. This new situation magnified the lingering doubts in the back of her mind. The new house they had planned to build "someday" seemed always to be one more summer away.

Each year they had planned and waited and made jokes about their present kitchen, big as all outdoors with the stove on one side and the fridge, a stone crock in the spring fifty yards away, on the other. The bathroom, too, was grand, one half a galvanized tub in front of the kitchen stove and the other half out yonder in the pines.

Now "someday" was upon them and they still had only the crowded, ill-lighted cabin. They both grew quiet in the days that followed, going about their work without the usual enthusiasm.

Kate spoke first. "If you could find work around Caroline, maybe we should move there for a while, see how it goes. Rob could go to school. I'm afraid I won't be able to keep up when the baby comes."

"I've been thinking about that, too," said Eric, "The end of the war seems nearer now. They've got the Philippines back now and Mussolini got himself shot. Maybe lumber prices will pick up a little."

Eric and I had a long talk last night. Funny how a piece of land, mostly rocks and trees, can be so precious, so hard to let go of. But it's not really the land we'd be leaving, it's the part of our lives we spent to acquire it, those years together side by side, working hard. We'll always have that with us where ever we go.

Then came that day in May when the war in Europe was over. Kate heard the message on the radio. When Eric came home from Caroline she met him at the door.

"Did you hear the news? The war's over in Europe!"

"Yes." He hugged her and kissed her on the cheek. "Sorry, I had a few beers. The whole town is celebrating. They're having a victory dance tonight and we're going."

Kate looked down at her bulging abdomen.

"Come on," Eric laughed. "We'll celebrate that, too."

They ate their supper amid excited conversation and short silences. Eric spoke again about leaving the homestead. They would be among the many families starting over, and besides the land was still theirs.

"There should be some construction going on soon," he said. "Those veterans and their families will need places to live. I hope they don't have to build more of those ugly wartime houses with narrow casings and no eaves. A man likes to feel he's created something besides wages when he works. I may have to go farther out to the settlement to work, but we'd always have the cabin for a refuge."

Kate's own plans were forming. She could work, too, after the baby was born, and when both children were in school, maybe a full time job. She would have to approach that carefully. Eric was a proud man. A woman's place was in the home, he maintained, but she remembered days of cutting brush and working at the mill. She knew, though, he made a powerful division between women working at home, and women working for wages. She would deal with future problems as they came.

Kate had been wearing one of Eric's shirts to cover her

unbuttoned skirt band. When they began to dress for the dance, she searched the trunk for a dress that would fit her now. The gray and black figured rayon would do if she took out the shoulder pads and put her rhinestone pin on the crossover neckline to hold it more discreetly in place. She looked down at her hemline.

"It's awfully short."

"It looks all right, Kate. You got nice legs."

She raised her skirt. The service-weight stockings hid the patches of skin darkened from kneeling to scrub the board floor. She stepped sideways and flirted her skirt at Eric. He laughed and Rob joined in. Rob had rarely seen his parents in such a playful mood.

The big community hall was packed. People came in various dress. Some men just off shift at the mills came in work clothes and hobnail boots. Parents picked up their children and whirled them across the floor. Kate thought, *it's for them—they wanted a safer world.*

A local pick-up orchestra made up in volume what it lacked in unity. Their repertoire was limited. Johnny, of an old and distant war, was marched home several times. Hidden sorrows surfaced in many eyes as the band laboured out "The White Cliffs Of Dover." The coffee was supplemented with the liquid innovations of resourceful people, their neighbours and their friends.

When they came home from the dance, Eric built up the fire in the cookstove and Kate made coffee. They sat and talked through the last of the night hours until daylight crept into the cabin. They decided to leave the homestead.

Eric tapped a forefinger on his cup. "That fellow who told me about driving a lumber truck said if I get the job we could rent his shack on the edge of town. It's small, three rooms, but it would do to start. If we sold the team and the cow we'd have something to go on."

They talked of the steady income, a school for Rob, the contact with other people they both needed. Eric had been lonely, too. And then they spoke quietly of the homestead,

Taffy, the funny mismatched team, Clarabelle, their first love. They would miss the silent woods, the animals, the clear spring and even the wicked river. Their words were like a requiem, a purge for their emotions, helping them to see more clearly the way ahead. At last they lay, still fully dressed, across the bed, and fell asleep until the sun wakened them.

Eric made two trips to Innisfail before his trucking job was assured. Kate, in her sorting and packing, made time to go up and see Martha. This parting saddened Kate. It would be a long time before she found another woman she could talk to as openly. She would still save magazines for Martha. Kate and Eric could come out sometime and see her and Jess.

The last evening was spent with Pa and Granny up on the hill. Miles and Leah came to share the farewell gathering. They sat at the kitchen table in the circle of yellow lamplight around a bowl of popcorn, the white kernels like the host of half-thoughts erupting in Kate's mind. Eric talked of their accomplishments, the harder times forgotten for the moment, and Kate told for the first time how she and Buck had both been frightened by a bear they never saw.

Granny laughed and said, "You tell such good stories, Kate. You should write them down. I always thought of doing something like that, but it's too late for me now. My hands are so crippled."

Kate looked over at her mother-in-law sitting so quietly, her crooked fingers twined in her lap, her stories untold. She recalled the pictures of Granny's first house on the prairie, and smiled at her mother-in-law. "I'll do it for both of us, Granny."

Kate felt the uncertainty of the challenge. Was this prospect just another carrot for her hungry mind, or would it be a feast? She put her hand on her side as the child inside her stirred.

The small house in town had a white enamel stove in the kitchen with a patch of linoleum in front of it. There were clothes closets with doors on them in each of the bedrooms.

The day they had the beds moved and set up, they stayed the night.

Kate woke at daylight and slipped out of bed to look out in all directions. She didn't have to stoop to peer out these windows. She could see part way down the main street to the Post Office and the general store beyond. A light came on in the restaurant and a woman's outline passed before a small window. Although there would be other women to talk to here, they would be strangers, and Kate did not make new friends easily, always waiting for them to make the first overture. The Hanover boys had not waited—they brought that quarter of moose, and a lasting friendship had followed. She would have to learn to be less reserved. Rob, who was to start school the next week, had already found a boy to play with.

Kate turned to reach up and tug at the string hanging from the ceiling, flicking the light on and then off. It still worked. In their own bedroom, she stood looking down at Eric. He had played for a wedding dance last night, and was sleeping the restful sleep of the artistically satisfied.

They made a last trip to the homestead to gather and store a few things in the cabin—the traps and their saskatoon fishing poles. Kate watched Eric whittle shavings and lay them on the stove in readiness for the next fire, a small tie to this place that had been their home for nine years. While he nailed slabs across the windows, Kate made a silent pilgrimage to the empty outbuildings. Lamb's quarter was beginning to grow in the abandoned pig yard, weeds to some, but had they stayed, it would have been tasty greens by summer. The sawdust pile had turned orange-brown from the sun, and the cardboard of Rob's tree house sagged from the rains. The spring was the only constant thing. She bent and scooped a handful of the clear, cold water and held it to her lips.

The homestead had been an article of faith with them, a link between centuries and generations, a place of peace and a deep unity with nature, a place of isolation and depression. It was the basis of community life, people thrown together who had helped one another through the Depression and the War. She owed to it all she had become, her resilience, strength, determination. She would tell her story, and the forest and the river would tell their story without end, without even trying.

Titles in the Polestar First Fiction Series

Mobile Homes by Noel Hudson
Mobile Homes is a brilliant first collection of comic offbeat stories. One of the stories received a Distinguished Story Citation in Best American Short Stories.

The Tasmanian Tiger by Jane Barker Wright
The Tasmanian Tiger is a multi-layered novel about mother-hood, mystery and murder set in both Tasmania and the West Coast of Canada. Ordinary people—an extraordinary tale.